THE OPERATIVE

JACK SILKSTONE

By Jack Silkstone

The Operative

The PRIMAL Series

PRIMAL Origin
PRIMAL Unleashed
PRIMAL Vengeance
PRIMAL Fury
PRIMAL Reckoning
PRIMAL Nemesis
PRIMAL Redemption
PRIMAL Renegade
PRIMAL Deception
PRIMAL Exodus

This book is dedicated to my boys, Bishop and Rook. A guy couldn't ask for more loyal companions.

Vinci Books

vinci-books.com

Published by Vinci Books Ltd in 2025

1

Copyright © Jack Silkstone 2024

The author has asserted their moral right to be identified as the author of this work in accordance with the Copyright, Designs and Patents Act 1988. This work is a work of fiction. Names, characters, places and incidents are the product of the author's imagination or are used fictitiously. Any resemblance to actual persons, living or dead, places and incidents is entirely coincidental.

All rights reserved. No part of this publication may be copied, reproduced, distributed, stored in any retrieval system, or transmitted in any form or by any means, including photocopying, recording, or other electronic or mechanical methods, nor used as a source for any form of machine learning including AI datasets, without the prior written permission of the publisher.

The publisher and the author have made every effort to obtain permissions for any third party material used in this book and to comply with copyright law. Any queries in this respect should be brought to the attention of the publisher and any omissions will be corrected in future editions.

A CIP catalogue record for this book is available from the British Library.

Paperback ISBN: 9781036702595

Prologue

HE WAS A GHOST, a highly trained operative with multiple identities, three languages, and two dozen confirmed kills. A man you didn't want to meet in a dark alley.

His latest mission didn't look at all challenging. The target was a middle-aged man living in the Australian city of Melbourne. In twelve years of working for the company, he'd taken three jobs in the land down under. It was a favored retirement destination for intelligence types. It was probably because it was miles from anywhere, but, as his kill count revealed, it wasn't far enough.

He checked his device and reread the short bio. Brian Schofield was fifty-six years old and in average shape, judging by the photo. There was a wife and a kid. Not a problem, murder-suicides were his specialty.

There was no historical data, not that it mattered. He wasn't here to pass judgment, only execute the sentence.

"Damien Broader, your vehicle is ready."

He glanced up at the hire car sales desk and saw the female attendant was holding an envelope. Slipping the phone into his pocket, he shouldered his backpack and went to the counter. Taking the envelope, he thanked her and exited the office. It took him less than a minute to find the allocated vehicle and throw his bag on the passenger seat.

It was a short drive from the airport to the suburb where his target lived. The streets were wide and tree-lined with open gardens that suggested minimal crime, an excellent place to raise a family.

He'd used a burner account to book an apartment nearby and planned to commence his recon that evening. Experience told him he wouldn't need to hang around. Most people's weekday routine was consistent. He'd check it out tonight, procure the required equipment, and do the job the following day. He'd be on a flight out before the bodies were cold.

The phone in his pocket vibrated as he pulled into the space allocated to his apartment. Killing the engine, he checked the screen. A single phrase appeared in his notifications.

Data has been corrupted.

It took a split second for the gravity of the situation to hit home. He tried logging into the secure application and confirmed that it was down. The system stored nothing locally. The phone was now a brick. He used a cloth to wipe his prints from the device and tossed it in the footwell. The sim was a burner purchased through a cut-out. Nothing, not the car or the apartment, could be traced. It was all expendable.

He grabbed his bag, left the vehicle, and walked onto the street. He was on his own now, burnt.

As he made his way to a main road to flag a taxi, his

earlier confidence evaporated. Mission forgotten, his only thought was survival. He needed to get out of Australia, and fast.

A passing taxi stopped, and he directed the driver to the international airport. He had a flexible airfare booked under a contingency ID. Exhaling, he reassured himself that his procedures were flawless. *The Entity* may have had a compromise, but the now bricked phone was his only link to them. He was clean.

By the time he was moving through the crowded departures concourse, he was back to his calm self. At the business class check-in, the attendant handed him his ticket with a smile.

"Alan Crete." The voice behind him was firm with an icy edge.

He hadn't heard his real name spoken out loud in almost a decade. Turning, he found himself face to face with a broad-shouldered, stern-faced man in a tailored suit. Backing him up were five similarly dressed men. His trained eye spotted the tell-tale bulge of a pistol on the hip of each of them.

"This is the end of the road."

Alan moved quickly, palming the man in the face and smashing his nose. At the same time, he threw an arm over his shoulder and spun him into a headlock.

As he went for the man's pistol, the others moved as fast as he had. The last thing the assassin ever saw was a pistol muzzle. A security officer's bullet punched a neat hole in his forehead and expanded inside his brain, killing him instantly. He dropped to the ground behind the officer he'd assaulted.

"Cordon off the area," the man croaked. "Don't let anyone near the body."

Chapter One

DAVID MARTIN STEPPED out of his rental SUV and squinted as he donned a pair of designer sunglasses. Dough-faced with curly black hair, he was an unremarkable-looking man with an unimpressive physique. At first glance, most people assumed he was an accountant or, worse, a real estate agent. In fact, he was a lawyer and fixer for a shadowy intelligence consultancy known as *The Entity*.

It wasn't his first trip to Texas, and he wasn't thrilled to be so far from the safety of the urban environment. This place is a dusty shit hole, he thought as he slammed the car door and surveyed his surroundings.

The Delta Ranch, such a lame name, he thought. It was smack bang in the middle of nowhere surrounded by thousands of acres of rugged, tree-covered hills. He imagined that they were crawling with rattlesnakes and spiders.

The ranch house was a short walk, but that wasn't where he'd find who he was looking for. Instead, he made for a sizeable open-ended barn, where boots poked out from under a tractor.

"X, is that you?" he asked between bursts of a rattle gun.

A leathery face appeared from under the machinery.

"Do I look like that behemoth? He's out back." The man gestured through the barn then slid back under the tractor.

"Thanks," mumbled David as he straightened his sports jacket and entered the barn, careful not to get horse shit on his loafers.

The structure had stalls on both sides and an open door at the back through which he could hear the crack of gunfire. Exiting, David made his way to an open area cleared between two low hills.

He spotted the man he was looking for crouched over a hefty tractor tire.

X, a massive lantern-jawed former CIA paramilitary officer, let out a grunt as he flipped the tire. Before it dropped, he sprinted toward a row of steel targets, unslinging the carbine that hung across his back as he moved.

Skidding to a halt, he rapidly engaged the targets in one direction, changed magazines then hit them in reverse before unloading. He slung the weapon across his back as he strode toward David.

"What's up?" his said, deep and abrupt.

David noted that despite the grey at his temples and the wrinkles on his face, the retired paramilitary officer looked as fit, if not fitter, than ever.

"Good to see you too."

"Niceties are for nice people. We ain't fucking nice!" X gestured to the barn. "I'm guessing we need to talk somewhere secure?"

"Preferably."

The Operative

David had known X for nearly a decade and knew the big man wasn't one for small talk, which was OK with him. He followed him back to the barn into one of the horse stalls, lined with cupboards to hold tack. X fished a device from his pocket and waved it over a wall panel. There was a click, and a cabinet slid sideways, revealing stairs that disappeared into a basement.

"Very 007," said David as he followed him down.

Lights flickered on, illuminating a bunker. X strode across to a line of lockers, punched in a code, opened the door, and placed his carbine beside a dozen other weapons.

"Rather well equipped," said David as he sat on a Chesterfield sofa.

"Beer?"

"Why not."

X grabbed two cold bottles from a fridge, twisted off the caps, and handed one to the lawyer. Then he lowered his hulking frame on to a couch opposite. "So, what have you got?"

"We've had a compromise," said David.

"How bad?"

"Four of our best field operatives."

"And the rest?"

"In hiatus."

"That's untidy."

"To say the least. Which brings me to my next point. We're enacting the plan."

X took a swig from his beer and swallowed. "What plan are you talking about? We had a lot of plans."

David smiled. "Plan Survivor."

X frowned. "No shit! The board approved it?"

"They did, and you and I will run it."

"We got a budget?"

David reached into his jacket and withdrew a folded piece of paper. "This is your contract." He handed it over.

X inspected the document and let out a long whistle. "That's a decent lump of treasure."

The lawyer nodded. "It's a big job. You up for it?"

X finished his beer and wiped his chin. "Ain't got anything else on."

JENNIFER MURPHY SAT in her cubicle on the eleventh floor of an office block in Charlotte, North Carolina. Middle-aged, she had shoulder-length curly brown hair and blue eyes. She was in reasonable shape, training three times a week at a local gym to maintain her figure. She'd described herself on a dating site as bubbly and a chronic oversharer.

Jen, to her friends, was a case manager for a multinational insurance company. A job she loathed, and subsequently, she spent a lot of time planning her holidays. Today, she was researching horse trekking in the Italian Alps.

"Jenny, have you wrapped up that O'Malley case yet?" her supervisor called across the office.

She minimized her internet browser, replacing it with a spreadsheet of her allocated cases, all of which were on schedule. "No, Neville. I'm still waiting on the photos."

Neville spoke from behind her. "Well, get onto it. I need that case cleared by the end of the week."

"They're an older couple, Neville. I'm waiting on their daughter to take better images."

"Jenny, I don't care. Get it done."

As he moved to the next cubicle, she shook her head.

"What the hell am I doing?" she murmured as she scanned her case files. Forty years old and working a crappy insurance job to fund holidays, which she went on alone. Not exactly where thirty-year-old her would have hoped to be.

Glancing over her shoulder, she saw Neville had returned to his office. Reopening her browser, she turned her attention back to the horse trek.

In her imagination, she was already there. She was cantering up a flinty hillside between olive-laden trees on a beautiful mare, spurred on by her handsome Italian guide.

Her fantasy was interrupted by a gentle cough. "That doesn't look like work, darling."

Her best friend and work colleague, Ben, leaned over her shoulder. "Does look amazing, though."

"Yeah, I know, and I've almost got enough leave."

"Did you see the email I sent you? I've got a better option."

She opened her email client and found his message. Opening it, she frowned. "What's this?"

"Perfect for you, is what it is. I found it on Facebook and thought Jen has to do this."

The email was a flyer for what looked to be a reality TV show called *The Operative*. She read the Tag Line.

From Zero to Hero. We're taking the average Joe off the street and turning them into James Bond.

"They're looking for people just like you," said Ben.

"You mean ordinary?"

He laughed. "Not ordinary, normal. Come on, babe, you'd crush this. Plus, it would get you out of this boring ass office. Even if it's just for a day to try out."

She opened the application form. "Ben, it's ten pages long. I don't have time for this."

"Of course not. I mean you've got to plan your horse holiday in Italy. So, I've filled out most of it already."

She scrolled down and saw that he'd done exactly that.

"Jen, fill out the gaps and email it in. Come on, what have you got to lose?"

"Fine! But you're buying me a triple-shot caramel latte. It's the only way I will get through the afternoon."

"Deal. You finish the application, and I'll run downstairs to Starbucks. But you better have that application in by the time I return."

He left the office as she started reading the application in detail. The first question asked why she would make the ultimate operative. She took a moment to think before typing her response.

Because no one would ever suspect me.

―――――

"NICK, your ex-wife is on line two."

Nick Liu looked up from his laptop and saw the pained expression on his elderly assistant, Magda's, face. "What does she want?"

She shrugged. "Money?"

The American-born Chinese lawyer stared at the flashing light on his desk phone as he exhaled. He'd been divorced for over six months, but the woman wouldn't leave him alone, and he couldn't say no.

"Stop giving that leech money," grumbled his father, the managing partner of the law firm, as he entered the office and dumped an armful of case files on his desk. "I want these annotated by the end of the week."

"Dad, one of the associates can do that."

"I'm not asking one of the associates. I'm asking you."

His father shot him a withering look as he left Nick's office, leaving him with the pile of folders and the flashing phone.

He stared at the light, which seemed to pulse in time with his heartbeat. His palms were sweaty as he picked up the handset and stabbed the call button.

"About time, Nick. That's why you don't have any clients, right? You keep them waiting on the phone all day."

"Anna, what do you want?"

"Want? What do I want? Is that any way to talk to the mother of your child?"

"Anna, it's a dog, not a child. Now look, I'm swamped. Can you tell me what you want?"

"He's not just a dog. It's bad enough that I had to raise him while you were at work. Now you don't want him to get the education he deserves."

"How much?"

"Three thousand dollars."

"Three thousand for dog training," he clenched his teeth. "Fine. I'll transfer it today." He placed the phone back in the cradle and sighed as he wiped his hands on his suit pants. Anna had divorced him to run off with some asshole personal trainer, which crushed his self-esteem. Something she had no problem exploiting at every opportunity.

It wasn't like he was in bad shape. He trained most days, watched what he ate, and tried to get enough sleep. But how was he supposed to compete with a ripped fitness instructor who worked out for a living?

His elderly assistant reappeared in his doorway. "Nick, the printer is broken again."

Well, at least he still had Magda.

"I'm going to have her number blocked," she said as he went to the law firm's common area print station.

"Thanks, Magda, but that's not necessary. Now, what's going on with the printer?"

"It's got some kind of weird glitch."

Nick checked the device's error code and identified a network problem. He opened the server cupboard and inspected the interface. A moment later, he'd rectified the problem.

The printer hummed, confirming the solution.

"If only you were as good with women as you are with computers."

"Wow, thanks Magda."

"This is for you." She thrust a printed page into his hands. "I think you should consider it." He frowned, examining the page as he returned to his desk.

Magda had printed what looked to be a social media post for a reality TV show called *The Operative*. The tagline caught his eye, and he immediately pictured himself dressed in a tuxedo, casually strolling into a casino.

"I thought you might be interested," said Magda from the door.

He laughed. "Magda, it's every balding middle-aged divorcee's fantasy. From Joe Schmo to James Bond."

"Then put in your application. If you're successful, you'll have to take three months leave without a call from that evil ex-wife, which is a holiday for me too. Then, when you win, we can go halves in the five hundred grand."

Nick typed the URL on the paper into his browser and opened the ten-page entry form. "You know what, Magda.

I'm going to do it, but if I win, I'm keeping all the cash. My days of handing all my money to women are over."

"SO FAR, we've had over nine thousand entrants. Based on your provided criteria, we've narrowed those down to a base of two hundred." A smartly dressed production consultant, Fiona Yang, gestured to a digital board displaying thousands of mug shots of potential candidates. On cue, most of them faded away, and the remaining hundreds came together into two blocks titled East Coast and West Coast.

David was impressed with the consultant. Two weeks earlier, he'd presented her with the concept documents that he and X had drafted, and already she'd set the ball rolling in precisely the direction he'd envisaged.

"Looks good." He glanced at X.

The former paramilitary officer sat wedged in a sleek white office chair dressed in a fitted suit that barely contained his massive frame. "Do we get the final sign-off?" he asked gruffly.

"Of course," answered Fiona. "I've sent David a link to our secure proprietary website. You will be able to access it easily. From there, you can approve the final hundred contestants for each pre-selection location."

"Excellent," said David.

"I'm excited about this project. It's a unique idea that has the potential to develop a great following. Thanks again for choosing us to help you put it together."

"We're very pleased to have you on the team," replied David. "Now, talk us through the pre-selection."

"Certainly. Again, I've used your direction to shape the program." She gestured to the screen, and the faces were replaced with maps. "I've got east and west coast teams preparing the locations and hiring the necessary crew. We should easily meet the timeline you've put in place. Fortunately, we have a standing relationship with a company we worked with on a similar project."

"What was the project?" asked X.

"Hunt for the Ultimate Ninja. You might have seen it."

"Nah, don't think so."

David hadn't either. He didn't watch television.

"Well, they used a lot of equipment that I think we can employ during the pre-selection. They also ran a fairly comprehensive command center setup we can utilize."

"Very efficient," said David.

"Thank you, the key component we needed to discuss was the budget for each location."

"Yes, what's the number?"

"I'm sorry?"

"How much do you need?"

She chuckled. "That's not usually how it works. I was expecting you to give me a number."

David turned to X, who shrugged. He had no idea what it cost to run something like this, and the board had given him carte blanche. "Funding isn't going to be an issue. Draw up a budget and have it sent to my assistant."

"OK, that's easy." She made a note on her smart device. "Right, next item on the agenda, the selection course. I've reached out to a company in New Zealand that specializes in this style of event. They're in the middle of drafting a concept that aligns with your requirements. I take it you would like me to negotiate the budget?"

"You got it," said David.

She made another note. "That brings us to the director.

Have you had a chance to look over the names I put forward?"

David took his phone from his jacket and found Fiona's email. His assistant had highlighted one of the five names. "Charles Chen looks good."

"I agree, he's done a lot of reality TV and will be a great fit for the project."

"Right, so that's a wrap!" exclaimed David.

"If you're happy, then I'm happy."

David rose and shook her hand before leaving the office.

"That chick's way too switched on," said X once they were in David's SUV.

"I agree. We'll part ways once the selection is over. I've had a background check run on the director. He's not going to be a problem."

"Do we need a director?"

David nodded. "It's essential that the project looks legitimate as long as possible. Don't worry; you will have complete autonomy to run the training how you see fit. Have you selected your team?"

"Yep, they're already at Camp X-Ray."

"X-Ray, isn't that the name of the prison at Guantanamo Bay?"

"Yep."

David looked sideways at the hulking operator. "We're trying to build something here, not destroy their will to live."

X shrugged. "Y'all gotta break 'em down to build 'em up."

"Come up with something more marketable."

"Fine, I'll call it The Ranch."

"Except the locals don't use that term. They call them Stations."

X rolled his eyes. "Fine, let's call it the goddamn Station."

As they left the production company, Fiona remained in the meeting room, consolidating her notes. She was updating a to-do list for her assistant when her boss appeared.

"How did it go?"

Fiona smiled. "Client is happy."

Her boss's eyes narrowed. "And you?"

"I've never had to work with people who have no idea how television production works. David seems like a smart guy, but he's no producer, and the other guy looks like a hitman."

Her boss shrugged. "Is their money good?"

"Yes, the escrow account has over a million in it."

He clapped his hands. "Well then, let's keep them happy."

JENNY GENTLY OPENED the door to her apartment and placed her gym bag on the floor. There was a broom leaning against the wall, and she grasped it in one hand as she hit the lights with the other.

"Buffalo, where are you, you little punk?"

Buffalo was her rescue cat, an athletic tabby whose mood was violently unpredictable. His favorite pastime was stalking her when she returned to their apartment.

She entered the living area and waited with the broom held high. The hairs on her neck rose as she heard a low growl from beneath the sofa.

"Buffalo, NO!" She braced herself for the onslaught.

He moved with lightning speed, a tiny tiger chasing

down its prey. She swatted him away with the broom, and he skidded across the kitchen floor. "That's enough," she scolded, waving the broom.

He sprang onto the countertop as she opened the refrigerator and found his food. His tail lashed the marble surface, and he growled again.

Tearing the lid off a serving of fish, she slid the container across the bench. "There, happy?"

He sniffed the expensive dish, tasted it, and let out a cheerful meow.

"Bipolar little shit." She stroked his fur as he ate.

Buffalo continued eating as she took her meal from the freezer. She gave his dinner a sideways glance then scowled at hers. "Yeah, you definitely eat better than me." She threw the portion in the microwave and poured herself a glass of red wine.

Five minutes later, she sat on the couch with an average lasagna and a passable glass of wine. Before starting her dinner, she checked her phone and spotted an email reply from *The Operative*. Probably a 'thanks but no thanks.'

Sipping from her glass, she tapped on the message and was surprised to see she'd been selected for a spot at the Eastern Seaboard preliminary selection in Richmond, Virginia.

"Holy shit!" She immediately called Ben and told him the news.

"That's fantastic, babe. You have to do it," he replied.

"I don't know. What if I make it through to the next round? Who would look after Buffalo?"

"You do know that cat hates women, right? He'd be much happier chilling here with me."

She laughed. "That's true."

"So, no excuses. You're going to kick ass."

"Yeah," Jen said with trepidation. "Yeah, I guess I am."

NICK FOCUSED on the timer on his phone as the numbers counted down. His heart felt like it would burst from his chest and sweat ran off the Asian American's forehead like rain, hitting the treadmill's deck as his feet slapped it relentlessly.

The timer hit zero, and the belt slowed. Gasping for air, Nick grabbed a towel from the arm of the treadmill and wiped the sweat from his forehead.

Sprint training was something he did when he'd had a bad day. It was therapeutic, pushing himself till he nearly puked. Self-punishment for allowing people to walk all over him.

His pace had slowed to a fast jog when an alert popped up on his phone. It was a message from Magda. The elderly assistant so rarely messaged him that he'd forgotten she was the only person not screened by his do not disturb.

Poking his phone where it sat on the treadmill console, he unlocked the screen to see the message.

Way to go, James Bond. You got a spot.

For a split second, he had no idea what she meant. Then he remembered the reality TV show and the ten-page application he'd submitted. Excited, he grabbed the phone. Hands slick with sweat, it slipped through his fingers onto the treadmill deck. He sidestepped as it shot under him and slammed into his garage wall.

"Damn it." He punched the stop button and dismounted, recovering the device from the concrete floor.

The Operative

Thumbing the screen multiple times, he failed to get any response from the spider-webbed screen.

"You're kidding me."

He wandered out of the garage, through his modest apartment and into his pokey office. Tossing the phone on his desk, he unlocked his laptop.

The alert from Magda was there too.

Opening his email account, he scrolled through the dozens of work messages, past one from his ex-wife and found the response from his application.

It was short, informing him that he'd been chosen for pre-selection for *The Operative*. While that didn't sound that impressive, it excited Nick. He hadn't won anything since college, much less been 'selected'. He pressed the accept button at the bottom of the email. It opened a webpage with the event's location and what to bring.

He'd never been to Virginia. Now all he had to do was convince his father to give him the day off. Even the thought of asking that made him nervous. Nope, he was going to call in sick. Not very James Bond, but at least he wouldn't have to deal with his father's scorn.

Chapter Two

VOMIT BUBBLED into Jen's mouth, but she managed to keep her lips closed and swallow it down as she dashed forward and threw herself across the line. The final siren blared, level fourteen of the beep test. Someone thrust a plastic cup of water into her hands, and she took it gratefully, using it to rinse the foul acidic taste from her mouth.

"Well done. You made it," the cheerful crew member announced. "Head over to the marquee for your next challenge."

Dragging herself to her feet, she glanced back at the contestants who hadn't been able to complete the fitness screening. The ordeal had consisted of a brutal strength circuit, Pilates session, mid-distance run, and finally, the ruthless beep test. She'd never worked so hard in her life.

Over a hundred hopefuls had turned up for the event, but over half hadn't made the grade. They now stood, pained, before a bubbly fitness instructor who thanked them for attending, while a film crew captured their anguish.

The Operative

Meanwhile, those who had passed the fitness test were ushered into a large tent.

A camera and a microphone ambushed her as she entered.

"How are you feeling?" asked an interviewer.

"Exhausted," she managed. "One of the hardest physical activities I've ever done."

She contemplated pushing past but remembered this was a reality TV show selection. They would be looking for contestants who were engaging and charismatic.

"There was a point where I didn't think I would make it. So I dug deep and managed to get across the line."

"Any particular motivators?"

"Yeah, my nephews. I'm doing it for them."

"Great stuff. You better get going," said the producer. "We'll catch up with you if you pass the next phase."

The words didn't seem like much. But, the 'if' hit home. Throughout the day, Jenny noticed that many younger, fitter, better-looking contestants had been breezing through the fitness test. She'd barely scraped through, and no doubt, it would get much worse.

Tentatively, she joined the others in a briefing area and waited for instructions.

"Hopefully, that's the last of the beep tests. That nearly did me in," said the man next to her. Asian, middle-aged, and balding, he had an easy smile and friendly eyes.

"Glad I wasn't the only one," she replied.

"Not many people our age made it through. Hopefully, life experience can prevail over social media reach and rock-hard abs. My name's Nick."

"I'm Jen, a pleasure to meet you, Nick."

"You as nervous as I am?"

She nodded. "God knows what they're going to do to us next."

"CAMERA TWO. Zoom in on those oldies at the back. They look terrified." Charles Chen, *The Operative's* newly appointed director, issued his instructions via radio from the control center. "David, we're getting some great footage here. It's going to come together nicely."

Chen and a team of technicians were monitoring the footage from three roaming camera crews in the comfort of a purpose-built semi-trailer. David sat observing the proceedings from a plush couch opposite a wall of monitors.

The lawyer had run a full background check on Chen, and the lightly built Asian had come up clean. His family was from Taiwan; parents emigrated in the late eighties. He was born in ninety-four, attended good schools, and cut his teeth shooting action TV commercials in a top advertising firm. When he went out on his own, he achieved limited success, until he got a break directing an adventure reality TV show. Not that David cared about any of that. More importantly, Charles Chen's parents were deceased, and he had no partner or siblings. He was a loner.

"The next part may not be as interesting," said David.

Charles glanced at his run sheet. "Right, the psychological profiling and intelligence testing. We'll get some facial close-ups and chase down some interviews later. The audience will be more interested in the contestants' feelings than anything else."

"But, we can see the results live?" he asked.

"Andy?"

One of the technicians gestured to a screen where each contestant was listed. "As they input their answers on the tablets, their scores will update here. A green bar indicates success, and a red failure."

"Makes sense."

The door to the trailer swung open, and X stepped inside. The Chief Instructor wore his standard heavy-duty tan cargo pants and a T-shirt declaring *Coffee or Die*. Accordingly, he held two cups in one of his mammoth hands. He spotted David and passed him one.

"X, I want to introduce you to our director, Charles Chen," said David.

"People call me Chuck. So, your name's Ex? Like as in ex-wife?" The director offered his hand.

David snorted into his coffee.

The big man scowled, ignoring the handshake. "It's just X."

"Ah, like the letter. Right. Got it. So, how do you fit in?"

"He's a producer and the Chief Instructor. You do exactly as he says," said David.

Chuck frowned. "That's not how this works. I'm used to having full creative control."

"X isn't going to get in your way. He's here for authenticity," said David.

"Right, so you're the real deal," asked Chuck.

X smiled. "You do your thing, and I'll do mine."

"Cool, cool. Oh, and for future reference, I drink quad shot lattes." The director gave X a cheeky wink.

"Can you drink that through a straw?" X asked deadpan.

Chuck's brow rose. "Huh, straw?" He glanced at David, who clenched his fist and mimed a punch to the jaw.

Chuck swallowed and turned back to the screens. "I'll get the coffee next time."

"How are our numbers looking on the psychometrics?" asked X.

David gestured to the screen. Most of the names had green marks alongside them. "So far, so good."

"Let's see how many get through the challenge course," said X. "Then we'll know what we've got to work with."

THE TOWER WAS at least three stories tall, with a wooden wall up one side against which a thick black rope hung. "I have to climb over that?" Jenny asked a male twenty-something fitness instructor.

"No, you climb the wall and then jump down."

"Jump?"

"That's what I said. Once you're back down, I'll give you the code."

"Can I look at the other side?"

The kid shook his head and pointed to the top of the tower.

Jenny moved across and grasped the rope. High above, she could see the top of the wooden wall. Remote cameras focused on her, attached to the frame.

Grasping the rope with both hands kept them from shaking. She swallowed and started pulling herself up the rope. Her muscles screamed with agony, and she kicked against the wall, taking some of the strain from her forearms and grip.

Halfway up, the only thing on her mind was fighting the urge to let go of the rope. The muscles in her arms had nothing left in them as she reached the top. She got a leg over the ledge and almost fell backward before rolling onto a narrow platform.

Her heart raced as she lay on her side, staring at the drop over the other side. Her stomach lurched as she rose to her knees and peered over the edge.

The bed of foam blocks looked like it was ten stories down. Jenny gripped a rail and stood as the instructor yelled from below.

"You've got two options. You can climb down the ladder and walk away from the competition. Or, you take the leap of faith."

So far, she'd completed tasks that ranged from navigating a maze blindfolded to folding an origami flower. Each time she finished, she'd earned a code. The drop below was her second last sequence to complete the challenge course.

She fought back panic as her legs nearly collapsed from under her.

"The ladder is right there," the instructor yelled.

Jenny heard the conceit in his voice.

Fuck you, she thought as she turned to one of the cameras. "I'm doing this for my nephews." She gripped the rail, took a deep breath, and let her body drop forward, rotating so that she landed back first into the bed of rubber squares.

"Well done!" yelled the PT from the side as he reached in and grabbed her hand. "That was awesome."

Jenny's heart pounded as he scrambled over the pit's edge and swung back to solid earth.

"Here's your code." He handed her a slip of paper. "You better get going."

Elation was quickly replaced with exhaustion as she ran through the parklands. She spotted a park bench through a gap in the trees and headed for it. Easing herself onto the wooden slats, she checked her watch. She had less than twenty minutes to reach her last challenge, complete it and make it to the finish line.

Examining her challenge map, she estimated it was at least another five hundred meters to her next task, then six hundred back to the finish. There was no way she could make it!

"Jenny!"

The voice startled her, seemingly coming from thick bushes. A second later, a figure emerged. It was the middle-aged man she'd met before the psychometric testing. She struggled to remember his name. "Nick?"

"Yeah, how's it going?" He made his way to the bench, looking worse for wear with a torn shirt and a coating of mud.

"Not good," she admitted. "I'm not going to make my last challenge at the lake."

"I just came from that. It's a hard one." He paused. "I'm in the same boat. I can't get to point eleven and back to the finish."

Jenny looked at her map. "I've just come from there."

There was an awkward silence.

Nick turned over his map and reread the rules. "There's nothing here about collaboration. It just says that contestants are to complete the activity on their own. It could be argued that we're achieving that as long as we cross the finish line apart."

Jenny frowned. "Are you a lawyer?"

Nick laughed. "As a matter of fact. Look, we've got nothing to lose. We're not going to make the timings as it is. You can be sure that the millennial crowd will have gotten them all done."

Jenny nodded. Fit athletes had passed her more than once in the last few hours. "What if the codes are different?"

Nick shook his head. "You've seen the kids running this thing. They'll be different for each activity, but that's it. Trust me, I know human nature."

Jenny checked her watch. She had even less time now. There was no way they were going to complete the task. Nick was right, there was only one option. She passed him the slip of paper from the wall. "This is your last one."

He did the same, and she scribbled the combination into the box on her map.

"I'll give you a head start," said Nick. "See you at the finish."

DESPITE THE FANTASTIC spread of food that adorned the marquee, Jenny could only bring herself to drink a few cups of energy drink.

Numerous other contestants who'd completed the challenge course were making short work of plates overflowing with BBQ meats and salads. Spotting Nick among the crowd, she shot him a nod.

She joined a small group of contestants gathered in one corner of the marquee.

"That was so much fun," said a tall African American woman whose figure suggested she could be a professional athlete. "The tower was a blast."

"Yeah, that kicked ass," said another fit-looking guy.

"Did you jump?" the first woman asked Jenny.

She nodded.

"Good for you," said the fit guy. "How did you go with

the lake? I see you managed to stay dry. What was the secret?"

"Ah-"

"Everyone listen up!" One of the organizers had climbed onto a stage with a clipboard in hand.

"I'm going read out a list of names. If yours isn't called, you haven't made the cut and can go."

"No fanfare. That's brutal," said the fit guy.

"Victoria Statten," announced the organizer.

"Hell yeah," said the African American athlete, punching the air.

"Mark Duncan."

The fit guy snapped his fingers. "Nailed it."

The organizer announced another dozen names. Jenny and Nick were not among them. She felt an overwhelming sense of disappointment, not only in her inability to complete the challenge course but also that she resorted to cheating in a futile attempt to get across the line.

"Well done to our fourteen. Unfortunately, the rest of you haven't been selected," said the organizer.

Jen lowered her head and joined the other disappointed competitors exiting the marquee.

"Hey, we gave it a red hot go." It was Nick.

She smiled at him and they angled away from the others, toward the parking lot.

"I guess they're going with a younger crowd," he said.

"Or they know we cheated."

"Jennifer Murphy, Nicholas Lui." The voice came from behind.

They turned and saw it was one of the organizers.

"Wait up." The man caught up with them, two clipboards in hand. "Do you know why you didn't make the cut?"

Jenny shrugged. "Because we cheated? Because we didn't complete the course? What does it matter?"

He considered her response. "They told me to ask how badly you want this."

"Who?" asked Nick.

"The producers. Technically, you broke the rules, but no one else had the balls to try that." He handed a clipboard to each of them. "This is an NDA. If you want in, sign and hand it to the team in the tent. You've got ten minutes to consider it."

Unknown to Jenny and Nick, they were being watched. A remote camera on the roof of the control truck zoomed in on them, and a microphone on the organizer's shirt picked up their voices.

"Why these two?" asked X as he watched the feed.

"They're relatable. They're not ripped cross-fitters like half of the others," replied Chuck. "They'll broaden the show's appeal to middle-aged Americans."

"They won't make it."

"That's not the point. They'll add drama, emotion, and character to the series. Trust me, they're going to be a real drawcard."

X turned to David and tilted his head, gesturing for them to leave the control trailer.

"They couldn't even finish the challenge course," he said when they were out of earshot.

"Does that bother you? I mean, they both scored well in every other facet of selection. They're not the most impressive physical specimens, but that could be good. Those two can blend almost anywhere. They're as vanilla as they come."

"They cheated."

"Come on, big guy. Don't be so naive. That's exactly why we want them."

X shrugged. "Hey, it's your rodeo. If you want to waste two slots, that's on you."

The door to the trailer opened, and Chuck appeared, grinning. "They all signed the NDAs. We've got a full cast."

"Fuck," said X. "There's no turning back now."

David slapped his shoulder. "Onward and upward, old friend."

———

"ARE YOU KIDDING ME?" Ben yelled at the top of his lungs. "You made it?"

"Keep your voice down." Jenny glanced nervously around their office. "I'm not supposed to tell anyone until it goes to air."

"I knew you'd get through. I knew it." He sat on the edge of her desk. "So, when does filming start?"

"I fly out Thursday. Are you OK to look after Buffalo for a few months?"

"Of course. No problems. Oh my God, this is so exciting. Where are you flying to?"

"I can't say."

"For how long?"

"Up to three months. It depends on how far I get."

"So, I guess Buffalo and I will be roomies for a while."

"Is that OK? It might not be long."

Ben winked at her. "Babe, you're going to kill it."

———

NICK FINISHED TYPING a short out-of-office message and took a moment to reread it.

Apologies, I am currently out of the office on extended leave. I anticipate returning to work in approximately three months. If your case is urgent, please contact my assistant Magda Wolf, and she will ensure that another attorney reaches out as soon as possible.

He hit submit and closed his laptop. Taking one last look around his office, he tried to think of anything he might want to take.

Nope, nothing in the tiny space would be useful for the challenge ahead. He assumed the show would be an arduous experience. That thought caused him a moment of concern. He hadn't put a lot of thought into this venture. He'd been caught up in being accepted and hadn't considered what it might entail. The only information provided was to report to JFK airport with carry-on luggage and an in-date passport.

"Extended leave! Who the hell approved that?" his father bellowed from the doorway. "Because the last time I checked, I didn't approve of any leave."

"I'm a partner, I don't need your approval to take leave."

"For the weekend. Not for three months."

"Yeah, well, I'm sure one of the associates can pick up the slack. That's all you've had me doing." Nick rose from his desk and stepped past his father. "I'll see you when I get back."

"If you walk out of that door, you might not have a job here when you get back."

Nick laughed. "Good luck finding someone to work for

the peanuts you pay me." He smiled at his assistant. "Magda, I'll see you when I get back."

Nick felt elated as he exited the building and made for his car. He hadn't even started this journey and was already feeling more confident.

"Nicholas Lui!" His ex-wife's voice evaporated the confidence.

The platinum blonde stood beside his BMW, dressed in figure-hugging active wear that left little to his imagination. "Why haven't you been answering my calls?"

"I've been swamped." He unlocked his car. "I'm on my way to a crucial meeting."

"Without your briefcase?"

"I've already emailed the documents. What do you want, Anna?"

She cocked her head seductively. "I've got an amazing investment opportunity."

"How much?"

"Only thirty-five thousand."

He opened the car door and climbed in. "I'm heading away for a while."

"Where are you going?"

He turned and looked her in the eye as he started the engine. "That's none of your business." Slamming the door, he put the car in reverse and backed out of his park. He gave her a wave as he drove off smoothly. Glancing in the mirror, he saw her standing with her hands on her hips. Yep, a month or two away was exactly what he needed.

Chapter Three

THE AIRCRAFT LURCHED sideways as Jenny clutched a vomit bag and prayed they'd land safely. She released a sigh as the wheels thumped onto the tarmac and the jet's reverse thrust roared.

"Folks, welcome to Queenstown," transmitted the pilot. Sorry about the bumps on the way in, but this is one of the most challenging approaches to an international airport. Thanks again for flying with us, and enjoy the fantastic weather."

She stared out the window at the sheer mountains towering over the airport. The jagged peaks looked like they'd been dusted with powdered sugar. It had taken two days and three separate flights to get here but the views alone made it all worthwhile.

The transition through immigration and customs occurred without incident, and within fifteen minutes she was heading for the bus stop designated in her instructions.

There were already over a dozen contestants waiting. She recognized some of them from the challenge course.

Nick was there, along with Mark and Victoria. Surprisingly, several new faces looked to be around her age. They were all carrying the same rubberized carry-on backpack that she'd been issued with her instructions. She was amazed at how much she'd been able to stuff into it.

Nick spotted her and approached with a smile. "How about that flight?" He mimed vomiting. "I nearly lost my lunch."

She laughed. "Me too, but how beautiful are those mountains? I can't believe we're in Queenstown. I've always wanted to come here."

"It's awesome," said Nick.

A bus arrived, and the driver stepped out holding a tablet. He checked names as people climbed aboard. Soon, they were driving alongside a brilliant blue lake on their way to an unknown destination.

"You nervous?" Nick asked as they drove past expensive hotels and hillside mansions.

"It hasn't set in yet. It feels like some crazy adventure," she replied from the seat beside him.

"That's because it is," he said. "And we've got no idea what comes next."

They gazed out the window at the mountains looming ominously on the other side of the lake.

Jenny eavesdropped on the conversations around her. Younger, fitter, and more photogenic contestants were boasting of their exploits, social media following, and how much they were going to 'crush it.'

Here she was, a middle-aged insurance agent, with zero social media and no skills that could translate into success on a reality TV show. The more she thought about it, the more she realized she had no place on the bus.

They arrived at their destination with a hiss of air

brakes and a curt announcement from the driver. As Jenny exited the bus, she saw they'd arrived at a marina where a luxury cruiser was nestled against the pier.

"Gather around, team." A tall bald man addressed them from where he stood alongside the gangplank to the boat. Dressed in combat pants and a maroon hoodie, with a khaki wrap around his neck, he spoke in a British accent. "My name is Peter, and I will be running the next few days of activities. I'd ask that you board the vessel in an orderly fashion, and we will get underway."

Jenny spotted a camera crew on the rear deck of the boat. They were filming each contestant as they boarded. She maintained a poker face as she crossed the gangplank onto the *Pacific Gemm*.

Once aboard, the gangplank was withdrawn, and the deck vibrated as powerful engines pushed it away from the marina and onto the lake.

"This is Lake Wakatipu, the third largest body of freshwater in New Zealand," announced Peter. Our progress marks the beginning of a significant journey for all of you. This is the start of *The Operative*.

Several contestants whooped, and they all started clapping and cheering. Jenny figured there were at least two dozen contestants crammed onto the deck.

"I now invite you inside to meet some key personalities taking you on this journey." He gestured to an open sliding door leading to the upper deck.

Up the stairs was a spacious lounge with a bar in one corner and expansive windows providing sweeping views of the mountains. Jenny saw four men standing alongside the bar, dressed similarly to Peter, who joined them.

"This is my team." He gestured to three men. "Dave, Craig and Edward. Together we have over forty years of elite military service. We will be running your activities over the next 48 hours."

Jenny swallowed. The veterans looked hard.

Peter gestured to the other man standing with the group. He was Asian and didn't have the same military bearing as the others. "Team, this is Charles Chen, your director."

The group clapped and cheered as Chen stepped forward.

"Hey, everyone, welcome to the show. Look, I'm not going to lie to you. For some of you, this will be the only interaction we have. But, for others, I will be closer to you than your mothers. Together we will make some of the most compelling viewing in reality TV history."

The contestants clapped again.

"Unfortunately, only ten of you will be making that journey. Which means we need to determine which of you will be going home."

There was silence in the group as Chen stepped back and Peter stepped up again. "Team, welcome to *The Crucible*, twenty-four hours of intense activity designed to weed out the weak and send them packing." He paused for effect, allowing the camera crew to scan their faces for reactions. "But, before we get started, I need to run through some administration to keep you safe out there. Let's start with what could go wrong, and trust me, plenty can go wrong."

"THEY'RE ALMOST IN POSITION," said X as he lowered a pair of binoculars and stepped away from the window of the alpine cabin. He and three hand-picked instructors used it as their base while they covertly monitored *The Crucible*.

Once Peter and his men had completed the culling activity, it would be up to X and his team to train the remaining ten.

"Where'd you find testicle head?" one of them asked in a thick Scottish accent. Steve, a former Royal Marine Commando, looked every bit the unarmed combat and weapons specialist he was. Medium height with a lean build, he sported short dirty blond hair and a permanent look of bemusement. In his early forties, he'd been working on and off with X for ten years.

"Knew you'd hate him. Peter's a former para and runs a local event company," said X.

"Bet you he's a Rupert," said Steve. "They all sound like bloody royalty."

The only woman in the room laughed. Bianca, an athletic brunette, was dressed in drab-colored outdoor gear, her lengthy hair tied up in a bun. Like Steve, she was a veteran, former military human intelligence operative turned CIA field agent. "He even looks a bit like that bald prince."

"Prince William," said the other occupant of the cabin. Raj Edwards was a British citizen of Indian descent. Tall and swarthy his most discerning feature was an immaculately trimmed mustache. The team 'geek' Raj was responsible for everything technical, including the digital radios and secure tablets they would use over the next 24 hours. He was sitting on a sofa, pen in mouth, computer on lap.

"Yeah, that's the one," Bianca replied.

"OK," said Raj. "Everyone's set up and online. You can all review each of the candidates. There are boxes for attributes and sections for comments."

X turned from the window. "Make sure you add comments. I need context when we take the final list to David."

"What about Prince Scrotum and his team?" asked Steve. "Are they capturing data too?"

"They're using a separate interface. We'll take their recommendations onboard, but this team will decide who progresses."

"Except David has the final say?" enquired Bianca.

"He and I," said X.

"Cool." She shrugged on her day pack. "I'm going to head out to my station."

"Give us a radio check on the way," said X.

"Will do. See you all tomorrow." She exited the cabin, leaving the three men alone.

"She's a good hand," Steve said as he checked his gear.

"I don't work with mouth breathers," replied X.

"Thank fuck. Right, I'm off too," said Steve. "See you when I see you."

X took one last look through his binoculars before stashing them in his pack and slinging it over his shoulder. "We all good here, Raj?"

"Yeah, mate." He closed his laptop. "I'm going to head to *The Station* and work on the setup."

"Right on." X left the cabin and walked along a narrow trail into a beech forest. He wasn't three hundred yards from the cabin when his phone rang; it was David.

"We underway?" the lawyer asked.

X could see the boat through the trees. Far below, it was rounding a rocky point with a rigid-hull inflatable boat (RHIB) in its wake.

"They'll be hitting the water any minute now."

The Operative

A LIGHT BREEZE caressed the New Zealand flag that fluttered above the *Pacific Gemm* as the contestants gathered on the rear deck. Jenny noticed that there was a black rubber-hulled boat tailing the yacht. A cameraman stood in the bow, and several men dressed in wet suits were also onboard.

Peter had positioned himself directly below the flag, his khaki checkered scarf wrapped tight. "There are only ten positions available," he said dramatically. "You're going to have to want it, bad."

As he spoke, the yacht rounded a headland and cut its engines. It glided into a glassy-looking bay and came to a stop.

"If you look at the shoreline, you'll see a flag," said Peter.

Jenny spotted it on the beach in front of thick trees. There was a figure standing alongside it. She estimated that distance from the boat as about three hundred yards.

"That flag is the entry point to *The Crucible*," he added. "Get to it."

Confusion rippled through the thirty contestants as they watched the RHIB cruise toward the shore and stopped about halfway.

"We have to swim," said Nick. "I'm not a great swimmer."

"We better get started then," said Jenny as she shrugged out of her polar fleece jumper and stuffed it into her backpack.

There was a splash as one of the contestants dove into the water.

"Should I take off my boots?" Nick asked as he followed Jenny's example.

"No. They won't hold that much water and you'll need

them on the beach. Just put your bulky stuff in your pack. It's waterproof, will give you some buoyancy."

"Good idea."

There were more splashes as other contestants jumped into the water.

"We gotta go," said Jenny. "Use the pack like a kickboard."

A dozen contestants were still on the *Gemm's* rear deck, in various states of undress as they prepared for the swim.

Jenny sat on the aft deck and lowered her feet into the lake. Ice-cold water flowed into her boots, and she suppressed a cry. Glancing toward the shore, she saw the first swimmers near the beach. They needed to get a move on. Dropping into the water, she hugged her pack tightly.

A sharp exhale sounded from Nick as he slid into the water alongside her.

"We need to get going," she said, kicking hard as she clung to the pack.

She focused on the distant shoreline and tried not to think about what could be lurking in the water below.

"Holy crap, it's cold," yelled Nick.

"Kick harder," she replied. "It will keep you warmer."

"Or swim faster," added Veronica as she swam effortlessly past them.

Jenny focused on the beach and saw the first swimmers emerging from the water. "Come on, Nick. We can do this." Glancing over her shoulder, she saw all the contestants had entered the water. The RHIB cruised a short distance away with rescue swimmers casually watching their progress.

Crippling pain shot through Jenny's right calf as the muscle cramped. She fought the urge to cry out, and let the leg hang, swimming with one arm and one leg.

Nick drew up alongside her and spotted that she was struggling. "You OK?"

"Yeah," she gasped. Her left leg sank as her forward momentum slowed. The pain was almost unbearable, and she clung to her pack, struggling to stay afloat.

Then, when it seemed she was about to slip under the water, her foot kicked a rock. Lowering her legs, she bounced forward off the bottom. "Nick, it's shallow."

They made faster progress wading than kickboarding with their packs. After three more minutes, she emerged from the lake's icy grasp and charged up the rocky beach.

"I can't feel my toes," said Nick as he stumbled, laboring for breath.

"We need to keep moving." Jenny glanced over her shoulder and saw that she and Nick were some of the last to leave the lake. They'd started poorly in an exercise designed to weed out the weak.

"You need to get going," gasped Nick. "You can't let me hold you back."

"I'm not going to leave you behind," she said, rubbing her hands together.

"Hey, this isn't a team exercise. It's everyone for themselves," he managed. "Plus, I'm pretty good out of the water. I'll be hot on your heels once I get my breath back."

"Get a move on, people!" yelled an instructor from the beach's edge. "This ain't no hike. You have to want this."

"Go!" said Nick.

Jenny slung her backpack and dashed up the beach, pumping her arms to get the blood flowing.

"Follow the tape into the woods," directed the instructor. He winked as she ran past. "And have fun."

Chapter Four

THE TRAIL into the forest was marked with white tape. It was tied to branches on either side of the narrow path. The first hundred yards or so were damp from the contestants before her. She knew she'd be hard-pressed to catch them. They were younger, fitter, and had a head start.

A gradual incline soon got Jenny's heart racing and her body warm. She followed the track through a muddy tunnel under a road and into an old-growth forest. The path wove around gnarled old trees, over slippery roots and moss-covered rocks as she climbed higher.

Despite her heart pounding and water squirting from her boots, she was enjoying the run. It had become more of a fast shuffle. The mountain air was crisp, and the peaty smell of the forest felt clean and renewing. It was precisely the sort of place she would choose for hiking.

The marked track led her up a ridgeline and turned into a narrow valley with a stream running through the trees. At one stage, she heard what she thought might be mountain bikers, glimpsing a flash of color through the trees as they ripped down a separate track.

Her legs were burning as the trail finally emerged from the edge of the tree line into a clearing. The track leveled off, and a small lake appeared as she broke into a run. At the far end of the lake she spotted another flag and what looked to be an activity station.

As she got closer she noticed a contestant standing with a show official and camera crew. There was a stack of heavy-looking crates by the water. In the distance, she could see two figures struggling to carry a crate.

"Oh, it would have to be you," said the waiting contestant. It was Veronica. The athletic African American stood alongside the boxes, hands on her hip, looking like she'd stepped straight from an active wear Instagram post. "Get the other end of the crate."

"The next part of the *Crucible* is a store's carry," said the instructor. "Working in pairs, you need to move one of the boxes to the next activity station. You'll note there is a trauma tag on each crate. If the tag turns red, you fail."

"Let's roll," said Veronica.

"No problem." She grasped the rope handle opposite and hefted the box to her waist. It wasn't overly heavy, but it was awkward. "I'm Jenny, by the way." She ignored the film crew as they angled in on the pair.

"Veronica. Now, let's get a hustle on."

They made their way, side-by-side, down the lake until the path narrowed and forced them to carry the crate single file. Jenny led, walking backward along the trail with Veronica facing her. She could see other contestants catching up over the athletic woman's shoulder.

"Can't you go faster?" asked Veronica.

"I'll try." She shuffled her feet. Her heel caught a rock,

and a moment later she was falling backward. She caught the crate in her lap, taking the impact on her tailbone.

"Fuck, check the tag," snapped Veronica.

"Yeah, I'm fine," Jenny said through clenched teeth.

Her partner checked the label. "It's green. We need to keep going."

Jenny slid the crate off her lap and stood. "I'll carry it behind me. It might work better."

"Anything would be better than this."

Turning, Jenny crouched and grasped the handle with both hands behind her back. "Ready to lift."

"Go."

Her shoulders screamed in agony as she hefted the box. She could feel it shoving her forward as Veronica pushed. Stumbling, she barely managed to stay on her feet as they moved forward.

For the first hundred yards, the new technique worked well. However, after that, Jenny started to lose feeling in her hands. She also had to force her shoulders back to stop the box from slamming into her bruised tailbone, which was agonizing.

As they crested a slight rise, Jenny spotted another pair struggling with their crate a short distance ahead. "Can we swap?" The pain was almost unbearable.

"Let's keep going. We can catch the guys ahead."

Jenny shook her head. "I can't hold it for much longer. I need to rest my shoulders."

"Fine. We can change."

They lowered the box, and Jenny moved aside as Veronica stepped in and took her position. "Come on. Let's get going."

Jenny wiggled her fingers and slapped her thighs. "Give me a second."

The Operative

"Hurry up."

She grasped the handle with both hands and hefted it to waist height.

Veronica dragged her up the hill as she struggled to keep up. It took them less than two minutes to catch and overtake the pair ahead, who'd pulled off the track to rest. Jenny met their gazes with a smile and a cheery hello.

Right as she felt she couldn't go any further, they crested a slight rise revealing another flag and what looked to be a rest station. As they approached, she saw they were somehow one of the first five pairs to arrive. The contestants were gathered around a trestle table, helping themselves to chopped fruit and water.

Peter was standing at the flag as they stumbled in. "Put your box in the stack and get some water. The next phase will start once everyone has arrived."

Jenny grabbed a bottle and a piece of apple, dropped her pack and sat on a boulder. Scanning the other nine contestants, she noticed a few familiar faces. Mark, the fit guy from the selection, was there with a blonde woman whose name she couldn't remember.

"Hey, you're doing pretty well," said another of the contestants, a tall steely-eyed Caucasian male with tattoos on his arms. "First of the older crew to make it in."

Jenny smiled politely as the man turned his attention to another contestant. Older crew, she thought. He had to be around the same age as her, but she was somehow classified as senior because she was a woman. She stewed on the comment when she noticed another pair approaching the finish. As they came into view she saw that one of them was Nick. The lawyer looked in much better spirits than when she'd left him on the beach.

Over the next ten minutes, the remaining contestants

arrived at the checkpoint. After the last pair arrived, Peter climbed onto the crates and issued their next challenge.

"Your job now is to construct a base camp from the equipment in these boxes. However, you're not allowed to talk. This is a test of your problem-solving skills and your nonverbal communication. Get to it."

IT TOOK the contestants two hours to construct the massive tent from the contents of the crates they'd carried up the hill. Tempers had flared, but eventually they'd bumbled through under the watchful eye of the Englishman and his tablet-wielding instructors.

When they finished, one of Peter's men led them to a nearby field where he ran them through a forty-five minute physical training session. They clambered through streams, crawled through mud and climbed over walls until they were utterly exhausted.

Returning to the tent, they found that Peter and his men had been busy. They'd decked it out with chairs, a screen, plastic gear cases and a row of packs along the back wall.

"Right, so this is the activity's instructional component, "Peter declared once they were seated. "Agents are selected based on their ability to retain, analyze and assimilate information. You will receive procedures, skills and data over the next few hours. It will be vital for survival when you're out in the field. I suggest you pay close attention. The first thing you are going to be taught is navigation."

Jenny, Nick, and the other contestants were bombarded with information for three hours. They started with basic map-reading skills and progressed to wilderness survival and first aid. Then, crates were dragged to the front of the makeshift classroom and opened.

Jenny had never handled a firearm before. The limit of her knowledge was distinguishing between a pistol and a rifle.

"This is an M4 carbine," announced the instructor, holding a sleek black weapon before him. "Also known as an AR15, it is one of the most common firearms worldwide. Today, I will teach you how to handle this weapon safely, and strip and assemble it. Pay close attention, you will need this information."

A quarter of an hour later Jenny was handling a weapon for the first time.

"It's not going to bite you," said an instructor.

Tentatively she took the weapon from atop an equipment case and accidentally depressed a button, dropping the magazine to the ground.

"I'm sorry," she mumbled as she made to recover it.

"Forget the magazine. Clear the weapon," said the instructor.

Jenny froze.

"Cocking handle to the rear, check the chamber," he prompted.

She fumbled through the actions and declared the weapon 'clear' in a soft voice.

"Now strip the weapon."

Her fingers felt like sausages as she attempted to push out the retaining pin behind the pistol grip.

"Not great under pressure, are you?" observed the instructor.

Jenny bit her lip and separated the lower part of the rifle and placed it on the equipment case. Then, she fumbled with the cocking handle and bolt, trying to remove them from the top half of the gun.

"Time's up. Everybody back in their seats," bellowed Peter from the front of the room.

Jenny sighed as she placed the piece of the weapon she was holding next to the rest of the rifle.

"You better partner up with someone who's got a clue," said the instructor as she turned to join the others.

"Listen up," said Peter. "You're about to enter the final challenge of the *Crucible*."

"THE MOUNTAINS WILL TAKE every opportunity to kill you," Peter told them. "Terrain and weather are by far the highest risk components of this test."

Jenny wasn't sure if the mission briefing was intended to strike fear into her soul or reassure her that the team had considered every risk.

Each contestant was issued a field pack containing 'contingency' supplies. They'd been instructed that they could use items and consume water carried in the side pouches but breaking the seals on the emergency package within the main compartment could only occur if their lives were in danger. Peter had shown them what was inside: energy rations, a first aid kit, an emergency beacon, and a bright orange shelter bag. Their personal gear bags would be left in the tent.

Jenny had carried the pack from where they were lined against the tent wall back to her seat. It wasn't light, only adding to the dread of what was to come.

"Right. In a moment, we will issue your maps and course routes, but first, there are certain cultural issues you need to be aware of. You will be operating in the lands of a tribe known as the *Hill Stalkers*. Now, while they're known to be openly hostile toward intruders, they operate under a strict code that, if followed, will keep you safe. If you encounter *Hill Stalkers*, you must ensure you do the following." He read a list of ten rules ranging from maintaining eye contact with the leader, no matter what, to constantly referring to oneself in the third person.

"How will we remember them all?" whispered the competitor sitting alongside.

"Link all the rules together into a story," she replied. "Recite it over and over."

"Makes sense."

"Team, that concludes the brief. Grab a partner and move to the table at the rear of the tent, where my colleague will issue your data pack. Get moving."

The contestants leaped into action, grabbing partners and sprinting to the rear of the tent. Jenny noticed the younger 'athletes' had already formed teams and the other middle-aged contestants had joined forces. No one was making a move in her direction. She felt like she was back in high school and was once again the kid picked last in every team.

"Come on, let's go." Nick grasped her elbow. "We can't give them a head start."

They rushed to the back of the tent, checked their names, and were issued an envelope. Then they hefted their packs and headed outside to plan their attack.

Nick tore open the envelope and removed a laminated map, positioning it so they could study the route.

"We've got to reach all the checkpoints and the endpoint," he explained.

"That's seriously steep terrain," Jenny observed.

"Yeah, we're going to have to get going." Nick checked his watch. "We've only got a few hours of light left. We want to get up that first hill before it gets dark."

Jenny rummaged in the side pouch of her pack and found a headlamp. "At least we won't be bumbling around in the dark."

Nick shrugged into his pack. "Something tells me that's the least of our worries."

Chapter Five

JENNY SET the pace as the pair followed a path away from base camp. They soon lost sight of the other teams as they set off on their routes to different destinations.

"Let's stick to formed trails as much as we can," said Nick. "Going off-road might look faster, but you're more likely to roll an ankle or get lost."

"Makes sense," said Jenny. She was happy that Nick had offered to take the lead on navigation. Aside from Google Maps, it wasn't something she had much experience with. "Where did you learn to read a map?" she asked as the trail turned into a steep valley.

"My dad made me join the scouts."

"But you didn't enjoy it?"

He laughed. "No, I wasn't exactly the outdoor type. But I did learn a few useful things. I can't start a fire with two sticks but I can tie a few knots and navigate."

"Well, I know how to sew and bake cookies." She laughed. "I grew up with my mom in the city."

"No father?"

"He left when I was young."

"Siblings?"

"Just me. How about you?"

"Mom and Dad are still together. I had an older brother, but he died when I was young. I don't remember him."

They fell silent as the track doubled back on itself, slowly climbing a steep grassy slope.

Every few steps Jenny would glance out over Lake Wakatipu and use the beauty of the landscape to distract from her burning leg muscles.

"Gorgeous isn't it," said Nick.

"So good to be out of the office," she replied.

"Tell me about it. What do you do in yours?"

"I'm an insurance claim investigator. You're a lawyer, right?"

"Yeah. Your days must be interesting. I mean, people try all sorts of crazy ass fraud, right?"

"My team primarily deals with storm damage. Pretty dry. Pardon the pun. What kind of law do you practice?"

"I work for my father's firm. We mainly handle family law, divorces and the like. Rather boring, to be perfectly frank."

"So we've both escaped the mundane and thrown caution to the wind," managed Jenny between breaths. The climb was growing steeper by the minute.

"Finally doing my own thing," mumbled Nick. "Hey, we're about halfway. Let's have a quick break."

As he checked the map, Jenny sipped from her water bottle and gazed west to where the sun sank behind a distant mountain range. The view was breathtaking.

"Our first checkpoint is along the ridge at the top of this hill," said Nick. "We should get there before it gets dark." He passed her the map.

Jenny could see the points on the map, but the terrain looked utterly alien.

"I find it easier if I orientate the map to the ground. The sun sets in the west, here, so you can use that."

She rotated the map. "How do you know which part relates to the right piece of ground?"

"You've got to read the contour lines. They join all the areas of the same height. Imagine slicing an apple, taking away every second slice, and looking at it from the top. The cuts are the lines."

"Oh, that makes sense." She found the track snaking its way back and forth over thin brown lines. Glancing at the ground, she could correlate the map to the terrain. She handed the map back to him. "We better get going."

It took them another twenty minutes to reach the top of the spur line, where they stopped to don their headlamps as the last faint glow of the sun disappeared from the horizon. Then they set off along the ridge toward the first checkpoint.

"Clear skies," said Nick as they approached a rocky outcrop that resembled a medieval fortress. "Visibility will be good, but it will get cold. We're looking for something on the southern side of this feature."

They followed a narrow footpath around the craggy outcrop and almost ran into a small camp.

One of the instructors was sitting in a folding chair with a light at his feet.

Jenny immediately spotted a tarpaulin with what looked to be a disassembled assault rifle on one half and a gun she didn't recognize on the other.

"I was about to send out a search party," said the instructor. "Right, your task is twofold. You must disassemble the AK47, and the other must reassemble the M4," he paused, "while blindfolded."

Jenny turned to Nick. "I'm not going to able to pull that other one apart."

He shrugged. "Well, I guess it's up to me then. You tackle the M4."

The instructor handed her a pair of blacked-out ski goggles. She knelt on the tarp in front of the disassembled weapon as Nick did the same with the AK. She took one last look at the parts and slipped on the goggles. She couldn't see a thing.

"The clock starts when I say go. Remember, the more time you spend here, the less time you'll have to reach the other checkpoints and deal with those challenges. GO!"

Jenny touched the parts until she found the familiar outline of the weapon's pistol grip. Her fingers grasped the buttstock and she placed it between her knees. Then she felt around for the T-shaped cocking handle and the piece that housed the barrel. This was the hardest part. She tried to visualize fitting the handle inside the groove in the... As she struggled to remember the name of the piece that held the barrel, she could hear Nick pulling the other gun apart.

"That's good, well done," the instructor said confirming that Nick had finished his task.

The pressure was on her now. She had the handle in the 'receiver,' that's what it was called, and then she felt for the bolt and carrier. She remembered to adjust the part so it would fit. Then, as she jiggled it, the cocking handle fell out. "Shit!"

"Slow it down," said Nick. "You can do this."

Jenny exhaled and slid the handle into its recess before feeding the bolt carrier over the top. The assembly slid easily into place, then she flipped it over. The hard part was getting the two halves of the weapon together. No matter how much she tried, she couldn't get the two pieces to align. Then she realized the retention pins were still in place. With deft hands, she popped them out, slid the lower into place, and locked it all together.

"Finally," said the instructor. "You got there in the end. You can remove your goggles."

Nick squeezed her arm. "Well done."

"Right, get your kit on and get the hell out of here."

They grabbed their packs and moved to the side to check the map.

"We've got some pretty average terrain to move over," said Nick. "We follow this ridge then head down a steep ravine." He paused. "Do you hear that?"

Voices floated on the cool night air, and up ahead, they could see lights bobbing along the trail toward them.

"Let's get going," said Nick.

A moment later, they met two other contestants on the trail; Veronica and Mark. The athletic pair had a cameraman following them.

"How are you guys doing?" Veronica asked. "We're about to hit our second challenge."

The younger pair still looked fresh despite moving faster than Jenny and Nick.

"We're doing well. Better keep moving," said Nick, letting them pass. "Good luck."

"Right on," said Mark.

For a moment, the cameraman looked as if he was going to join them, but then he continued after the athletes.

"Two already!" Jenny exclaimed. "They're crushing it."

"Not necessarily," added Nick as they continued along the trail. "Our first leg was the longest. We're making good time. Plus, let's see how they go with the weapons."

"Are you OK to pick up the pace?" asked Jenny.

"Yeah, let's do this."

"WATCH YOUR FOOTING. This is pretty loose," said Nick as he led the pair down a steep slope. Turning, he used the beam of his headlamp to highlight a section of rough terrain.

Jenny was thankful she had taken a friend's advice and bought quality hiking boots. They'd already saved her from no less than a dozen potential ankle sprains.

A whirring sounded from above, and Jenny paused to scan the night sky. She spotted a flashing red light.

"Using drones to film us," Nick said. "That's cool. Probably why there aren't crews following each of us."

"They saved them for the younger photogenic pairs," said Jenny.

"Are you saying we're not 'insta' hot?" He laughed.

"I think it's TikTok hot now." She chuckled.

"Another day, another platform…" Nick's voice dropped off as a rock slid out from under him, and he slipped sideways. Landing with a heavy thump, he let out a sharp cry.

"Shit, are you OK?" Jenny asked.

He exhaled. "I've rolled my ankle."

Jenny dumped her pack and helped Nick out of his. Then she focused her headlamp on his foot. "If you've twisted it, then it's going to swell up fast. We need to get some cold onto it."

The drone above zoomed down and hovered a short distance away as she scanned the slope below with her headlamp. Only twenty yards away, there was a stream running down the valley.

"Can you get to the stream?"

"Yeah. It's not too bad."

Leaving their packs, she helped him walk to the stream. "Get your boot off and get that ankle in the stream."

"Yes, ma'am."

"I'm going to check what's in the med kit," said Jenny as she returned to their packs. Grabbing one in each hand, she shuffled back to the bank of the stream.

"I didn't think we were supposed to open them unless there was an emergency," Nick hissed between his teeth as he held his foot in the icy stream.

"And what would you call this?"

"Good point."

As Jenny rifled through her pack, it wasn't only the drone watching her. X sat a half-mile away, observing through a thermal night vision scope.

He was quietly impressed with how efficient the middle-aged woman was. He opened her profile on his tablet, carefully keeping the screen under his jacket.

Jennifer Murphy was a forty-year-old insurance investigator from Charlotte, North Carolina: no partner, no children, and one sister with two nephews.

X was pleased with the interface that David's people had developed. He could check on a candidate's overall progress with a glance at a graphic highlighting each of the broad assessment criteria: physical, cognitive and skills. He could break down each assessment area into more detail with a touch of the screen.

Murphy's profile had amber indicators for physical. Not surprising, considering her age. Still, she was performing well in both skills and cognitive.

Closing her profile, he opened her partner's. Nick Lui was a lawyer from Florida. His profile read like a classified;

boring, middle-aged man seeking a partner for some semblance of excitement in his dull-as-fuck life. Like Jenny, he was struggling on a physical level. However, his problem-solving and mechanical aptitude were off the charts. He'd be very interested in seeing how he tracked with EQ. He'd seen smart guys like this before, geeks. They usually lacked the social skills to work effectively in a team and blend in.

Turning his attention back to the scope, he watched Jenny apply a compression bandage to Nick's leg. Her quick action impressed him, but he doubted they would last much longer, much less make the final twenty.

His radio crackled. "Hey X," transmitted Bianca.

He thumbed his mike. "Send."

"Peter's guys are saying one of the teams is lost. They haven't checked in at their next activity."

"Foxtrot team. Yeah, I'm looking at them now. The clumsy fucker rolled his ankle. They'll make the first aid stand in the next ten to twenty. Get Peter's guy to check them out."

"You wanna axe them?"

X watched the pair as they continued down the valley. Lui only had a slight limp. "Not yet."

NICK'S LIMP was barely noticeable as they approached their next activity station. Jenny had done a solid job strapping the ankle with tape to the point where he could walk on it with little pain, albeit with restricted movement.

They spotted a light at the edge of a tree line. Angling toward it, they saw it was another of Peter's instructors. He was waiting under a camp light with a camera crew.

"Drop your packs here" the man ordered. "They said one of you might be injured."

"Just a sore ankle," replied Nick. "We've got it under control."

"Right, well, you're not making great time. So you'll want to get into this next challenge quickly."

"Have all the other pairs been through?" asked Jenny. The camera was in her face.

He shrugged. "Maybe. Follow the green chem lights into the forest. You will encounter a medical situation that you must resolve using this equipment." He tossed a medical pack from a trestle table at their feet. "Your time starts now."

Jenny grabbed the pack. "Nick, you lead."

"Right on." He headed straight for the first green chem light at the head of a trail. Jenny could hear moaning from ahead as she followed Nick into the trees.

Emerging into a small clearing, they were blinded as a bank of floodlights snapped on. As their eyes adjusted, they were confronted with the wreckage of a light helicopter. Five casualties were strewn around the twisted fuselage, in varying states of injury. Two men were screaming; one with a piece of aircraft stuck in his side, the other's leg shredded beyond recognition. A dazed woman, blood streaming down her face, cradled an older man with waxy features. The fifth body was lying on its back a short distance from the chopper.

"Right," said Nick. "There's only two of us. We need to work out who we can help."

"Triage," Jenny murmured as she lowered the medical pack to the ground. "It's called triage."

"You've done this before."

She shook her head as she unzipped the pack. "No,

work made us sit through an active shooter brief. Bleeding kills people quicker than anything. We need to check who's bleeding and stop it."

"The guy with the leg," said Nick.

Jenny pulled what looked like a belt from the pack and ran to the wounded man. "Nick, check the others."

"Help me!" screamed the man with the mangled leg.

"That's what I'm going to do." Jenny reminded herself the wound was fake as blood poured through mangled flesh below the knee. She slipped the tourniquet around his thigh and pulled it tight. Almost immediately, the flow of blood slowed to a dribble.

Her patient grabbed her by the shirt. "Don't let me die."

"You'll be OK. Others need our help."

"This one's not breathing," yelled Nick. "I need help with CPR."

"No. Check the others first. We need to help the ones we can save." Jenny bent over the man with jagged metal stuck in his side. A strut had punched clean through the man's lower intestine.

"Please, you've got to help me pull it out," the man begged, his voice faint but frantic.

"If you do that, you will die," she said. "I'll make a bandage, but if you sit still, you'll live."

Nick checked on the other two casualties as Jenny grabbed bandages from the med kit. "I'll bandage the woman's head," he said. "That old guy's pulse is pretty weak."

Jenny handed him bandages and found a space-blanket tucked into the pack. "He's going into shock. You need to keep him warm. We need to keep all of them warm." She found another of the metallic blankets and took it and a handful of bandages with her back to stabilize the victim.

Weaving two bandages into donut-like rings, she reached behind his body and slipped one over the metal strut. Repeating the procedure on the front, she wrapped another bandage around his torso to secure her bandages. "You're going to be OK. I need to check on your friend."

He grasped her arm and wheezed. "Don't leave me."

"I need to check your friend." She gently removed his arm and turned to face the man with the mangled leg.

The cameraman filmed her closely as she checked his pulse and breathing. He was unconscious, but his vitals were strong. Checking the tourniquet, she saw that it had effectively stemmed the blood flow. Then, tentatively, she bandaged as much of the mangled leg as she could.

"This guy is trying to breathe!" Nick yelled from the fifth victim.

Jenny rushed across to join him and saw that it was a first-aid dummy. The mouth was opening and closing as it gasped. She dove in and turned the mannequin onto its side, clearing the airway. Then she tipped its head back and exhaled two vital breaths into it. "Check the pulse."

"There isn't one."

"OK, we need to start compressions."

A whistle blast sounded, and they turned to the instructor. "OK, job done. That's it. Move back to the tent and grab your gear. You need to get a hustle on if you're going to finish the course."

The cameraman followed them, shoving his camera in Jenny's face as she put her pack on. "How did that go?"

Jenny shrugged. "I think we did OK. I've got a good feeling about it."

"What about you?" he asked Nick.

"Jenny was all over it," he said. "She nailed it."

They left the cameraman in the tent and walked a short distance from the site before checking the map.

"How's your ankle?" asked Jenny.

"Tight, but no pain. I meant what I said back there, you're awesome at this."

"And you're killing the navigation. We make a good team. Now, let's see if we can finish this thing."

OVER FIVE HOURS, Jenny and Nick managed to complete another two challenges successfully. One of them involved assembling Ikea furniture without instructions or speaking. The other was a terrifying climb from the bottom of a canyon to a suspension bridge, up a tiny caving ladder, followed by an abseil back down to the valley floor.

Jenny had been terrified, but working in the narrow beam of her headlamp had allowed her to focus on the ladder and not the horrific fall below.

Having left the abseil site, they had climbed back up a tussock-covered slope onto a spur line. According to their map the final activity was on a plateau less than a hundred meters away.

"God, I don't think I've ever been this hungry," said Nick as they trudged up the hill.

"Or tired. I can't keep my eyes open," added Jenny. "How's your ankle doing?"

"Aching, but I won't let it slow me down. We don't have far to go."

They walked on.

"Is it just me? Or is it getting lighter?" said Jenny.

"I noticed that too. We've been on the go for over twenty-four hours. No wonder our eyes are hanging out."

The Operative

They'd moved another hundred yards when Jenny spotted lights ahead. "That has to be it."

A round structure grew out of the gloom as they approached.

"STOP!" A loud voice froze them in their tracks.

Two hulking figures appeared from behind a boulder.

"Turn off your headlamp," Jenny told Nick as she killed hers.

"Who are you?" the men asked.

Jenny remembered that the predominant tribe in the region had a strict code of hospitality once initiated. "We're travelers seeking permission to move through your lands." She avoided eye contact and remembered not to stare at their weapons.

"You must go back the way you came," the other man ordered.

"Please," said Jenny. "My colleague is injured and needs help."

The two men talked in whispers. "We will take you to our chief," one of them responded.

"Good thinking," whispered Nick as they followed the two men toward the round building, a canvas yurt.

They saw four other contestants sitting outside the yurt as they got closer. The scornful looks on their faces indicated that they may have been waiting a while.

"Wait here," said one of the men. He left his colleague to guard the entrance to the tent and stepped inside.

Jenny dropped her pack and slumped to the ground next to it. Nick did the same. The other contestants were sitting in their pairs talking. She assumed they were strategizing for the upcoming meeting.

"So what's our game plan?" asked Nick.

"Do you remember all the rules?"

"Yeah, most of them. The big ones were only making eye contact with the chief, always talking in the third person, rapport is king, and wait for the chief to ask you what you want."

"They told us it's a patriarchal society. So, you better take point," she said.

"Right, and we've run out of checkpoints, so, ultimately, we're looking for safe passage and a destination. It's a pity we don't have a gift to offer."

A guard threw back the yurt's door flap. "The chiefs are waiting, come in."

Jenny and Nick were closest to the door and entered first. The guard gestured for them to sit on the far side.

There were three people inside. Two fearsome-looking middle-aged men were sitting cross-legged. Behind them, an older woman was seated, working on what looked like an embroidery frame. There were several cameras and microphones fixed to the structure of the tent. She figured that the crew was hidden outside.

Jenny noted all the tribe wore modern outdoor clothing, cargo pants, T-shirts and flannel shirts. The only traditional-looking items they wore were large jade pendants hanging from leather thongs around their necks.

Nick emulated their sitting position, and Jenny followed suit, waiting as the other contestants entered. They quickly filed in and sat facing the tribal chiefs.

"The *Hill Stalkers* welcome you to our lands," said one of the men.

Jenny noticed that he was the older of the two.

"Brian and Adriana, thank you for your hospitality," said one of the other male contestants.

Jenny noticed that the man ignored the comment.

"Daniel and Naomi extend their thanks also," the other male contestant added.

The man ignored their remark too.

Then, as Nick was about to speak, another man entered the yurt, carrying a large tray that he placed in front of the contestants.

"You must be hungry," said the chief. "Please eat."

A gasp from one of the other contestants, Naomi, triggered Jenny to inspect the culinary offering.

She fought the urge to gag. The tray held crackers, each topped with what looked to be cheese and an eyeball. She turned to Nick, who was struggling to hide a look of disgust.

"I... I mean Nick and Jenny, thank you for your hospitality," he managed to stammer. He reached for a cracker and handed it to Jenny before selecting another for himself.

The other contestants watched in horror as she raised it to her mouth. *It's just an olive*, she told herself as she took a bite. It had the consistency of jelly but a salty taste, and the more she chewed, the less it felt like an eyeball.

Glancing at the chief, she noticed that he had turned and shot a questioning look to the older woman, who nodded. He then rose and took a bottle from a box by the door. Crossing the tent, he unscrewed the lid and passed it to Jenny.

As she raised it to her lips, the light bulb came on. They'd been misled, the tribe wasn't patriarchal, and the woman was literally calling the shots.

Strong whiskey burned her throat and warmed her stomach, flushing any trace of the eyeball from her mouth. She offered the bottle to Nick, who took a healthy slug.

Locking eyes with the grey-haired woman Jenny took a gamble and spoke. "Chieftess, Jenny and Nick thank you for your time and hospitality."

The woman smiled. "Manaia of the *Hill Stalkers* welcomes you to our lands and compliments you on your iron stomach. The all-seeing snack is not for everyone."

The other contestants immediately helped themselves to the crackers, and Nick passed them the bottle.

"Daniel and Naomi, also thank you for your hospitality," added Daniel, after a swig of whiskey.

The Matriarch ignored the remark. "Jenny, why do you choose to travel our lands?"

She maintained eye contact with the woman. "Jenny and Nick are on a quest. They are nearing the end and only need to find one more place. They seek your permission to pass through your territories to complete their task."

She paused in thought.

"Alex and Brian also…"

The Matriarch held up her hand. "You will wait your turn. Or you will be thrown out."

Alex blushed, and Jenny caught the venomous look thrown sideways at her.

"The *Hill Stalkers* admire courage, Jenny. You have Manaia's permission to pass through our lands. And –" She gestured to the box, "a gift to see you on your way. You may leave."

"Jenny and Nick, thank you again, Chieftess Manaia." They rose, and as they passed the box, one of the men reached inside and handed Jenny a small hip flask-shaped bottle.

Outside, they returned to their packs, where a camera crew was waiting.

"What's in the bottle?" asked Nick.

Jenny activated her headlamp and shone it on the flask. "It's whiskey, from a local distillery."

"Well, at least it will keep us warm," said Nick.

"The coordinates to the distillery are on the bottom of the label," said Jenny. "Could that be the end point?"

"Maybe. Let's check."

Jenny read the coordinates from the bottle.

"They're just off the edge of this map. Like, maybe three or four hundred meters. We traverse down this ridge line through a forest, and then there's a track that looks to be heading in the right direction."

"Risky move?" asked Jenny.

"I think it's a no-brainer. The chief gives us a bottle with coordinates for a nearby distillery. It would seem like a good place to end the challenge."

"OK then. Shall we have a swig?"

"I think it would be rude not to. Plus, it'll take the edge off my ankle."

The camera crew positioned themselves to catch the sunrise behind the pair as they passed the bottle between them.

Nick finished his slug when the next two contestants appeared outside the tent.

"That's our cue," said Jenny. "Let's get moving."

———

X HAD COMMANDEERED an office at the distillery for his team to meet. Lavishly appointed in leather and wood it had a view over the copper stills down into a courtyard where Peter, his team, the film crew and Charles were receiving the contestants.

"You've all seen the results on the app?" X asked.

"Yeah, I've inputted all my comments," said Bianca. "I think the final ten look good. *The Crucible* managed to weed out the weaker ones."

"I agree," added Steve. "The Rupert's crew seem to have scrubbed most of the muppets. The top ten looks pretty strong."

X reached for his phone. "Right, I'm going to ring David and get his approval to lock them in."

He established a secure connection and put the device on speaker. "David, Steve, and Bianca are here with me. Have you had a chance to review the *Crucible* results?"

"Team, good to have you onboard. I concur with the results except for the final ten. I've got strict instructions to provide a diverse workforce. Your top ten are all under the age of thirty. I want to elevate the Foxtrot team to position nine and ten."

X examined the listing on his tablet. Foxtrot was the middle-aged pair. "The woman, Jennifer, is reasonably capable. The male, Nicholas, has physical limitations."

"He managed to finish in the top twelve, despite an injury," interjected Bianca.

"He's smart," added Steve. "Stripped down the AK faster than anyone else."

"Who are we losing to bring them in?" asked X.

"Drop eight and nine and sub them in," said David. "That's not negotiable."

X sighed. "Roger." He opened the final listing and made the changes. "It's done."

"Right, I'll see you at *The Station* in the next few days," said David before hanging up.

"You can always fuck them off later," said Bianca. "You're only going to get two or three through the wringer."

"Yeah, but what if eight and nine were our two?"

She shrugged. "That's life."

X exhaled and then rose. "Right, let's get out of here."

The Operative

As the three instructors left the distillery, Peter and his team were concluding their part in the process.

As the pairs of contestants reached the distillery they'd been welcomed with a gourmet breakfast. Wooden tables had been set up on the lawn, loaded with bacon and egg rolls, pastries, coffee, and juice. Starving and tired, each team had descended upon the buffet like starving wolves. Only an hour and a half separated the arrival of the first pair from the last, although it was rumored the final teams had not completed their activities.

Jenny and Nick sat on a patch of lawn with some of the other contestants. They'd eaten their fill and removed their boots to air their feet.

"So what was your favorite part?' asked one of the contestants, the heavily tattooed man around her age.

"This bit right here," said Jenny, her hands wrapped around a piping hot cup of coffee.

"Amen to that," said Nick.

"I loved that bridge climb," said another of the contestants. "That was crazy stuff."

"The meeting with the Chief was pretty intense," added another.

"You mean the Chieftess," said tattoo arms. "That caught me off guard."

"You're not the only one," added Jenny.

"OK, team, gather around." Peter had jumped onto a raised stage before the open doors leading into the distillery. A camera crew focused on him and the barrels stacked high, branded with the distillery's logo.

Great product placement thought Jenny as she stood with the others under the lens of another three cameras.

"You should all be very proud of yourselves for getting this far," said Peter in his clipped British accent. "It has been my team's absolute pleasure to guide you through *The Crucible*." He paused. "Unfortunately, this is the end of the road for most of you."

On cue, a bus rounded the corner of the building and hissed as it halted.

"If your name is called, dump your field packs over there, and get on the bus. Marcus O'Brien."

The guy with tattoos strode for the bus ignoring the cameras focused on him. Immediately everyone started whispering and assumed the winners were getting on the bus.

Peter kept calling names, and to Jenny's amazement, he included Nick and her. She followed Nick to the bus and sat beside one of the younger contestants. Jenny recognized her as Amanda from the meeting with the *Hill Stalkers*.

As the bus filled she soon realized she and Nick were in with the losers. Mark, Veronica and a half-dozen of the fittest contestants remained outside.

"Well, we made a good go of it," said Amanda.

"Wasn't there supposed to be ten contestants?" said someone else.

Suddenly Peter strode across to the bus and leaped inside. "Sorry, there's been some confusion. Jennifer Murphy and Nicholas Lui, you're both in with the other crew."

Chapter Six

JENNY HAD NEVER FLOWN in a helicopter before. Clutching the edge of her seat, she took a deep breath as the tiny aircraft lifted from the ground and clawed skyward. She could feel it tremble and shudder as gusts of wind buffeted it. The aircraft quickly gained altitude and leveled into smooth flight once clear of the mountains.

The insurance investigator from North Carolina gazed at the rugged landscape in disbelief. She'd never really thought she had a chance of getting selected to compete on *The Operative*. Yet here she was, through the first challenge and on her way to a secret location.

Glancing sideways at the other two contestants in the aircraft with her, she noted the grins on their faces. They didn't look like they'd just completed an intense twenty-four-hour challenge. Like her, they were fueled by a big breakfast and the thrill of helicopter flight.

The pilot transmitted over their headsets as they followed a vibrant blue river weaving through a steep canyon. "Right, we're about three minutes out from the first drop. Once the bird touches down, I'll get out and open the door. I'll unload your pack from the pod, and you will carry it clear of the aircraft. Once we lift off, you can open your instructions."

Jenny reached into her jacket and checked the envelope the crew had given her at the distillery was tucked safely into a pocket.

As the helicopter crested a high range, she noticed the terrain beyond was different. There were no trees or houses. Fence lines and dirt tracks crisscrossed rolling hills and rocky outcrops. Farming country, she assumed as the chopper descended.

"OK, the first stop is coming up."

The pilot brought the aircraft down on a small hill covered in long brown grass. Jenny watched as the rotor wash whipped the grass into a frenzy before the engine decreased power and the pilot climbed out. It took him a moment to unload the first contestant before they were airborne again. Less than three minutes later they put down in another equally remote location and offloaded the other passenger. Then, it was Jenny's turn.

As they touched down she removed her headset and unbuckled her harness. When the pilot opened the door, she climbed out, hunched, and strode a dozen paces from the aircraft. She watched as the pilot took her pack from a container strapped to the helicopter's skids and dumped it on the ground. He secured the latch on the container, and climbed back inside his machine.

She squinted as the engine screamed, and the downwash launched dust and debris into the air. Then, as agile as a bird, the helicopter leaped into the air and disappeared over a ridge.

As the thump of the rotors and the roar of the engine

faded, Jenny was overwhelmed by silence. Standing, she turned in a circle, surveying the landscape.

She was surrounded by hills devoid of trees. Rocky outcrops, grass and low bushes stretched in every direction. She'd never felt so isolated in her life.

Tearing open the envelope, she removed a map and printed instructions. She had five hours to move from her location to a designated point. Failure to reach the rendezvous would result in termination from the program.

Opening her pack, she removed a GoPro given to her at the distillery. They'd taken the field pack from *The Crucible*, and returned her small day pack with some water and food. They'd also supplied her with a compass and an emergency beacon. She noticed that there was a green flashing light on the device.

She took the compass out and used it to align the map on the ground. First, she needed to work out where she was relative to where she needed to be.

There were two prominent features in the area, and thanks to Nick's training she knew how to translate their unique shapes into contour lines. Finding them both on the map, she studied the ground between them and quickly identified a large outcrop of rock to her west.

Her destination was roughly four kilometers north of her location on the edge of the valley floor. According to the map, it was a cluster of buildings alongside a waterway. Tracing Moa Creek, as marked on the map, she found it joined a tributary that wound its way up the hills to a position just east of her. She could follow it all the way if she walked across to it.

Gathering her things, she stuffed them in her pack and set off. Hopefully, Nick and his ankle were doing OK, she thought as she trudged across the hills.

X STEPPED out of the Hughes 500 helicopter as it touched down in a grassy paddock. Striding across to a sweeping ranch house, he crossed the raised porch, shoved open the front door and entered. He paused momentarily, taking in the organized chaos of a functioning television production, and then made for the staircase that led to a loft apartment.

The Station, what they called a ranch in New Zealand, had been purchased through a production company established by David. The five-thousand-hectare property was remote, well-equipped and perfect for running a clandestine training program.

X tossed his gear bag on the couch in the loft apartment's landing, removed his tablet and entered the planning room.

"OK, Raj, where we at?" he asked his tech guy, who was sitting at the central table with a tablet.

X took the seat opposite.

The open-plan office comprised most of the upstairs space, along with X's bedroom and ensuite. Dormer windows on both sides of the roofline gave views over the farmyard and the field to the front. Raj had fitted screens to almost every square foot of wall. They displayed everything from training schedules to mapping software and feeds from cameras and drones.

"All our gear is up and running. The production team is finishing their setup now."

"Good. Do you have a track on the candidates?" X asked pointing to a screen displaying a map.

Raj tapped his fingers on the tablet, and a series of markers appeared on the screen, showing each candidate's location.

The Operative

"What's the green icon?" X gestured to a marker that was moving along a track.

"That's Bianca and Steve. They're out with a camera team and the director. He wanted to get some long shots."

"And the reception?"

"I've got all their gear laid out in the barn. Did you want to go through the candidates now? Or wait for Steve and Bianca to get back?"

X glanced at the map and saw that a few markers were moving reasonably quickly toward the ranch. "Let's get it done."

Raj nodded, flicking his tablet contents onto one of the screens. "I'll start at the bottom of the deck, Nicholas Lui." Nick's profile appeared on the screen.

"I've read his profile. He won't be with us for long," X said with a grunt.

Raj advanced to the next candidate, Jennifer Murphy.

"Same same," said X.

They progressed quickly through the profiles. The top four were the ones that interested the chief instructor. The extras were dead wood that needed pruning.

"Righto, in slot four, we've got Veronica Bloom," continued Raj. "She's the CFO of a successful tech start-up, twenty-seven, cross-fit regional champion and speaks three languages."

X recognized the athletic African American. He'd picked her as a standout during *The Crucible*. She was a highly motivated alpha female with something to prove. A lethal combination that made her highly receptive to his training and influencing methodologies.

"Third position is Natalie Garner."

An attractive, grey-eyed blonde appeared on the screen.

"This one's right up your alley, X. She's a twenty-nine-year-old Texan real-estate agent. Former model and a state-level triathlete. She's got a black belt in karate and comes from an abusive family."

X nodded. When his psychologist arrived, they'd thoroughly review each profile and identify strengths and weaknesses, leveraging them to shape each character.

"Number two," said Raj. "Mark Dunstan, a Virgo from Boston who enjoys working out, bow hunting and selling luxury sports cars."

X rewarded the humor with a chuckle. Dunstan had been a bit of a dark horse during the pre-selection and *The Crucible*. A quiet professional, he'd performed well in every aspect. Average looks, average height and in his early thirties, Mark could breeze through a security check at an airport without sparking the slightest interest. If X was a betting man, that's where he'd have his money.

"And finally. Our star player Captain America himself, Eric Anderson. Former infantry officer turned banker. Thirty-two, six foot, benches three fifty and works in finance."

X had seen Eric's type before. The military was full of them. Cookie cutter officers. Smart, physically capable, and cocky. He'd enjoy breaking Anderson down over the next six weeks. He pried his hulking frame from the office chair. "I need a cup of joe."

Raj followed him downstairs into an expansive country kitchen, recently upgraded with commercial appliances to handle the show's catering. A pot of hot coffee was on a bench, and he poured a hefty slug into an enamel mug. X waited for Raj to make himself a cup of tea before striding along the bustling corridor that split the residence. Deftly maneuvering around crew and equipment, he exited the rear of the building and stepped into the farmyard beyond.

The Operative

A sizeable, graveled square separated the primary residence from the barn, shearing and equipment sheds. For the production team, it would serve as a parking lot for vehicles ranging from pickups to earthmoving equipment and side-by-side buggies.

The barn was the largest structure on the property and was paramount to the training programs. Multi-level it had an upstairs area for lessons and planning, and a lower operational section.

Raj led him through a code-protected side door into a caged section serving as the Q-store and armory. The tennis court-sized area was stacked high with crates of tactical equipment, weapons racks and boxes of clothing.

"We got everything, Raj?"

"There are a few outstanding orders. Nothing critical."

"Excellent."

They left the Q-store and entered the area formerly housing the farm's heavy equipment. The open workshop would now serve as a flexible training area. There was a gym setup at the far end, massive mobile TV screens, and equipment stacked against the rear wall.

X strode across to a rubber fight mat where ten large duffel bags were arranged. Kneeling, he placed his coffee down and unzipped one. Inside was the uniform and equipment each of the trainees would be wearing. He found the wearable tech David had insisted they use in a side pouch.

X had to admit that the smartwatch was a great idea. It allowed his team to track and communicate with the trainees and monitor their vitals. It would be an excellent addition to the observations of his instructors.

"Raj, how long have we got till the first trainees arrive?"

The technician checked the tablet that seemed to be glued to his hand. "A little over an hour."

X returned the watch to the bag and zipped it closed. "Excellent." He downed the last of his coffee. "I'm gonna hit the gym. Get Steve and Bianca to check in with me when they're back. Also, can you find out where the hell Jacquie is? If I'm going to start fucking with heads, I'll need my shrink."

NICK'S ANKLE throbbed as he crossed a small stream and pushed through a patch of thick prickly shrubs that tore at his clothing and skin. He could hear voices and the rumble of an engine. As he emerged from the bushes he spotted the reception committee at his destination.

An open-backed military-style truck was parked alongside an SUV. He spotted the other contestants, including Jenny, sitting on the truck's bench seats. He'd made it. A camera crew filmed him as he limped to the truck. One of the male contestants, tall and wiry, reached down and helped him onboard. "You OK?"

"Rolled my ankle. It will be fine. Thanks."

The tailgate slammed shut and the truck started with a rumble.

"Don't mention it. My name's Adrian."

"Nick. How did you go out there?"

Adrian smiled. "So far, so good, right?"

The truck crunched into gear, and they turned onto a rutted track. In a field to the east, Nick spotted what looked to be a construction site. A crane was moving a shipping container, lifting it over stacks of timber.

"Probably one of the sets," said Adrian.

Nick spotted Jenny at the front of the truck and gave her

a wave. She'd done well, arriving at the checkpoint earlier than most.

The truck's engine growled as the driver downshifted, and they entered a narrow gorge. As they rounded a bend, the terrain opened, and a cluster of buildings appeared.

Passing over a cattle grid, they swung into a gravel square bordered on three sides by buildings and came to a halt with a hiss of brakes.

"Get out of the bloody truck."

The voice was loud, piercing and heavily Scottish.

Nick and Adrian didn't hesitate. They reached over, unlatched the tailgate, and let it drop. Dropping from the vehicle, the contestants gathered in a huddle.

"Move into that hangar and stand behind your bags," yelled the Scotsman, who'd strode into view. Medium height with a wiry fighter's build, he wore a fierce scowl. He didn't look like a man anyone wanted to cross.

"Fucking today, people!"

Nick followed the others as they moved into a massive shed and started reading names off bulky kit bags. They were in alphabetic order; his was front and right.

One of the women unzipped her bag and peered inside, earning the ire of the Scotsman.

"What were you told?" he asked.

"Move inside and stand behind your bags," she said quietly, immediately realizing her error.

"Listen carefully, do as you're told and clarify if you don't understand."

Nick stood behind his bag and glanced around the hangar. A whirring noise from above drew his attention, and he spotted a camera mounted on a rail. A second camera on a rolling dolly was operated by a cameraman he recognized from *The Crucible*.

A door opened at the far left of the building, and a half-dozen people entered. Nick spotted the director, Charles. He was the only one who didn't look like they could kill you in a heartbeat.

The group joined the Scotsman in front of the assembled contestants. A muscled brute with short grey hair and a lantern jaw stepped forward. Like the others, he wore outdoor clothes devoid of brands or labels. His chest and arms strained at the fabric of his T-shirt.

"Candidates, welcome to *The Operative*. My name's X, and I'm the senior instructor here at *The Station*."

His accent was southern, and Nick guessed he was Texan.

"Ya'll need to understand that this isn't some kind of bullshit boot camp. My staff and I are here to turn you into field operatives. We will impart information, enhance your capability and ultimately test you. You won't call us, sir, and we won't yell at you. The burden to deliver is on you. I, for one, do not give two fucks if you fail. Hell, that makes for good television." He turned to the director. "Right, Chuck?"

The director nodded.

"You've already met Steve," continued X, tipping his head toward the Scotsman to his left. "He's our head of lethal effects. Hand-to-hand combat, weapons, explosives, booby traps. If it's deadly, then Steve's our man. To his left, your right, is Bianca."

The sandy-haired woman dipped her chin. "Hi."

Nick guessed her age as mid-thirties. Like the others, she had an air of lethality about her.

"Bianca is a certified badass. She's our clandestine operations expert. A goddamn ghost and master of manipulation. She's also an expert marksman and a dab hand at driving."

Bianca gave a little curtsey, and one of the contestants laughed.

X smirked. "And also, a regular goddamn comedian. This guy to my right is Raj. He's our tech guru, quartermaster and electronic surveillance expert. Without a doubt, he's the smartest human here. Right, Raj will handle the issuing of equipment, and then Steve will familiarize you with *The Station*. I'll see you at your first training session tomorrow morning."

X and the director exited the room, leaving his instructors with the ten contestants.

Raj was tall and dark, and Nick guessed of Indian heritage. He was holding what looked to be a tablet computer, possibly the latest generation iPad.

"Ladies and gentlemen."

The crisp British accent caught Nick by surprise.

"The bag in front of you contains your training uniform, toiletries, underwear, socks, footwear and most of the things you'll need during training. You can request anything else through the Q-store." He pointed to a kiosk desk alongside the door X had departed through.

"Excuse me?" One of the candidates raised her hand, an attractive blonde called Natalie.

"Send," replied Raj.

"Is there a makeup department? I mean, this is a TV show, right?"

Raj looked to the director, Charles, who shook his head. "No, we're shooting this as it is. If you want to wear makeup, that's on you."

Natalie looked a little irritated. "Can I ask for makeup from the Q thingy?"

"Certainly, we'll do our best to get what you need. Now, I've got one piece of equipment to talk you through. In the side pocket, you will find a smartwatch." He waited for the contestants to locate the device. "This device acts as a safety mechanism. It lets us know where you are and gives you access to the training program."

"Additionally, in the event of an incident, it will allow you to request emergency support. The interface is relatively simple; I'll leave you to work it out. The device itself is waterproof and charges through magnetic proximity. Please ensure you keep them on at all times." Raj watched as they fastened the watch-like devices.

"Even when showering?" asked a contestant.

"I'd recommend washing it. Otherwise, it will get a little funky," said Raj. He rechecked his tablet. "If there are no more questions, I'll hand over to Steve." He paused. "No? I look forward to working with you all." He turned and exited via the door to the Q-store as Steve moved to the front.

"Right, no doubt you bastards are looking forward to a hot shower and some scram. So, grab your kit bags and follow me."

AS STEVE LED the candidates around *The Station*, Raj made his way to the shearing shed. A large sign on the door of the former farm building barred entry to everyone other than the production crew.

Inside, despite extensive renovations, the oily scent of wool still hung in the air. Raj didn't mind the smell. It reminded him of childhood visits to his uncle's farm.

For a tech guy, the shearing shed was now heaven. The

crew had converted the space into a state-of-the-art production facility. Cables ran from server racks to editing terminals. Benches were laden with charging batteries and temporary shelves were packed with cameras and sound gear.

At the rear of the shed, the crew had turned what was usually a shearing break room into the production control room. Like X's planning room, it had screens on the walls and a large central table.

As Raj walked in, he noted that a drinks fridge and an expensive-looking coffee machine had been added since his last visit. "All of the smart devices are online," he told X, who was sitting with Chuck, discussing the next twenty-four hours of training, filming and production.

"Can we get that on screen?" X asked.

Raj used his tablet to flick the interface onto one of the wall screens.

A green figure represented each candidate. Under it was a readout showing their heart rate, blood pressure and oxygen saturation.

"That's fantastic," said Chuck. "We can cut to the heart rate when you're doing high-intensity stuff. The audience will get a real feel for how scared they are."

Raj glanced at X and caught the big man's eye roll. "Chuck, you called this meeting, what is it you wanted to discuss?"

"We need to set a time for the daily production meeting. I thought it could be after dinner, say seven o'clock?"

"Add it to the calendar," said X.

"Excellent. Can you or one of your people brief the next day's activity schedule? That way, the crew can work out exactly what they need to prepare."

X gave him a thumbs up. "That all?"

"Yeah, really looking forward to working with you guys for the next few weeks."

"Yep." X rose from the chair and exited the office, leaving Raj and Chuck behind.

"He's a bit of a hard ass," said Chuck.

Raj laughed. "Sir, you have no idea."

"WELL, ISN'T THIS HOMELY," said Veronica as she tossed her gear bag at the foot of a canvas stretcher. "The genuine cow shed experience."

Their accommodation was an old equipment shelter with no windows. Jury-rigged lighting hung from the exposed metal framework that supported a rusted tin roof.

"People would pay good money for this," added Eric as he followed suit, laying on a stretcher.

"They can have it," added Veronica. "When did you ever see James Bond sleeping in anything other than a five-star hotel?"

"In *From Russia With Love*, he slept in a truck filled with straw," said Nick as he selected a stretcher.

"Yeah, that's true," added Mark. "Although, he did have the company of a gorgeous woman."

"Well, y'all can tick that box," said Natalie Garner from the stretcher she'd chosen between Eric and Mark. She shot the former military officer a pout and a wink.

Jenny was the last to choose a bed. As a result, she got the one closest to the bathroom door. It clanged as one of the women swept through it. A moment later, she reappeared looking shocked. "You guys have to see this."

Jenny joined the others as they filed through the door and into their bathroom facilities. A shade cloth fence surrounded a pair of portable toilets, two free-standing open showers and a sink with a mirror nailed to a post.

"Is this five-star enough for you, Veronica?" asked Eric, with a laugh.

"Are we expected to shower together?" asked Stacey. "Out here in the open?"

"I guess so," said Mark. "We can allocate different times for men and women."

"Or we could check our hang-ups at the door and get on with it," said Eric. "Once we get started, I bet free time will be limited."

"I saw some fence pickets outside the shed and more shade cloth. We can throw up a screen around the showers," offered Nick. "Be good to have somewhere to hang your towel."

"I'll give you a hand," said Jenny.

"Suit yourself," said Eric. "I'm going to get my head down while we can."

Two other contestants offered to help, and the four left the others in the accommodation shed. Nick untied one of the bathroom corners so they could drag the supplies in.

"Hey, I'm Stacey," said the woman who'd first discovered the bathroom. She was relatively young with husky blue eyes, short brown hair and a robust, compact build.

"Jenny," she replied.

"Must be a little intimidating being the oldest here. I'm so impressed that you made it this far."

"Thanks." Jenny grabbed an armful of metal pickets from a pile next to the shed. She noticed that Stacey followed suit, picking up twice as many.

"Yeah, I'm Troy," said the other contestant, helping Nick with a shade cloth roll. Like Stacey, he was well built, in his thirties and good-looking.

It took them less than ten minutes to secure the makeshift shower screen. Everyone else was fast asleep on their stretchers when they returned to the bunkhouse.

Nick glanced at his watch. "We've got twenty minutes till dinner. Good idea to get our heads down."

Jenny exhaled as she lay on the sleeping bag atop her stretcher. A week ago, she would never have been comfortable on a saggy pillow or a rock-solid stretcher. Yet, here she was, sleeping in a tractor shed in clothes she'd been wearing for two days.

As she closed her eyes, the smartwatch on her wrist vibrated. She glanced at the screen and saw that tomorrow's first training session was at six am. Her body seemed to ache in response to the message. This was the beginning of the actual training. She hoped it would be a slower pace, but something told her that wouldn't be the case.

Chapter Seven

"GOOD MORNING, you glorious bastards. What a day to be alive." Clouds of vapor shot from Steve's mouth as he bellowed.

The time was zero six hundred, and the contestants were gathered in a field a short distance from the barn. Dawn was still an hour away, but powerful floodlights threw light across the frost-laden grass. A cameraman dressed in a heavy fur-lined jacket was filming the contestants, who wore cargo pants and long-sleeved T-shirts.

"It's so damn cold," murmured Nick, folding his arms across his chest.

Jenny rubbed her gloved hands together.

"So, this is your first training session. I better make it one to fucking remember. Let's get you warmed up and ready to rock. Jogging on the spot, go."

Steve ran them through a vigorous routine of static exercises, including star jumps, burpees, pushups and high knees. Once warm, he ran them in single file into the barn and onto rubber mats.

"Form a half circle," he directed.

They gathered around.

"My job here is to turn you floppy-eared fucks into cold hard killers. This morning, we're starting with the art of the fist. Does anyone here have any experience with martial arts?"

Jenny glanced around as several contestants raised their hands. Natalie, Veronica, Mark, and Eric indicated they had some training.

Steve pointed to Eric. "Big guy, what's your flavor?"

"I wrestled in the Army, and I've done a little kickboxing."

"Right. Cool, well, step out here and show us what you've got." Steve cricked his neck and gestured for the bigger man to approach.

Eric didn't move.

"Are your ears painted on?"

Eric left the half-circle and raised his hands in a traditional fighting stance.

"Right, what have you got?"

Eric launched a conservative volley of punches at the instructor.

Steve rocked back on his rear foot and easily avoided the combination. "OK, not a bad stance. Good timing, but slow as fuck. What else you got?"

The bigger man tried again. This time he punched at full speed before adding a front kick.

Steve easily avoided the onslaught. "Any slower, and you'd be growing moss."

Eric's eyes narrowed as he circled the wiry Scotsman. With a yell, he launched a devastating volley of sidekicks.

Jenny couldn't believe how fast Steve moved. Avoiding the kicks, he struck like a cobra, his fist clipping Eric's jaw.

Then, as his opponent was stunned, he snaked an arm under his chin and brought the bigger man to the ground.

Eric slapped the mat with his hand, submitting. Steve ignored it, maintaining the choke-hold for a few seconds longer. "First lesson. There is no submission. The engagement is complete when your target is neutralized."

Releasing his hold, he let Eric slump to the mat.

"Is he OK?" asked Jenny.

"No, he telegraphs his kicks. That's why he's sleeping. Now, I want you to partner up, grab gloves, pads and get back on the mat."

Eric groaned as he sat upright. Steve offered him a hand and hauled him to his feet. "Get your shit together, pretty boy. I'm going to teach you a couple more things before your next nap."

JENNY PEERED through a clump of long grass and identified her next position. Inching slowly through the grass, she ignored the damp seeping through her pants and shirt. Having moved a few feet, she paused and waited.

Their instructor, Bianca, had outlined the principles of camouflage, 'why things are seen.' Then she'd shown them how to weave natural vegetation into shaggy sniper outfits called gillie suits. They'd smeared camouflage cream on their faces and headed for the hills to practice their new skills.

In a scene reminiscent of a Tom Clancy novel, the ten contestants had been split into two teams. One group of five was positioned on a scaffolding platform with binoculars. The other team, Jenny included, attempted to make their way down a sparsely vegetated rocky gulley to a flag without being spotted.

Jenny froze when she heard a rustling through the bushes to her right. Out of the corner of her eye, she spotted a staff member striding through the shrubby grass.

A radio crackled. "That's it. Right there. Seeker at your feet."

She held her breath.

"At my feet?" the searcher confirmed.

"Yes."

She recognized Eric's voice over the radio.

"There's no one here," reported the staff member.

"You sure?"

Jenny could understand Eric's frustration. He was one of three contestants who hadn't reached the flag during their attempt. Nick had spotted him and sent in the seekers.

'The human eye is drawn to movement,' Jenny remembered from her training. The seeker moving away from her would distract the observers, allowing her a window to crawl into a patch of thick brush.

Inching forward, she entered the bushes where she could move to a crouch. She could see the flag, her target, through a gap in the branches.

As she made to crawl, she felt something tug at her shaggy camouflage covering. The sniper suit had gotten caught in a thorny bush. As she attempted to wriggle out of it, more strands seemed to weave themselves into the needle-like thorns. "Shit!"

There was a commotion a short distance to her right. The hunters had found one of her teammates. Glancing at her watch, she saw that time was running out. She had less than a minute to make the flag.

The Operative

It took her a moment to unsnap the fasteners and tear off the Velcro straps that held the bulky gillie suit in place, without dislodging the GoPro camera attached to her shoulder. Sliding out of the garment, she crawled through the bushes into a shallow muddy stream.

The water was putrid, and she gagged. Sliding in the mud, she scrabbled through another section of bushes and into the grassy area where the flag fluttered. Scrambling forward, she touched the flag and jumped to her feet. A split second later, an air horn sounded, indicating the end of the activity.

The remaining two contestants in her group, Nick and another man, Troy, joined her at the flag.

"Good work, Jen," said Nick.

"You guys got so close," she replied as a camera crew focused in on the three of them.

"Close, but no cigar," added Troy as they made their way to the observation platform where the rest of the contestants were waiting.

"Right," said Bianca as they arrived and stood with the others. "You can see now how formidable camouflage can be. You knew they were out there and still only managed to find two. Imagine if you were simply going about your daily activities. Do you think you'd spot them?"

The candidates shook their heads.

"What about the urban environment?" asked Nick. "Do things change when everyone is moving?"

"That will be covered in later lessons. Now, we will build an observation post and conduct surveillance."

"Will we be tested on it?" asked Troy.

Bianca smiled. "You're going to be tested on every detail of everything you learn."

There were groans from the candidates.

"What?" she continued with a smile. "Did you think this was going to be easy?"

———

"ALL RIGHT, sleepy heads. Get out of your chairs, punch out ten pushups, and grab a coffee. You've got two minutes," bellowed X.

It was a little after nineteen hundred hours, as the instructors called it, and Jenny and the other contestants were upstairs in the classroom above the barn. Their day, so far, had been a whirlwind of training, focused on remaining hidden and gathering intelligence. Jenny enjoyed it, but it had been seriously taxing. Like everyone else, she struggled to stay awake in the warm classroom.

Jenny managed to pump out eight pushups before dropping to her knees. Forearms wobbling like jelly, she completed the set of ten before falling to the carpet. As she struggled to her feet, Nick placed a mug of black coffee on her desk.

"How did you do your pushups so quickly?" she asked.

"I haven't done them yet." He placed his coffee down and dropped to the ground. Fifteen seconds later, he'd pumped out the pushups and taken his seat. "Hey, Jenny," he said once his breath returned. "Why do you think there's no crew filming this?"

Glancing around, she saw that he was right. Throughout the day, at least one camera crew always filmed the activities. Additionally, she'd been wired for sound and worn body cameras.

"This probably doesn't make for exciting viewing," added Nick.

The Operative

"Right, plant your asses in your seats," yelled X from where he sat on a table at the front of the classroom with his cup of coffee. He gave them a moment to return to their desks before continuing. "Now, I've got four hours to teach you guys how to devise a workable plan. While that might not sound exciting, I can assure you that it's the skillset that will get you through the series. In fact, I can almost guarantee that the fucker who takes away the most from this period of training will be our winner. So, without further ado." He finished his coffee, rose from the table, left his cup, and grabbed a dry-erase marker.

"How many of you know this acronym?" His hand slashed across the whiteboard, spelling the word KISS.

"Keep it simple, stupid," said Eric. "I think we've all heard it before."

X tossed the pen into the corner of the room. "Fuck, well, I guess I'm done here. You guys can head back to your rooms and get some rack."

The candidates glanced at each other to ascertain whether he was joking.

"KISS is the most important consideration for any plan," he continued. "The clandestine operating environment is already complex enough. If you try to implement multiple moving parts, *Ocean's Eleven* style clusterfuckery, something will go wrong." He paused. "And in this business, that means mission failure."

"But what about the Israeli mission to undermine the Iranian nuclear program? That seemed complex," said Eric.

X let out a snort. "I've got three hours and forty-five minutes to teach you how to plan small-team intelligence collection and target neutralization operations. I'd leave undermining the Iranian nuclear weapons program to

Israel's Joint Intra Agency Effort." He winked. "They've got a little more time and resources." He grabbed a tablet from the desk and activated a flat panel screen. "Right, let's get this shit show started."

Words appeared on the screen.

Know your operating environment.

"A simple well-informed plan that is well executed, that's the gold standard," said X. "By the time I'm finished, you guys are going to be all over it."

Hours later, at one in the morning, the candidates were heading to their accommodation for much-needed rest.

"That was intense," said Mark Dunstan. "Who would have thought there was so much to consider."

"That man is beyond impressive," added Nick. "Big as a house, but smart as all hell."

"I know, right," added Jenny.

"Come on," said Eric. "None of that is rocket science. It's just basic planning. We did stuff way more complex than that in the Army."

"Well, not all of us have been in the Army, bro," added Mark. "I was pretty impressed too."

"Yeah, so was I," added Jenny.

Eric laughed. "Well, you guys are easy to impress. A couple of acronyms and a cool story or two and I'll have you eating out of my hand."

They were a short distance from the shed when everyone's wearable pinged. Jenny glanced at it and saw that the training schedule had been updated. Their first session was at zero six thirty. She groaned. Five hours sleep. Hopefully, they'd get a chance for a nap later in the day. Although, something told her that wasn't going to happen. Exhausted was a state they were going to have to get used to.

———

AS THE CANDIDATES collapsed onto their stretchers X and the rest of his team assembled in the upstairs training room. Bianca, Raj and Steve were there along with a new face.

Jacquie Semenov was the program's human behavior expert. Russian-born, she'd immigrated to the US, where she'd studied psychology before consulting with the Department of Defense, CIA, and now the private sector. She was petite, with a teardrop-shaped face, long brown hair, and dark soulful eyes. Jacquie wore the same uniform as the rest of the team: combat trousers, hiking boots and a fleecy hoody.

"Jac, I think you know everyone here?" X asked as Raj slid a tablet across the table.

"Thank you. Yes, it's good to see you all. I'm looking forward to working on the project with you," said Jacquie, in a neutral accent with only a hint of her native Russian. "I'm sorry for my delayed arrival. Unfortunately, I had to finish up a series of lectures at Stanford. I did read all the candidate profiles on the trip. So, at least I'm not coming in cold turkey."

"You haven't missed much," said X. "The selection process ran smoothly. We got at least four good candidates out of it. There's a little dead wood to cut out, but we have plenty of time for that." He gestured to one of the screens that listed the current ranking. "Right, so this is the first of our debriefs. We will review the rankings daily, discuss any issues, and lock in the next day's program. It's early in the game for rankings, so let's start with any issues and tomorrow's program. Steve, you got anything you want to raise?"

"Nah, mate," the Scotsman replied. "Things went well today, and I'm good for tomorrow."

"Good work readjusting Anderson's attitude," said X.

"Yeah, I thought you'd like that."

"Bianca, you had them for most of the day. Any standouts during your field training?"

"You won't like this, but your old bird, Jenny Murphy, is a bit of a natural," said Bianca. "Good eye for detail and picks things up quickly. Anderson's got a head start on everyone because of his military training, but that won't last. I'm all good for tomorrow."

"OK, Raj, any technical issues?"

"No mate, not on our side. The crew has had some problems with their wireless gear. I'll deconflict their channels tomorrow."

X nodded. "That leads us to the final piece for tonight. The director wants to introduce some kind of video room for the candidates. A place where they can tell the audience how they're feeling about the training and possibly record messages for their family. I don't give two fucks so long as it doesn't hamper training. What are your thoughts?"

Raj, Bianca and Steve all shrugged.

"Will I be able to review the footage?" asked Jacquie.

"Of course. Raj has full access to their servers."

"Then, I think it's an excellent opportunity to get insight into their motivations and vulnerabilities. I can draw on that information to develop their profiles for later training serials. It will help me shape them toward accepting certain behavioral changes."

"When does that start?" asked X.

The Operative

"Shaping starts tomorrow. Every day I will inch them closer to the behavior we need from them. For the candidates who make it through to the end, taking of human life, any human life, will be as normal for them as drinking coffee."

"And I do love coffee," said X.

Chapter Eight

BREAKFAST AWAITED at the shooting range when the contestants arrived, jogging along a farm track. Drenched in sweat from a five-mile run along goat trails and rutted dirt roads, they devoured bacon and egg rolls and drained an urn of coffee.

With breakfast out of the way, they were briefed at *The Station's* makeshift range complex. Three shipping containers were positioned in a field. They held weapons, ammunition and targets. Alongside were parked several older vehicles to be used in different scenarios. The range consisted of a firing point and an impact area stretching down a long valley.

"Team, we're going to spend most of today working on basic weapon handling and marksmanship," said Steve. "I've got fuck all time to get you up to speed, so pay attention. Despite what leftist twats will tell you, guns don't kill people, bullets kill people, and all the ammunition we're using is live. Number one rule. Always point the weapon in a safe direction. We only point guns at people we intend to shoot, and we'll get to that later. First things first, we're going to rehash weapon safety."

It took the former Royal Marine less than thirty minutes to run through the safety aspects of each firearm. During that time, a vehicle delivered X and three of his instructors. They set up the range as the candidates finished their initial briefing. From there, Steve partnered them off and allocated each pair to an instructor. Jenny was assigned to Bianca along with Stacey, a candidate she'd had little to do with.

"Morning, team," Bianca said pleasantly. "I've got you each a set of active ears and eye protection." She passed them headsets and glasses. "We're going to be firing a lot of rounds today, let's make sure we stay safe. Now, have either of you done much shooting before?"

Stacey, a stocky blonde with husky blue eyes, raised her hand. "A little. Friends of ours had a farm when I was growing up."

"Cool, what about you, Jenny?"

"No, I've never fired a gun."

Bianca smiled. "Well, today's your lucky day." She led them to their firing point, where a trestle table was laden with at least a dozen weapons.

"We're going to shoot all of these?" Jenny asked tentatively.

"Yep," said Bianca. "We'll start close and work our way out." She took a tablet from the table. "If you look down range, you'll see all our targets pop up."

Jenny flinched as a pink humanoid shape snapped up twelve feet to her front. More figures appeared behind it, spaced every hundred yards to a half mile. "There's no way I can hit those."

"Sister, by the time I'm done with you, it'll be head shots out to five hundred." Bianca deactivated all the targets except the closest one. "Right. Jenny, let's get you started on the pistol. Pick up the Glock."

"It's OK. Stacey can go first."

"It wasn't an offer, pick up the gun."

Jenny swallowed and took the pistol from the table. Remembering what Steve had told them, she checked there was no magazine and pulled the slide back, ensuring no bullet was in the chamber. "Weapon is clear," she said softly.

"OK, first things first. I'm going to teach you how to grip and aim the pistol," said Bianca. "Then we're going to do some dry firing before we get you chucking lead, OK."

"OK," echoed Jenny.

She paid close attention as Bianca ran her through the basics of the pistol. They worked on grip, stance, loading, sight alignment, and trigger control.

"In my opinion, the pistol is the most difficult weapon to master," the instructor said as she handed Jenny a magazine stacked with live rounds. "Because it's short, it is unforgiving. The slightest miscalculation and you will miss the target. The key is to build a strong grip, align with your target and control the trigger."

Jenny inserted the magazine and racked the slide. She could feel her heart pounding as she held the weapon in both hands, tucked in against her chest, as Bianca had shown her.

"OK, let's do this. Fire two rounds at the center of the target."

Swallowing, she pushed the weapon towards the target, extending her arms until they were locked out and the gun's sights were on the humanoid shape. The end of the barrel trembled as she squeezed the trigger.

The gun jumped in her hands as it fired. She shot again, before returning the weapon to her chest.

"You can breathe now," said Bianca. "Unload the weapon."

She exhaled as she dropped the magazine and ejected a round from the chamber.

Bianca caught the bullet. "That wasn't so bad. Was it?"

"I suppose not."

"Wow, check out the target," said Stacey.

Jenny placed the pistol back on the table and checked the twelve-yard target. The pink human shape had two neat little red holes in the center of the chest.

"You're a natural-born killer," said Bianca. "We'll have you popping headshots in no time."

The comment chilled Jenny to the bone. In seconds, the apprehension of firing a gun had been replaced with pure adrenalin. Had it been real, her target would be dead. She caught herself wondering if she could do it. If, given the right circumstances, she could squeeze a trigger and end a life. She fixated on the two red marks. Suppose that man had threatened the life of those she loved. Then, she could kill him.

"THAT WAS THE BEST DAY YET," said Nick, scrubbing black grime from his hands in the sink outside their dining facility. Jenny stood next to him, doing the same. They had spent the entire day at the range, stopping only for lunch. They progressed from shooting various weapons at a static firing point to shooting from behind cover and working in pairs. They even had the opportunity to shoot from inside a stationary car.

"I never thought shooting could be so much fun," said Jenny. "Once I'd built my confidence up, that is. What was your favorite gun?"

"I loved the submachine gun. It's like a little jackhammer," replied Nick as he dried his hands.

"Who would have thought it was such a dirty sport," added Jenny as she did the same.

Their dining facility was a large, air-conditioned tent a short distance from the ranch house. Dinner was a self-service affair, with the contestants free to sit wherever they wanted. As they entered, Jenny noted that Mark, Eric, Veronica and Natalie were already seated at one table, eating and chatting.

She and Nick joined the rest at the food station.

"You get the feeling that we've been relegated to the B team," Nick whispered as they waited.

"There's strength in numbers," said Jenny as they got their food and joined the other candidates at a separate table.

"How did everyone go today?" asked Brianna. The short-haired brunette was one of the few contestants Jenny had yet to interact with.

"Nailed it," said Stacey. "Jenny and I were dropping tangos like pros."

"Tangos?" queried Brianna.

"Yeah, that's what they call bad guys in the business."

"Learning new things every day," added Troy as he sat. "Hey, has anyone used the diary room yet?"

"Has there been time?" asked Nick. "They've been running us ragged."

"A friend of mine was on a reality TV show. She said the diary room was the key to becoming a star. You get in there and get emotional," said Brianna. "I guarantee they will air it. More airtime is what wins reality TV shows. It's that simple."

"Well, you know those guys will be all over it." Troy gestured to Mark and Veronica's table. "They'll do anything to win."

"I like the idea of being able to send a message to my family," said Jenny. "They must be wondering how I'm doing."

"Do you have kids?" asked Brianna. "A teary message to your kids could get you even more screen time."

"Two nephews. My sister's kids."

"That will work."

"I've got three nieces," added Stacey.

"No kids and no siblings," said Troy.

"Same here," added Adrian.

"That's interesting," added Nick. "I don't have kids either. I wonder if that was part of the selection criteria?"

"Mothers and fathers probably make crappy assassins," joked Troy. "Right, I'm going to shower and get some rest. No doubt tomorrow is going to be just as brutal as today."

―――

X GULPED from his protein shaker as he climbed the stairs to his apartment and the operations room. He wasn't surprised to find Jacquie sitting in front of a tablet with headphones on.

A glance at the status board told him that most contestants were asleep. Their wearables registered a lack of movement, low heart rate and steady breathing. Interestingly, Jenny was still awake. He checked the map and saw that she was in one of the diary rooms outside of the mess hall.

He turned to Jacquie and tapped his ear, gesturing for her to remove the headphones. She slipped one side off. "You listening in on the old bird's diary time?" he asked.

"If she's old, then you're prehistoric, buddy. Yeah, I'm getting some interesting insights into Miss Jennifer Murphy. She recorded a very heartfelt message for her sister and nephews. She's having a hard time, but she'll stick it out for them."

"Good for her." X took another gulp from his shake and slumped into a chair.

"She's got a lot of potential," continued Jacquie. "She's made significant improvements in her physical profile, and she's got the emotional intelligence we're looking for."

"There's a saying, Jac. You can't teach an old dog new tricks."

She snorted. "I think that says more about you than her."

X shrugged. "Yeah, but at the end of the day. Do you really think a middle-aged aunty is going to be able to pull the trigger and get the job done? She might have the skills, but what about the will?"

"That's why I'm here. To help her find that will."

"Yeah, but even your psycho-manipulation has limits. Some people just don't have the killer instinct. Have any of the others been using your diary room?"

She nodded. "All of the top four. They've all recorded something."

"Heartfelt crap, no doubt."

"Pretty much. But it's all useful and gives me interesting insights into what makes them tick."

"Looking forward to seeing what you can do with that info." He drained his shaker. "Right, I'm going to get some sleep. Big day tomorrow. We'll see how our contestants shape up one on one."

"That sounds very interesting. You mind if I observe?"

X smiled. "I'd be disappointed if you didn't."

―――――

JENNY FLINCHED as paint projectiles hit the side of the car she was crouched behind. Gripping her M4 carbine tightly, she turned and looked back at Stacey, who was a dozen yards away at the corner of a building. Behind Stacey was the rest of the squad: Troy, Mark and Brianna.

"I'm stuck," she yelled as more rounds struck the vehicle. "I need covering fire."

Stacey gave a thumbs up and stuck her weapon around the edge of the building, firing blindly.

As Jenny made to dash back to the wall, a volley of bullets peppered the car. Whoever was out there had not been perturbed by her teammate's efforts.

"You need to find a better position," she yelled. "You gotta try and hit them."

Another thumbs up.

Jenny sighed; she had volunteered to take point in their first 'force on force' training activity, a decision she regretted. With the contestants decked out in combat vests, helmets and carbines, they'd been split into two teams. Their objective, to hunt down and 'neutralize' the opposing team.

The battleground was a makeshift village surrounded by hills. The crew had configured shipping containers into buildings, and wrecked cars littered the streets. The opposing force, consisting of Natalie, Eric, Veronica, Adrian and Nick, had started on the far side. Jenny had suggested that they wait and ambush them as they came hunting. Mark, their squad leader, had instead taken the fight to them. "Fortune favors the bold," he'd said.

"The others are getting into position," Stacey yelled.

"Tell them to hurry," she responded as more rounds slapped into the car.

"I'll give you more cover."

"No, stay back," yelled Jenny.

Stacey stepped around the corner and raised her carbine. As she made to fire, the wall alongside her was peppered with orange marks. She shrieked as pellets hit her chest, and one slapped her helmet, leaving a splash of paint. "I'm hit," she screamed, slumping to the ground.

"Stacey is down!" Jenny yelled. The rest of the team, now on top of the building, opened fire.

Over the crack of their weapons, she heard a yell from the enemy. They might have hit one. Suddenly, she wasn't taking fire. She crouched and sprinted for the building. As she passed Stacey she grabbed her teammate, dragging her behind the wall.

A quick check revealed that she'd have been instantly killed had the rounds been live. "Thanks for covering me."

"Fuck you," Stacey hissed. "Do not get shot. It hurts like hell."

"I'll do my best."

"They're pushing around on your side," bellowed Troy from the roof.

She glanced back at the car and spotted figures through the paint-splattered glass. Bullets snapped over her head as she hugged the wall.

"We're exposed up here," yelled Mark. "We're pulling back."

Jenny's heart raced. With the team withdrawing off

the roof, she was the only line of defense from the attack coming from her side. She dropped the magazine from her weapon and took a full one from Stacey's vest.

"Hey, that's mine."

"Sorry, I think I'll need it more than you."

"YOU SEEING THIS, BOSS?" Raj directed X's attention to the primary screen in the control room, where a drone shot was displayed. He and X had joined Chuck and his production team to observe the training activity. They were in radio contact with Steve and the others running the safety measures on the ground.

On the screen, Alpha team was making an audacious flanking maneuver, having neutralized at least one of Bravo's operatives. Currently, all that stood between them was candidate Jenny Murphy.

"This will be over in less than a minute," said X. He keyed his radio. "Steve, Alpha is assaulting from the right flank. Get ready to reset the activity with teams at opposite ends."

"Roger."

"Tighten up that drone shot," ordered Chuck, the director. "And get a ground crew onto Jenny."

"I've got fifty bucks that she breaks and runs," said X.

"I'll take that bet if you make it Euros," said Raj.

"You fuckers left the EU."

"Doesn't mean I don't travel."

"Fine. Deal!"

They watched Alpha's three strong assault force break cover and charge Jenny. The other two operatives were firing at the rest of Bravo, pinning them on the roof where they were exposed.

"Here we go," said Raj.

On a separate screen, the feed from a camera crew focused on Jenny. She looked terrified as she stood at the corner of the building, her carbine held ready. X glanced at his tablet and saw her heart rate was 135 beats per minute. "That cash is in the bank," he murmured.

The assault force reached the wrecked car without having a shot fired at them. They paused, and then as they made their dash for the building, all hell broke loose.

Jenny spotted them and opened fire. Her initial barrage peppered one of the attackers, dropping Natalie. The other two skidded to a halt as Jenny knelt, pumping the trigger of her assault rifle. Paint projectiles slapped the car as the men hid behind it.

"Mag empty," said X. "They'll get her now."

Almost on cue, the two men, Eric and Adrian, surged forward for the kill.

X expected Jenny to panic and run. She did the opposite. Before the magazine she'd ejected had hit the ground, she'd inserted a fresh one, slapping the bolt release as paint rounds exploded around her. Then, eyes wide and jaw set, she shot Adrian in the face, paint splattering across his shoulder camera. Seeing his partner fall, Eric fired several shots before retreating.

"You go, girl," exclaimed Raj as he slapped X on the shoulder. "I'll message you my account details."

X shook his head in disbelief.

"Can I get some comments on camera?" asked Chuck.

"No!" snapped X. "The mission isn't over. Both teams lost three combatants in that engagement. That leaves four on the field. Raj, double or nothing?"

"Terms?"

"You win if she does."

Raj glanced up at the screen. The sole surviving member of Jenny's team, Mark, had joined her behind the building. On a separate screen, Eric and Veronica huddled, discussing their plans. "Yeah, OK. I'll take that bet."

"Right on. Now it's time to up the ante." He spoke into his radio. "Steve, let them know they've got three minutes to finish their mission. The winner gets indemnity from the first elimination."

"Hey, look, decisions like that need to be discussed," said Chuck. "I'm trying to direct a television series."

X shut him down with an icy look as he transmitted again. "Steve, three minutes on the clock."

JENNY FLINCHED as Steve's voice boomed over a megaphone, declaring that the round would be complete in three minutes and the winning team would have indemnity from the first elimination activity.

"Veronica and Eric are going to come at us hard," said Mark. "We should set up an ambush."

"I don't think so," said Jenny. "They're two of the toughest competitors. They'll assume we'll want the indemnity more than them."

"Well, they're not wrong. We've got about two and a half minutes. What's the plan?"

"We get after them. We've got nothing to lose."

Mark nodded, checking the magazine on his carbine. "Let's do it. I'll take point."

"Two minutes," bellowed Steve as they made their move.

Mark led them away from the building and the paint-splattered car, pushing along the right-hand side of the battleground, their weapons aimed inward.

Jenny spotted movement toward the center of the makeshift village. "They're in the middle."

She aimed her weapon as he turned, and they progressed down a street lined with wrecked cars. Suddenly, Mark opened fire. "Flank them," he screamed, waving his arm to direct her to the right. Jenny sprang into action, running to the side of the cars. Raising her carbine, she aimed it in the direction that Mark was firing.

Catching a glimpse of a figure hiding behind a stack of tires, she fired twice before moving cautiously up the street. 'Keep your head on a swivel,' Steve had repeated during training, constantly reminding them that a threat could come from any direction.

She could see that Mark was fixated on the figure behind the tires. He had them covered and was waving for her to flank them. She paused. There was a second shooter out there, and Veronica and Eric had proven themselves to be slippery adversaries.

'One minute," bellowed Steve.

"Cover me!" yelled Mark.

He lurched forward as Jenny peppered the tire stack with paint rounds, keeping the shooter pinned behind it.

Suddenly, Mark yelled and raised his arms in the air. He was hit. Jenny searched frantically for his assailant. She spotted him as paint rounds slapped into the car's roof alongside her. A figure appeared on a shipping container opposite. Jenny fired as they jumped onto a burnt-out van.

She was on her own now and knew it was a matter of survival. Earning immunity was well and truly out of her reach. Sprinting from the car to a stack of tires, she heard rounds hissing past her.

"Just give up, Jenny," screamed Veronica.

Gritting her teeth, Jenny shoved her carbine back around the corner and fired off the rest of her magazine. Then, as she ran, she ejected it and fumbled her last mag into the weapon. Weaving between car bodies, tires and barrels, she sprinted for the building where Stacey had been shot. Rounds splattered a drum to her left as she ducked past a car and reached the building. Legs burning and breathing hard, she turned and hugged the corner of the wall, her weapon ready.

"Thirty seconds," Steve yelled.

Veronica and Eric broke cover and came at her across the street with their weapons blazing. Jenny fired in response, targeting Veronica, who was closest to her. Pellets struck the wall and whistled behind her as she lined up the athletic contestant and pulled the trigger.

Her efforts were rewarded with a cry as pellets struck her target's face and chest. Flecks of paint splattered her mask as Eric zeroed in on her. Jenny ducked behind the wall and turned, narrowly avoiding a camera crew.

She dashed for a cluster of shipping containers. All she needed to do was stay out of Eric's sights for a few more seconds. There was mud surrounding the makeshift city block. Trucks had churned the soil into a slick paste. Jenny slipped as she reached a container and fell heavily on her shoulder.

Winded, she lay still for a moment before scrabbling into one of the containers. Inside, she wedged herself into the far corner, behind a desk and aimed her barrel at the door. A shadow flashed past the doorway. Jenny panicked and fired the last of her rounds. Then, as the carbine locked back on empty, Eric stepped in through the opening.

"Trapped like a rat," he snarled. The infantry officer turned banker had a twisted grin on his face as he squeezed the trigger.

His killing shot hit Jenny on the lens of her face mask, blue paint splattering across her vision.

"Guys, we need to reset and film that shot again." One of the film crew appeared from behind Eric. "Great one-liner and a great kill. We need to take a few minutes to get it right."

It took ten, and Jenny had to relive the humiliation of the death blow repeatedly. Finally, when the crew was happy, she was allowed to join the others at the edge of the battleground, where Eric's team greeted him with high fives.

"Right, I want your weapons cleaned and secured in the container," barked Steve. "You've got half an hour to get back to camp, clean up and report to the classroom for a full debrief. Get moving."

"What about my indemnity?" asked Eric.

Steve's eyes narrowed. "What the fuck are you talking about?"

"I won the challenge. I get indemnity from the elimination."

The instructor shook his head. "You didn't win, champ. When the buzzer sounded, there were still two of you in play."

"That's bullshit," said Eric.

Steve shrugged. "Got no one to blame but yourself." He turned to the others. "Key takeaway for the day. In combat, there's no room for pithy one-liners. If you've got the shot. Take it. Right, get a fucking hustle on."

As they lined up to return their weapons, Jenny found

herself behind Eric. As they entered the container, he turned to face her. "You fucking know I won. You should have surrendered when we got Mark."

"That wasn't the objective," whispered Jenny.

"Yeah, well, you know I won. You could have said something."

"Jenny couldn't have changed anything," Nick said from behind. "They've got us covered with sensors, cameras and drones."

"Shut your face, Nick. You got taken out by a chick. You're not even in this game."

Nick stepped past Jenny and positioned himself in front of the bigger man. "Yeah, well at least I'm not a complete asshole."

"Tactitards, stow your shit and get on the road," ordered Steve. "If you're late to my debriefing, you'll be running the hills till midnight."

Eric glared at Nick then Jenny before shoving his weapon into the rack. He and Veronica left.

"Man, that guy's intense." Nick turned to Jenny. "I thought you did a great job out there. I mean, you shot me right in the face."

"Yeah, sorry about that."

"All's fair in the art of war," said Nick as they joined the others on the road back to camp.

Jenny noted that Eric and his 'squad' hadn't waited for the rest of them. They were already a few hundred yards away.

"Well, that was fun," said Nick as they started jogging. "I wonder what they've got for us next."

"They offered indemnity," said Jenny. "We have to be heading into an elimination."

"Yeah, that's right," said Stacey. "You know the others have formed a pact. They see us as the weak ones."

"We should do the same," said Troy. "We do everything we can to help each other get through."

"And we do the same to bury those assholes," said Stacey. "It's our only chance of making it through any elimination rounds. Troy's in, what about the rest of you?"

"Yeah, OK," said Nick.

"Is that fair?" asked Jenny.

"You can play fair," said Stacey. "Or you can be eliminated. It's your choice."

Chapter Nine

JENNY'S LEGS trembled as she spooned scrambled eggs into her mouth. The morning's training session had been a brutal one. A seven-mile trail run broken up with hill sprints, sandbag carrying and lunges. Steve said they'd put in the goods and earned an extended breakfast.

"I think they're setting us up for the elimination round," said Nick, as he tucked into a plate laden with bacon and eggs. "This is the first reward we've earned since we got here."

The 'B' team, as Eric called them, were seated together. Their group consisted of Stacey, Nick, Adrian, Troy, Brianna and Jenny.

"You think?" asked Jenny, glancing at the other table where Eric, Veronica, Mark and Natalie were eating and laughing.

"After Steve ripped into us at the debriefing last night, I thought we'd roll straight into it," added Troy. "Anyone got an idea what elimination will look like? Do you think they'll use some kind of obstacle challenge like on *Survivor*?"

"This is a lot more sophisticated than that," said Nick, between mouthfuls. "I think, somehow, they're going to test us on everything we've learned. Maybe we will plan and then execute some kind of mission."

"On our own?" asked Jenny.

"No, I think it will be a team thing," said Nick.

"Well, hopefully, we won't have to work with those guys," added Troy.

"Remember our pact," said Stacey.

Jenny felt her wearable buzz and glanced at the screen. "Looks like we're about to find out." The message required them to report to the upstairs classroom immediately.

"Here we go," said Nick.

The team exited the dining tent and crossed the equipment park to the barn. Jenny felt trepidation building in her stomach as she climbed the stairs to the classroom. X was standing at the front of the room as they filed in and sat.

"Listen up," said X as he scanned the candidates with a steely gaze. "This next phase of your training will be your opportunity to test the skills and knowledge you've developed. In the business, we call it a full mission profile. You will receive a detailed briefing in a moment. Then, you'll be split into two teams and isolated in separate planning areas. You'll have three hours to prepare for your mission before you execute. I'd wish you good luck, but that shit is for people who don't plan. Bianca, you have the floor."

Jenny glanced sideways at Nick, who shrugged. He was right on the money with his guess on the elimination program.

As Bianca replaced X at the front of the classroom, screens behind her blinked on, revealing two aerial photos of separate residences. "Team," said the athletic brunette. "The mission is simple. You will be given the coordinates for

The Operative

a target. Your job is to gather as much intel as possible on the persons and activities conducted at that location." She paused. "Compromise, failure to gather intelligence and poor performance will be terms for elimination."

Stepping to the side, she advanced the screens. "There are two locations. Working in teams of five, you will plan and execute your intelligence-gathering mission against your allocated target. These are the teams."

Jenny found her name on the slide. She was in team Romeo with Nick, Stacey, Adrian and Eric. She felt like she'd been punched in the stomach. The worst possible scenario had come to fruition. She was heading into an elimination round with a man who wanted to destroy her.

"Right," continued Bianca. "Bravo team will report to the training floor downstairs. Romeo, you will stay here. Everything you need to plan this operation has been given to you on tablets accessible via your wearable. Get to it."

The candidates moved fast. Bravo team exited the room along with Instructor X, leaving Romeo behind with Bianca.

"Tablets are here," said Nick from the back of the room.

"There's a Q-store inventory on them," said Bianca. "If it's listed, you can draw it for the mission. I'll also be here to answer any questions."

Nick handed out the tablets. "There's a library of documents on the home screen," he observed. "I think we should take the time to look through them and then convene a planning session. What do you guys think?"

"Yes, that's what we will do," said Eric. "Let's say fifteen minutes to review, and then we can start planning."

Jenny glanced at Nick, who shrugged. They could both see what was going to happen. Eric would try to railroad his plans on the rest of the team, sidelining the 'weaker' competitors. They would have to hold their own if they wanted to stay in this game.

"SO EXACTLY WHAT IS OUR MISSION?" asked Stacey as Romeo team gathered around a single table, tablets in hand.

"Simple, it's a recon job," said Eric. "We get in. Get as much info on the place as possible and then get out."

"One of the documents listed some priorities," said Jenny, thumbing through the pages on her tablet. "Here we go, Priority Information Requirements."

"Clearly, we need to plan our mission around getting as many of those as possible," said Eric.

"Without risking compromise," added Stacey. "Compromise is almost certainly going to mean elimination."

Eric's gaze lingered on Jenny, "Yeah, we wouldn't want that to happen." Then his eyes dropped back to his tablet. "If we want to win, we'll have to take some risks."

"True, but I think we can mitigate risk with some of the tech in the Q-store," said Nick.

"You're pretty good with that stuff," admitted Eric. "You and Jenny can run low-risk standoff surveillance with Stacey. Adrian and I will look at opportunities for close target recon and possible infiltration. That plays to everyone's strengths and maximizes our chance of success."

Jenny was caught off guard by his approach. She'd expected him to take charge but also anticipated being put in a position where elimination was highly probable. Evidently, he planned to sideline the team's three 'weakest' members and take all the glory for himself.

The Operative

"I think I'd be better working with you," said Stacey. "I'm not really into all the geek stuff."

Jenny pursed her lips. Stacey had seen the writing on the wall, and the blonde had already jumped ship; so much for their pact.

"SO, the next thing we need to do is decide the outcomes of the elimination round," said the director, Chuck, as X and his team were about to leave the production meeting.

While the two teams were planning, the production and training crew had ironed out the finer details of the challenge. Role players, safety staff and camera crews had been allocated and X had given his orders. However, there was no mention of who might be cut.

"That depends on how the contestants perform," said X.

Chuck shook his head. "That's not how it usually works. The eliminations are our opportunity to guide the show. We can use it to remove undesirable talent. I've got some notes we could go over."

X's eyes narrowed. Raj and Jac waited for the explosion they thought would follow. "How about we let the crew finish their work, and we review your notes."

Chuck nodded enthusiastically. "You heard the man. Let's get to work, people."

X gestured for Raj and Jac to stay as the assistant producers and camera crews filed out of the shearing shed. "OK, what have you got?"

"My list doesn't depart much from the current rankings." Chuck directed their attention to one of the wall-mounted screens. Raj updated the listing twice daily, based on contestants' performance across various metrics. "However, some interesting relationships are emerging that I don't think we want to lose. For instance, Stacey isn't performing well. However, she is part of a compelling dynamic that creates tension between Eric, his supporters, and the others. I think we need to make sure we keep her in play."

"Is that how this is usually done?" X asked.

Chuck laughed. "Yeah, nothing about reality TV is left to chance. We manipulate every aspect of it."

"Interesting. So, who do you think we should," X accented his words with air quotes, "eliminate?"

"Mark Dunstan and Adrian Paulson. They're both run-of-the-mill white guys who don't add any real drama to the show. If we scrub them, we've got a higher percentage of diversity and better viewing."

X gave a thumbs up as he rose. "I've got a call with David later tonight. I'll make sure he gets your recommendations."

"Boss, you feeling OK?" asked Raj as they returned to their office in the ranch house.

The facility was a hive of activity as staff loaded trucks and vehicles in preparation for the pending elimination.

X laughed. "Why? Because I let Chuck think his opinion counts? That guy's about as relevant as a one-legged man in an ass-kicking competition."

"There isn't even a call with David, is there," said Jac once they'd arrived in the office.

"Nope. Not till after the Full Mission Profile. I want to see how they perform in the field before we start culling."

"So, not all about the drama?" she replied with a chuckle.

"Fuck no, ain't no room for drama in a gunfight." He

slumped into a chair. "Right, Raj, how we lookin' with comms and overwatch?"

"THERE'S A WHITE VAN APPROACHING. Can you confirm the writing on the side?" asked Nick as he observed the driveway to the target location through binoculars.

He and Jenny were manning a camouflaged observation post on a distant hill overlooking a luxury estate. They'd hiked in and set it up overnight, leaving the rest of Romeo team a few hundred yards away on the other side of the hill in a lay-up point or LUP.

Jenny adjusted the focal point on her powerful spotting scope as the van stopped at the outer security gates. "Hirepool," she reported as the driver spoke through an open window to a security guard. A moment later, the gates swung open, admitting the vehicle.

"So far, we've got a hire company and a liquor delivery service," transmitted Nick over his radio.

Jenny tracked the van as it continued along the drive that rose through lines of green vines. Panning past the van, she focused on a stone mansion that adorned a slight rise, surrounded by lawns and gardens. She zoomed in on two men trimming a hedge and loading clippings into a side-by-side buggy. Past them another man operated a ride-on mower. "They're giving the gardens a tidy-up," she said. "I think they're getting ready for a party."

"You get that?" asked Nick.

"Yep," replied Eric. "All this activity is perfect cover for a CTR. We're getting ready to head in."

"The noise from the mower would mask a drone. That would let us get closer with less risk," said Nick.

"Yeah, but that doesn't give us the flexibility to send someone inside. But don't worry. You'll be safe where you are. OK, we're moving. Make sure you keep us updated on any activity."

"Will do," replied Nick.

Jenny watched the gardeners as Nick focused on the driveway and perimeter fence. Both men looked to have radios attached to their belts. "Nick, I think the gardeners are doubling as security."

"That makes sense. The intel package said there would be at least five guards on target, and so far, we've only seen the one at the gate."

Jenny continued scanning the residence, past a swimming pool to a double garage. As she watched, the roller door on one side rose, revealing a side-by-side with what looked like a radar dome perched on its roof.

"Nick, look at this." She moved away from the spotting scope so he could slide across and take her place.

"Oh, wow. That's some kind of security buggy with a thermal camera and scanners," he said, adjusting the focus. "This could be a security fast response element. We need to warn the others."

As Nick reported what he was seeing to Eric and the others, Jenny used the binoculars to scan the approach route they were using. She spotted them and their camera crew a short distance from the target's outer perimeter fence.

"You know, if that were us down there, Eric wouldn't have warned us," said Jenny.

"Yeah, but we're not like him," replied Nick. "Now, how many of the information requirements on the list have we ticked?"

Jenny checked her notes. "Not many."

"We should have launched the drone. It would have

been able to sniff out the wireless networks and see over those hedges."

"Too late now." She watched as the mower returned to the garage.

"Guys, we've found a good entry point," transmitted Eric. "There's a culvert here that gets us under the perimeter fence. Adrian and I will see how close we can get to the residence. We're taking all the surveillance gear. If we get a chance, we're going to enter the building. Stacey is going to remain at the perimeter. Let us know if any security, especially that buggy, moves."

"Will do," replied Nick.

"Wow, he's going for glory," said Jenny. She watched as the men slipped through the security fence. Then, she lost them in thick bushes as they headed toward the residence with a cameraman in tow.

"It's telling that they didn't assign a camera crew to us," said Nick.

"Well, at least they gave us body cameras and mics," said Jenny as she watched the sweeping drive. "Nick, do you think it's weird that the show doesn't have a host?"

"I was thinking about that the other day. I think they'll add the host's commentary in post-production. Plus, I don't think X would put up with some over-energized influencer type sticking their nose everywhere. I mean, he barely puts up with the director."

"True." Jenny spotted a vehicle approaching the road leading to the residence. "We've got incoming," she reported. "Black SUV with heavily tinted windows."

"We've also got movement at the garage. They've driven the buggy outside," added Nick. "I can see it is a security vehicle. It has multiple sensors, including optics that could be thermal."

"That SUV could contain a HVI," whispered Eric, referring to a High Value Individual. "If we can positively identify them, it could seal the win."

Jenny tracked the SUV as it passed through the security checkpoint then along the paved drive to the residence, where it stopped. The driver exited and moved to the opposite side, out of her view. "I can't see the occupant."

"Me either," confirmed Nick.

"If we push forward a few more yards, we can get eyes on," Eric reported, his voice low over the radio.

"That's not a good idea. There are two guards in the buggy. They're leaving the residence," said Nick. "That sensor suite may be able to spot you."

Jenny turned her binoculars to where Eric, Adrian and the cameraman were hidden. Scanning the gardens, she failed to spot them. "They might be OK." At that moment, she heard the distant roar of an engine.

"No, they're on to them," snapped Nick. "You're blown. Get out. Get out now," he transmitted.

"Pulling back," replied Eric.

Jenny's pulse quickened as security personnel gathered around the SUV, while the buggy raced along the driveway. She caught a glimpse of movement near the fence as Adrian and Eric made their escape.

Meanwhile, the buggy exited through the security checkpoint, turned onto a small trail that paralleled the fence and skidded to a halt. One of the guards left the side-by-side with a rifle in his hands. Jenny could see the sensor on the vehicle's roof panning back and forth.

"Could they spot us?" she asked.

"Not from there. A small unit like that only has a few hundred yards range. Also, I doubt it could see our heat through the bushes and netting."

The Operative

The guard jumped back in the buggy. It reversed to the main road before driving down to a track that ran along the vegetated valley that Eric had used to infiltrate. Again, it stopped, conducting a scan.

"Guys, you need to get out of there. The security teams are moving up the valley doing scans. If you stay put, they're going to find you."

"We're with Stacey. We're heading back to the LUP." The radio did little to mask the frustration in his voice.

"OK, we will continue to monitor the situation from here. If we get an opportunity, we will launch the drone."

"X, half of Romeo have reached their LUP," reported Raj. He and the senior instructor were monitoring the activity in the production studio.

"We got some great footage from that close shave," added Charles. "It's going to be edge-of-the-seat stuff, with the overlaid audio from the two in the hideout."

"OP, it's an observation post, not a hideout," said X. "Did the guards positively ID any of the CTR?"

"Yeah, Adrian was eyeballed by the close protection team," replied Raj.

X cracked his knuckles as he contemplated the information. "Tell Romeo team that Eric, Adrian and Stacey will move to the alternate RV and await extraction. Their mission is over."

"Wait," said Chuck. "We can get more out of this. Surely they wouldn't just give up?"

"They've still got two team members in play," said Raj.

"Yeah, but they're the oldies. They're not going to give

us the same kind of action that Eric can produce," said the director.

"Well, I guess this is their big chance," snapped X. "Raj, where are we at with Bravo team?"

"They're playing it real safe. So far, they've established two OPs and are watching the target. They're discussing the merits of a CTR. My gut feeling, they won't make a move till after dark."

"We could order them to go in," said Chuck.

"That's not the point of the activity," replied X. "There are vulnerabilities built into each target. The teams need to find them and exploit them."

"Got it. But the endgame is television. We can make this better."

"Just film it, Chuck. Leave the training outcomes to me and my team."

———

"WHAT DO WE DO NOW?" asked Jenny. "We're out here on our own."

Nick shrugged as he adjusted the spotting scope. "I guess we continue to monitor the target and extract as per the original plan."

Jenny focused the binoculars and saw the buggy and the black SUV had returned to the front of the garage. The grounds staff had also resumed work, erecting a marquee alongside the villa. "Yeah, they're definitely preparing for a party. We need to get closer to see who's attending. Do you think the drone would work?"

He shook his head. "No, they're going to be on alert now. They'll spot it."

"Nick, I think they've left us out here to fail."

"What makes you say that?"

"Just a gut feeling."

Nick paused in thought. "What if it's actually the opposite?"

"What do you mean?"

"What if X has left us out here to prove ourselves? We need to look at this as an opportunity."

"OK, maybe." She lowered the binoculars and turned to Nick. His brow was furrowed.

"We need to be bold."

"What are you thinking?"

He smiled. "How do you feel about infiltrating their party?"

THE VAN MARKED *Alpine Catering* pulled off the main road and drove along the gravel drive leading up to Romeo's target compound.

"What's going on here?" said the driver, a middle-aged woman dressed in a white chef's jacket with a name tag that read *Margaret*.

"Looks like she might be lost," said her passenger, a younger woman whose tag read *Izzy*.

The caterer brought the van to a halt and lowered the window.

"Hello," said the woman. "I was wondering if you could help me out. My car is parked just off the road, and it's got a flat battery. I need a jump."

The woman was a little younger than Margaret, had a kind face and was dressed for a hike. She checked the clock on the dash. They had plenty of time. "Sure, we can help. Lead the way."

"Thanks so much. Follow me. It's not far."

They drove slowly, following her off the road and down a track into a clearing.

"I can't see the car," said Izzy as they stopped. Her door was yanked open, and she was suddenly staring into the muzzle of a pistol.

"Get out of the truck, and no one gets hurt," ordered an Asian man, also dressed in hiking gear.

Margaret's door opened, and a second weapon appeared in the hands of the woman. "We're not going to harm you. We just need to borrow your van and jackets," she said.

"Please, please don't hurt us," stuttered the caterer.

"Out of the van," the man repeated.

They exited slowly with their hands held high.

"Please don't..." Margaret's whimper was cut off by an approaching car. An SUV skidded to a halt, and the two assailants aimed their weapons. The driver's door opened, and a woman wearing a fluorescent vest and a baseball cap stepped out. "OK, candidates. Time out."

Jenny immediately recognized Bianca and lowered her weapon as a camera crew appeared from the vehicle's rear.

"Stay here," said the instructor. "Ma'am," she addressed the caterer. "You and your colleague have inadvertently stumbled into a reality television show. If you step over to the car, I'll explain everything."

Nick and Jenny waited at the rear of the van. "I think we might have broken their scenario. I wonder what they're going to do."

Bianca spent a moment talking to the caterers before joining them. "OK, so you've got five minutes with Margret and Izzy. You can use whatever is in the van or on their persons. Assume that you have physically detained them."

The Operative

"Are they OK? We assumed they were part of the scenario," said Jenny.

"They're fine; a lack of foresight on our behalf. Lesson learned. Stay flexible, right? Now, get to it."

Eight minutes later, Jenny was at the van's wheel as it approached the villa's security checkpoint."

"You guys see anything suspicious on the way in?" asked the guard as he checked a tablet for the truck's details.

"No," replied Jenny. "Why, what's going on?"

"Had a few people sniffing around. Probably journalists looking to snap some photos of the high rollers. Which reminds me, I'll need you guys to check your phones. You'll get them back on the way out."

Jenny handed over the phones she'd taken from the caterers.

"Someone will meet you at the house and show you where to park. You have a good one," said the guard.

"You too," replied Jenny before driving toward the villa. The guard had almost certainly spotted the camera crew in the truck's rear. But that was all part and parcel of being in a reality TV show. Funny, she thought. They didn't make it seem any less realistic. Her pulse quickened as the massive stone mansion came into view. One of the grounds staff directed them along a side road to what she assumed was the kitchen entrance.

Nick opened the glove compartment and glanced at a device inside as she parked. "We're picking up half a dozen networks and a bunch of IP addresses," he said excitedly.

"We'll get even more once we're inside." She turned to her partner. "I should have asked before. Do you have much cooking experience?"

Nick smiled. "Yeah, I love cooking."

She exhaled. "OK, we've got this."

Chapter Ten

"WHAT THE HELL happened to you guys?" asked Eric as Jenny and Nick stopped for coffee. He'd spotted them as soon as they entered the dining tent. "We've been waiting here for hours."

Nick poured him and Jenny a black coffee. "We made a move after your extraction."

"A move? What the fuck does that mean?"

"It means we managed to get on target and gather more information," replied Nick.

"How?"

Nick's wearable buzzed, and he glanced at the screen as Eric and Jenny did the same. "We've got a debrief in fifteen. I guess you'll find out then. Like everyone else."

"You guys better not have fucked this for me." The square-shouldered contestant stormed out of the tent.

"The nerve of that guy," said Nick. "We've probably saved the team's bacon." They took their cups and headed for Stacey and Adrian's table.

"Hey, you guys took your time getting back," said Stacey. "You get lost?"

"No," said Nick. "We managed to find a way to get up to the villa."

At that moment, Bravo team entered the tent. Troy and Brianna spotted them and approached.

"How did you guys go?" asked Jenny.

"Nothing special," said Brianna. "Veronica and Mark ran the show. We set up a couple of OPs and sent in a drone to collect electronic data. We managed to answer some of the info requirements. Not many of the high-value ones, though."

"So much the same as us," said Stacey.

"Well, we better head to the debriefing. Everyone ready for four hours of berating for 'how shit' we are?" said Nick.

The group left the tent and crossed the vehicle park to the upstairs lecture room. They'd reached the stairs when Stacey and Adrian stopped and glanced at their wearables.

"I've got to report to medical," said Adrian.

"Me too," added Stacey.

"Debrief starts in ten minutes. They're probably going to check on all of us after our first mission," said Jenny. "I'd hate to know where my heart rate was."

"We'll see you up there," said Stacey.

Jenny paused at the top of the stairs and watched the two contestants enter the medical post. Then she followed everyone else inside.

STACEY OPENED the door to the medical hut and entered the reception area with Adrian close behind. They waited a moment before the inside door opened, and Steve appeared.

"This way."

She shot Adrian a look then followed Steve into the treatment room. Inside, Steve handed them each a black hood. "Put these on."

"What's going on?" asked Adrian.

The instructor didn't reply. He continued to hold the hoods. Stacey sighed, took one and slipped it over her head. She heard a door open, and footsteps as at least two more people joined them. A hand grasped her shoulder and guided her out of the building into a vehicle.

"Where are we going?" she asked.

No one answered.

The hum of tarmac soon replaced the crunch of gravel beneath the tires. They drove for fifteen minutes before the vehicle pulled off the road and a door opened.

"Get out. Count to twenty and then remove the hoods," said Steve.

Doors slammed shut, and the vehicle left as Stacey counted. Reaching twenty, she tore off the hood and saw that Adrian was with her. A glance revealed they'd been dropped at a tin shed on a long stretch of road. A peeling, hand-painted sign declared it was a bus stop.

"What the hell," she murmured.

"I think we've been scrubbed," Adrian said quietly.

Their original backpacks had been left by the side of the road. Recovering hers, Stacey sat on the shelter's weathered bench, hugging it to her chest. "So that's it then?"

"I guess so," said Adrian.

"No ceremony. No last diary entry to tell the audience how we feel? What the fuck." Stacey had tears in her eyes. "They didn't even tell us why we got cut."

The Operative

Adrian shrugged. "We didn't make the grade, and X is not the kind of guy to mince words."

They sat in silence until Adrian spotted a vehicle approaching along the road. As it got closer, they could see it was a small bus. It stopped before the shelter, and a folding door opened with a hiss.

"Get in," ordered the driver, a wizened silver-haired man who looked like he had stepped straight from behind a horse-drawn plow.

"Where are you going?" asked Stacey.

"Does it matter? You gonna stay here?"

"That's a fair point," said Adrian as he shouldered his backpack and stepped on board.

Stacey followed.

"There's a fare," said the man.

"We haven't got any money," replied Adrian.

"That fancy watch will do."

Reluctantly, he removed the wearable and handed it over. The driver passed him a large envelope in return.

Stacey did the same, taking her envelope and sitting alongside Adrian. Inside, she found a copy of the non-disclosure agreement she'd signed on day one, an airline ticket home, her passport, phone and a fifteen-thousand-dollar cheque.

She glanced across at Adrian and saw that he was smiling.

"Not bad for a week's work," he said.

Holding the cheque in both hands, she slumped into the seat. The first thing she would do when she got home was book a week at a day spa. Her body ached in ways she never thought possible.

———

"THIS IS MORE LIKE IT," said Eric, tossing his gear bag onto a full-sized single bed.

"Not quite five-star," added Natalie as she claimed the position beside his.

Following their debrief, the contestants were rewarded with a few hours of downtime and an upgrade to their accommodation. They'd farewelled the shed, swapping it for a renovated workers' bunkhouse with a modern bathroom.

Jenny counted eight beds in the room as she chose one. That meant that two of the contestants were always going to be scrubbed. There was no doubt in her mind that the only thing that had saved her was the successful infiltration of the party and the information it had revealed. If that hadn't come off, she would have been going home.

Nick took a bed to one side, and much to her surprise, Veronica took the other next to her.

"What you and Nick achieved out there was pretty cool," Veronica said as she stretched out. "You guys make a good team."

"Thanks, you guys did well too."

Veronica shrugged. "We played it safe."

"We would have nailed it without the catering stunt," said Eric. "If that idiot Adrian hadn't fucked it up."

"In his defense," said Nick, "security was set up to counter the sneaky peaky approach. We just didn't identify that during our initial planning and assessment."

"You came out of it smelling like a rose, though," said Bianca. "Didn't you?"

"What are you trying to say?" asked Nick.

"We warned them that the buggy was approaching," said Jenny. "The only reason they got out without being captured was because of us."

"And yet they're not here, are they? And you," she tipped her head in Jenny's direction. "Most certainly weren't the odds-on favorite to make it through the first elimination."

"Take it easy, Bianca," countered Veronica. "Jenny has more than held her own. Adrian and Stacey didn't make the grade. Eric probably didn't go down with them because he's the golden boy."

"Quick to jump ship," snapped Bianca.

"Get over yourself, sweetheart and read the room. X and the rest see everything. If you don't make the grade, they'll bin you. My suggestion, rest up. Because we've got no idea what's coming next."

Chapter Eleven

"THE MOST POWERFUL weapon that any operative has in their arsenal is the ability to convince someone else to assume all the risk," their lecturer opened.

Jacquie, as she'd introduced herself, was unlike any of their previous instructors. Softly spoken and petite with a tear-drop face framed with perfectly groomed mouse-brown hair, Jenny thought she looked like a news reader.

According to the training schedule, Jacquie would lecture them all day on 'soft skills.' Jenny had assumed this was communications related. She hoped her experience in sales would allow her an edge over some of the other candidates.

"My job here," continued the lecturer, "Is to arm you with the tools to do just that. I'll show you how to select a target, evaluate them, develop a strategy and then execute it."

"Sounds pretty complicated for something that women do naturally," said Eric, shooting a grin toward Mark and Troy, sitting to his right.

Jacquie shrugged. "It's true that many women and men can manipulate with ease, primarily using their sexuality to target the underlying insecurities that men tend to manifest. What makes it even easier is that men are terrible at hiding their insecurities. They tend to flag them with easily identifiable overcompensations. Like, for example, particularly flash and expensive cars, like a BMW X6, perhaps," she said, with a smirk.

Eric's eyes narrowed as the other candidates laughed.

"Over the next few hours, we're going to explore a broader range of psychological tools, including emotional and cognitive empathy, to deception, insecurity, trust and fear. When I'm finished, you'll all understand the mechanisms of manipulation and how to apply them. After that, the real fun can begin."

JENNY SIPPED a green tea as she read her first target briefing. It was less detailed than she'd expected: only a photo, a short bio and the information she was expected to elicit. During their training, Jacquie had warned them about achieving the correct balance between being attentive and prying. According to her, nothing would shut down a first contact like pushing too hard.

The contestants were in the dining facility, waiting to be summoned and taken to their training scenarios where they would be required to establish contact with their target. Jenny had opted for peppermint tea over coffee. She tended to come on a little intense when she was caffeinated.

Glancing around the mess tent, she saw that others had opted for coffee as they read their briefings. The door swung open. Her anxiety peaked as four production assistants entered.

Each of them called a name. Hers was second. She followed the young woman out of the tent and across the vehicle park to the gym. Jenny noted the roller doors were all down, concealing what was within.

"Once you're through that door, your scenario begins," said the woman as she handed Jenny a shoulder bag. "These are your props."

"OK, thanks." She looked inside and found a laptop, phone, water bottle and a clutch. Taking a deep breath, she grasped the door handle. "Here we go."

A camera crew was the first thing she spotted as she stepped inside. Pausing, she looked past them and saw a set had been constructed on the gym floor. Where they usually practiced unarmed combat, there was now a cafe, with uniformed staff and customers.

She spotted her target sitting in a booth as she moved to the counter and ordered a latte. Then she approached him with her order number in hand. "Excuse me, hi. Do you mind if I sit here? I need to charge my laptop." She gestured to the power outlet.

He glanced up from the paper he was reading and smiled. "Go for it."

"Thanks." She slid into the seat, removed the laptop from her bag then rummaged inside. "That would be right," she exclaimed with a sigh.

"Everything OK?" the target asked.

"I left my charger in the office. The battery went flat on the plane. You don't happen to have one?"

He shook his head. "No, sorry. I don't carry a laptop. I guess I'm a bit old-fashioned like that."

The Operative

She smiled. "You don't say. Still reading print media and all."

A chuckle. "I sit in front of a computer all day."

"Tell me about it. Between my phone, tablet and laptop, I spend all my time behind a screen. The joys of working in sales." Jenny's coffee arrived. She thanked the waiter and took a sip. "Wow, great coffee. Is this your local?"

He nodded. "I work around the corner. Drop in most days."

"The worst thing about traveling all the time is how hit and miss the coffee is. Seriously, one day you get a place like this. The next, you're sipping lukewarm swamp water from a polystyrene cup in a truck stop."

He laughed again, lowering his paper. "Truck stop coffee sucks."

"Not always. You'd be surprised how far coffee culture has penetrated the Midwest. Last week, I had a great cup at a truck stop outside Pocatello."

"What were you doing in Pocatello?"

"Meeting a client. Insurance claim on a barn fire. Nice little town."

"I grew up in Wyoming."

"Country boy?"

"Yeah, parents ran a farm."

"Mine too. My name's Jenny, by the way."

"Paul."

"I miss the land. What do you do here in, Boston, Paul?" It took Jenny a moment to remember the city from the scenario briefing.

"I'm in software development, specifically forensic accounting software."

"You mean like FBI fraud tracing type stuff?"

"Well yeah, I guess that's one use for it. I'm mainly

involved in developing the algorithms that drive the software."

"That's very interesting. It's amazing what's being achieved with algorithms now. All the quoting for insurance premiums has gone that way. When it started, I had to check each one for accuracy. Now, they're almost always spot on, remarkable."

Paul smiled, adjusting his glasses. "Most people have no idea how many algorithms touch their lives daily."

THE CONTROL ROOM was a hive of activity as Chuck and his team managed four crews and multiple remote cameras capturing the interactions occurring on two separate sets. Jenny and her target occupied the cafe in the gym. Upstairs in the lecture theatre the other set was a cocktail bar, where Mark was attempting to establish rapport with his target.

Jacquie was in the thick of the chaos, sitting alongside Chuck, watching the screens and giving directions to her role players via radio. "Make him work harder for it," she told Mark's target. "He's missed at least two opportunities to establish further rapport. If he misses another one, I want you to clam up."

"Brilliant," Charles said. "That's raising the stakes with him. Now, what have you got for Jenny?"

"She's doing reasonably well," Jacquie replied. "She came in a little hard but softened once she found her rhythm. She's established common ground, mimicked his body language and shaped the conversation without making it unnatural."

Chuck gestured to one of the screens that showed the

biometrics from the contestant's wearables. "Her heart rate was high at the start. It's leveled out now."

"To be expected."

"Still, it would be great to raise her stakes as well. Maybe we could also send one of the other contestants in like a double team. We could pit Natalie against her. There's some real tension between those two."

Jacquie smiled. "I like the way you think, Chuck. But let's build them up a little more before cutting them down. Each of them has a number of these scenarios to get through in the next twenty-four hours. Plenty of time for you to raise the stakes."

Chapter Twelve

THE HUMIDITY HIT David in the face like a wet sponge as he stepped out of the air-conditioned comfort of the Toyota Landcruiser. "Fucking tropics," he murmured as he grasped his briefcase and followed his security detail into low-slung concrete structure adorned with vines, mold and flaking paint.

The back of his linen shirt was already damp with sweat when he reached the office of the man he was there to see.

The Governor of the Eastern Highlands Province of Papua New Guinea, Jason Makura, was overweight with a massive bald head and deep-set eyes. He held a phone to his ear and shot David a nod as the lawyer entered his office. The security detail remained outside as David waited for the Governor to finish his conversation.

"You must be David," the Papua New Guinean Official asked once he finished his call.

"Yes, Governor Makura. In the flesh." He stepped forward and shook the man's hand.

"Take a seat." The Governor directed him to one of the

plastic chairs on one side of his desk. "I'm sorry about the heat. The air conditioner has broken again."

The Eastern Highlands province was a poor region, even by PNG standards, which was one of the reasons that David had selected it for the project. Money went a long way here, and everything was for sale.

"I can have one of our people come and sort that out for you."

"I'd appreciate that. How is the construction of your facility going?"

"I inspected it earlier today. It is almost complete."

"That is good news. Although, I know the workers would want it to last longer. Is there scope for future projects?"

David nodded. "There certainly is. Once we've got the training center up and running, we will look at expanding our presence. There are several community projects that we will continue to develop. Another school and a new police station in Lufa."

"Your company has been very generous. But I know you're not here today to discuss community projects and air conditioners."

"True. I take it the police chief has mentioned our request?"

"He has, and he said there would be significant benefits if we were to help."

David unlatched his briefcase and removed a thick envelope. "Our charity would like to start by making this contribution to your election campaign. We want to continue seeing the Eastern Highlands prosper under your leadership."

The Governor licked his lips as he took the envelope and placed it on his desk. "Your support is most welcome. I have big plans for the area. Consider your proposal accepted."

David rose and offered the man his hand. "We look forward to continuing to do business with you and supporting those plans."

The lawyer's phone rang as he was climbing back into his Landcruiser. He answered the secure application over a Bluetooth earpiece. It was X. "You should see the state of my loafers."

"David, who the fuck wears loafers in the field? Get yourself a decent pair of boots. How did it go?"

"He agreed."

"Good, and the facility?"

"Nearing completion. One of your colleagues, Hartman, is overseeing the project."

"Yeah, I know Hartman. Guy's a fucking savage; they booted him from DEVGRU for brutality. Guaranteed he'll put together a good product."

"How are our trainees progressing?"

"They're finishing soft skills with Jacquie. Then they'll progress to vehicle handling and tech. Following that, the next full mission profile."

David activated the training app that Raj had downloaded onto his phone and opened the rankings. He noted that there had been a reshuffling since he'd last looked at it. "Jenny and Nick seem to have moved up from the bottom."

"To be expected, they're better talkers than trigger pullers. Let's see what happens in the next phase."

"Well, in case they don't, I want Jacquie to develop a specialized behavioral modification program for them."

"That's a waste of time."

"Indulge me, X. I am cutting the cheques."

"Fine. But I'm telling you, I might be able to train

them, but you can't change who they are. When push comes to shove, they're not going to have that killer instinct."

"Let's see what comes out in the wash."

"SO WHAT ARE you going to do, Jenny?" Bianca asked calmly from the passenger seat of the high-powered SUV as it rounded a corner.

Through the windshield, Jenny had spotted large plastic barricades blocking the road. Masked gunmen stood on each side of the barrier.

"J-turn. I'm going to execute a J-turn," she stated, drawing on the training she and the other contestants had received earlier in the day.

"OK, let's do it."

She applied the brakes, slowing the car as they approached.

"Brake harder," instructed Bianca. "Hand on the gear selector."

Jenny winced as she pumped the brake, and the car came to a standstill fifteen yards from the obstacle blocking the road.

"Move faster! Any second now, they could start shooting."

The gunmen raised their weapons.

She slapped the selector into what she thought was reverse and applied the gas. The engine roared, and they leaped forward.

"Reverse is up, not down. You're in first gear."

Paintball rounds slapped the top of the windshield.

"I'm going through," she yelled.

They closed the distance to the barriers as more paintballs slapped the car.

"Remember what you learned."

Jenny waited for the bumper to contact the barriers then accelerated hard. She caught a glimpse of the two shooters diving out of the way as the SUV's engine roared, and they shoved the barriers, breaking through. She remembered to drop the car back in drive, and they accelerated away.

"Monumental screw up, but a decent recovery," said Bianca. "Let's go around again and try that J-turn."

"Well, that's one way to fuck it up," said Eric from where he and the other candidates were watching.

"You're such a dick, Eric," said Veronica. "Jenny rarely drives. This is a steep learning curve for her."

"Oh, and we're all pulling J-turns and running blockades on our way to work, are we?" snapped Natalie.

"No excuses for being weak," added Eric as he and Natalie left the group and headed toward the catering tent with Mark and Troy in tow.

Nick, Veronica and Brianna remained, watching as Jenny's SUV navigated the race circuit, engine roaring and wheels squealing.

"Getting faster," observed Nick.

"She just needs to build up her confidence," said Veronica. "She's got killer hand-eye coordination. Just needs to back herself."

"Here we go. Come on, Jen," said Brianna.

As the powerful SUV rounded the final corner, they heard it growl as Jenny downshifted, slowing it. Then, the tires screeched a hundred yards from the blockade as she braked. The rear wheels spun before it had lost all forward momentum. Coming to a halt, it immediately lurched rearward before Jenny slammed on the brakes and wrenched the steering wheel. The nose swung almost entirely around, about a hundred and sixty degrees from the checkpoint. Then, with a roar, the SUV took off in the opposite direction.

"Fuck yeah, way to go, Jenny," exclaimed Nick.

"There we go," murmured Veronica as she turned to follow the others. "Now she's developing into a real threat," she added, walking away.

"Does that mean she's going to join team Eric?" asked Brianna as they watched Jenny park the SUV. "I mean, he's already got the boys and Nat."

"No," said Nick. "Veronica might be ruthless, but she's fair. It just means the gloves have come off. She's not going to cut us any slack."

"I didn't know she was," said Brianna.

The two of them waited till Jenny joined them.

"Good work," said Nick. "You got there in the end."

"So much harder than it looks," added Brianna.

"Sure is. Any idea what we're doing next?" Jenny asked as they approached the race circuit building complex.

"No idea," said Nick, gesturing toward the two helicopters in the parking lot. "Those came in while you were driving. So, I'm guessing we're heading to a new location."

―――

THE HELICOPTERS DEPARTED the Highlands Motorsport Park and climbed north over rugged brown hills. After a short flight, they circled what looked to be a winter sports facility perched atop a barren mountain before touching down a short distance from a colossal hangar.

Steve and a camera crew met them in front of the structure's twenty-foot-tall sliding doors. The instructor wore khaki coveralls and a broad smile.

"I hope you all enjoyed this morning's training," he barked in his Scottish accent. "Because now you're going to be putting those skills into action. Follow me."

As he approached the doors, they rumbled open, revealing the inside of the massive structure.

"Hell yeah," exclaimed Troy as they walked between two rows of brightly colored side-by-side buggies. "This is going to be a blast."

Nick counted sixteen buggies lining the walkway to the rear of the hangar, where X and his staff were waiting. The ones on the left were red, and the ones on the right were blue, with candidates' names stenciled on them in yellow.

"These are Polaris Razor ATVs," explained Steve. "And they're going to be the culmination of your driver training. But this isn't going to be no Driving Miss Daisy."

They reached the end of the line of vehicles, where X and his staff were waiting beside a large flat screen on the wall. Like Steve, they were dressed in khaki one-piece suits.

As the candidates gathered in a huddle, Bianca stepped forward. "Team, this challenge will pit you against your instructors." She paused. "Each of you will be allocated a side-by-side. In it, you will find a digital display. Outside of this hangar is an off-road environment peppered with virtual gateways. Your job is to pass through them and earn points. Our job is to stop you. It's that simple. From here, you will move to your allocated Razor, put on your safety gear and familiarize yourself with the vehicle. Once you're happy, head outside and get a feel for how they handle and how the virtual environment works. You've got ten minutes. After that, we're coming to get you. Any questions?"

"What are the rules?" asked Brianna. "Can we damage the vehicles?"

"There are none," Bianca answered.

"Drive fast," added X. "Because my team is going to smash you off the road."

Nick looked around. The contestants all look a little startled, except Eric. He was staring at Jenny with a smirk on his face.

"Your time starts now," barked X.

Nick sprinted for the row of blue buggies. His was second from the end. A jumpsuit was hanging on the driver's side. A helmet with his name on it lay on the seat. It took him less than a minute to suit up and climb in; the hangar was already rumbling with engines.

The cockpit of the ATV was relatively simple. He fastened the racing harness, started the engine and shifted into drive. Tentatively pushing the accelerator, he followed the first of the Razors outside.

As soon as he was on the gravel, the touch screen in the center console lit up, displaying a timer. He had two minutes before the challenge started. Two minutes to get a feel for how the side-by-side handled and get a read on the terrain.

Several tracks led away from the shed. He aimed for one and stomped on the throttle. The buggy lurched, its knobby tires scrabbling for traction as the turbo-charged engine screamed, rocketing him forward. Heart racing, he backed off the power, reigning in the ATV as he ripped along a track.

He checked the clock and saw he had little time to get his bearings. His chosen track led to a high point a few hundred yards away. Racing to that point, he skidded to a halt and unfastened his harness. Climbing onto the driver's seat, he stood up through the roll cage and looked around.

The 'proving ground' was a network of tracks that wound through hills and around structures. Despite intersecting and looping back, they all returned to a massive lodge and the hangar. In winter, it probably served as a cross-country skiing area. Currently, the contestants were blasting around the tracks at various speeds.

The speakers of his side-by-side started beeping, and he glanced at the center console. It was counting down ten seconds. Dropping into his seat, he fastened his harness and waited.

An extended beep announced the start of the challenge. A map appeared on the screen with icons to denote the gateways.

"It's Pokémon Go on steroids," he said as he searched for the closest checkpoint. There was one a short distance away, back toward the hangar. He gunned his engine, spun the wheel and swerved as another ATV blasted past. He caught a glimpse of Jenny's name on the side and grinned behind the visor of his helmet.

He ate dust as he followed her along the track but quickly caught her and pulled in alongside. Her visor hid her face, but she gave him a nod and a quick thumbs up as they blasted toward their first checkpoint. This was, by far, the best challenge yet.

———

GRAVEL BOUNCED off the fenders of Jenny's ATV like hail on an iron roof as Nick roared past her, covering her in dust. She slowed, leaving enough space to let the wind clear the worst of it.

The Operative

She wasn't feeling particularly confident about this challenge. This was her first time in a high-powered racing buggy. Through the dust billowing from Nick's tires, she spotted a line of red buggies leaving the hangar. X and his team had joined the game. Now, things were going to get real. As she followed Nick through the first checkpoint, a chiming sounded from her speakers. On-screen, a spinning icon revealed that she'd earned ten points.

That's easy, she thought, as she checked the map for another gateway. There was one a short distance away. Engine roaring, she ducked out of Nick's dust trail and took a separate route. As she slowed to negotiate a sharp S-bend, she felt her buggy lurch. Glancing in a wing mirror, she gasped. One of the red buggies had rammed her, hot on her tail.

Pushing the gas harder, she split her focus between staying on the track and avoiding the buggy behind her. Another nudge confirmed her worst nightmare. The driver was positioned to execute a pit maneuver, using their bumper to spin her off the road. It was one of the techniques they'd learned to counter on the track. "You got this," she snarled through clenched teeth. She eased off the throttle, waiting for the red ATV to nudge the rear right corner of her buggy. When she felt it touch, she spun her steering wheel in the opposite direction and gunned the engine.

The back end of her buggy whipped away from the attack then fishtailed as she fought to keep it under control. A glance in her mirror revealed that the move had been successful. The red ATV was off the track and bouncing through rocks and grass.

Grinning, she raced through another gateway, earning ten more points. Confidence growing, she gunned the buggy harder as she lined up another gateway and blasted past one of the other candidates.

She knew she'd done well in the 'soft skills' training and testing. If she could finish somewhere close to the middle of the pack, she'd be less likely to be eliminated.

She avoided contact with any red buggies for eight minutes and accrued ten more points. Jenny was speeding to another checkpoint when the speaker system chimed, and a computerized voice announced two minutes were remaining. She checked the screen and saw it displayed a list of the candidates' points. Nick was on top with fifty points. Good for him. Eric was sitting in second place with forty, and everyone else tied with thirty.

Checking the map, she saw there was one gateway that was worth twenty points. However, it was slightly further than the rest and located on a trail that switch backed down a cliff. Risky, if the staff managed to block you, there was nowhere to go. Still, if she made it, she'd be in second place. That was incentive enough to go for it.

She raced across a wide-open area, aiming the buggy for the track that led to the 'jackpot.' As she neared the cliff, she saw another vehicle in her mirror. Through the dust, she spotted the ominous red of one of X's hunters.

"Stay focused," she murmured as the track narrowed. "Get to the target."

The dirt road started high and cut back and forth as it descended toward the valley floor. Jenny reached the first hairpin corner and took it a little fast, her back end sliding out. Overcorrecting, she sent the Razor into a savage fishtail. Heart pounding, she managed to get it under control, but it had cost precious seconds.

A glance in the mirror revealed there were now two buggies directly on her tail; one blue and one red.

The Operative

The red buggy was glued to her as she entered the next turn. She felt it contact her outside as she cut the corner right. It wasn't much of a push, but enough to send her inside tires off the track. The steering wheel shuddered as the ATV bounced through rocks and shrubs. She hung on to it with white knuckles, wrenching the vehicle back onto the road.

She was behind the instructor now. Dust filled the air and gravel pinged off her visor as she tried to maneuver from their wake. She had nowhere to go, hemmed in by a steep drop-off on one side and the blue buggy to her left.

To make matters worse, her steering was pulling to the right, the wheel shuddering in her hands.

Slowing, she glanced sideways and saw the name on her fellow competitor's buggy, Eric.

"NO!" She wasn't going to be beaten by that bastard. A glance at the screen told her they were almost on the gateway. All she had to do was stay on the track, and she would get the points.

She glanced sideways and saw that Eric was watching her. He lifted one hand from the wheel and waved. Then he wrenched his steering wheel toward her.

Jenny reacted quickly, but there was nothing she could do. Her damaged wheel strut collapsed, and her buggy slid off the narrow track and tipped. She clung to the wheel as her world rotated. The racing harness held her tight as the ATV gathered speed. Her view became a blur of sky and dirt.

She was strangely calm as the buggy continued its destructive course down a hundred yards of slope. A single statement was the last thing that passed through her mind before a rock smashed into her helmet. Fuck you, Eric.

"CAN YOU HEAR ME?" The voice sounded muffled and distant.

"Jenny, can you hear me?" the voice repeated louder. A hand grasped her shoulder, and she opened her eyes. She instantly regretted the move. A wave of nausea swept over her, bile filling her mouth.

"Jenny, can you feel your fingers and toes? Do you have any back or neck pain?" The voice was clear now, and Jenny recognized it as Bianca's.

She swallowed, then wriggled her fingers and toes before rolling her head from side to side. "I think I'm OK. My head hurts, but everything else is fine."

"The fuel tank is leaking. We need to get her out of there." This time, it was Steve's voice, followed by a sound like whipped cream shooting from a can.

"OK, Jenny," said Bianca. "We'll roll the buggy back upright and get you out of the harness."

As the fog of the accident cleared, she realized she was on her side. She winced as the buggy was slowly rolled upright. Bianca released the catches on her harness and Jenny slumped back into the seat.

"I need you to cross your arms and grasp the shoulders of your jumpsuit. We'll turn you and slide you out of the buggy."

She followed the instructions, and a moment later, she was lying on her back, looking up at Bianca.

"Follow the light," the instructor said, shining a small torch into one eye and then the other.

"Can I take my helmet off?"

"Yes, but if you feel any pain in your neck, I want you to stop."

She unbuckled the helmet, gingerly sliding it off her head. "That's better."

"You've had a pretty bad knock, Jenny," said Bianca. "We're going to transport you up to the chalet where one of the medical team can check you out, OK."

Jenny fought the urge to vomit as she sat in the rear seat of an SUV. She closed her eyes, but Bianca squeezed her leg.

"Gotta keep those eyes open till the doc can check you out."

As Bianca handed Jenny over to the medic, the other ATVs arrived. X climbed out. "How bad is it?" he asked, removing his helmet and gloves.

"Wait to see what the doc says, but I'm pegging it as a mild concussion," she reported. "Give her half a day's rest, and she'll be fine."

"Do we know what happened?"

"Not sure," replied Bianca. "I didn't see it first-hand. I'd already passed her. I assume the contestant behind her made contact. The crew will know."

They walked to the production truck parked behind the chalet. The director, Chuck, was waiting outside, wearing a concerned look. "Is she OK? That crash looked bad."

"Concussion. She'll be fine," said Bianca.

"A head injury? Shouldn't we get it checked out? She could have internal bleeding or something."

"The doc is with her," said Bianca.

"Show us what happened," said X.

"Yeah, of course."

One of his crew had already cued up the footage from a drone. It was paused at a point where Jenny's ATV was still on the road.

X pointed at the buggy behind her. "Who is that?"

"Eric," replied Chuck. "We can play it at half speed."

They watched as Eric's buggy overtook Jenny's. X grunted approvingly as the carts made contact, and Jenny slid off the track and rolled.

The accident looked even worse in slow motion. The ATV shed plastic as it tumbled down the slope, slamming into a boulder before coming to a halt on a lower track.

"Eric, what a ruthless prick," murmured Bianca.

"That's a big impact. We need to send her to hospital," added Chuck.

"We will see what the doc says," said X. "We're pushing the training back by half a day. You can take your time packing up and returning to *The Station*."

"What are you going to do?" asked Bianca once they were clear of the truck and back at X's SUV, where Raj, Steve and Jacquie were waiting.

"Boss, David wants an update," said Raj.

"Of course he does." He took his smartphone from his coveralls and dialed. A moment later, David's face appeared via an encrypted link.

"Did you kill a trainee?" he asked.

"No, we had a minor incident resulting in a concussion. The medic is on it."

"We've got a call scheduled for your time tonight," reminded the lawyer. "I expect a full update then."

"Roger." X ended the call before turning to his team. "Choppers will be here in the next few minutes. Steve will go with the candidates. They've got the rest of the day off. Jenny will remain with the doc under observation. We'll get things packed up here and head back."

"What happens if we need to send her to a hospital?" asked Bianca. "Chuck's right. It was a big hit."

"You know the rules," said X. "If anyone leaves the

program, for whatever reason, they're immediately scrubbed."

"HOW'S THE HEAD?" asked Bianca as she entered the treatment room.

Jenny was sitting on a stretcher in *The Station's* medical aid post. "My head's not too bad. It's my neck and shoulders that ache."

"That will be soft tissue damage. The crash tossed you around. Look, Jenny, I need to discuss something with you."

"OK," she replied apprehensively.

"When you joined the program, you signed a legal agreement with several clauses. You're eliminated if you require medical treatment external to the show."

Jenny's face dropped. "So, this is the end for me?"

Bianca shook her head. "No, not necessarily. Both the medic and I are of the opinion you've suffered a mid-level concussion. While an MRI would give you a definitive answer, we don't think it's necessary. However, I do need to provide you with the option of additional medical care."

"Which means I'd be eliminated?"

"Correct."

She winced as she shook her head. "If you guys say I'm OK, I want to stay."

"Right, I'll get the medic to have you sign a waiver. Rest up today. Tomorrow doesn't look like it's going to be too rough."

"Can I join the others soon?"

"Yep, as soon as you sign the waiver." She glanced at her wearable. "I'm due in a meeting. Rest up."

Bianca left the treatment room and walked into the medics' office. "Once she's signed that waiver, she can go."

"Cool."

As she left the aid post, she almost ran into the director.

"How's Jenny?" Chuck asked.

"Almost back to normal. Just needs rest."

He frowned. "So, we're not going to send her for an MRI? I think that's almost negligent."

"Chuck, we offered her the opportunity, and she declined. She's signed a waiver accepting all responsibility."

"We have a duty of care."

"As far as I'm concerned, we've more than met that responsibility. Look, I've got a team meeting to attend. If you want to discuss it later, we can."

Leaving him at the aid post, she passed the mess tent, where trainees were talking and laughing, and into the ranch house. X and the rest of the trainers were waiting for her upstairs in the loft office. "Sorry, I'm late."

"You're good," said X. "We're still waiting on David."

"He's connecting," informed Raj.

A moment later, David's face appeared on the wall-mounted screen. "Team, how many trainees have we killed today?"

"None," replied X. "Bianca was about to update us on the injured candidate."

"Jenny will be fine. She has declined external medical treatment and will be re-joining the others," reported Bianca.

"A shame," said X.

"She's very determined."

"Her and the other oldie are a waste of time," snapped X. "They don't have what it takes."

"The results say otherwise," said David. "Both of them are sitting in the top five."

X shrugged. "They're not killers. Need I remind you all exactly what we're doing here. The organization lost four top-tier operators and we need to produce their replacements."

On-screen, David glanced down at a tablet. "I had accounting pull some numbers. Only two of the last thirty-five missions were targeted assassinations. Over half were covert intelligence collection activities. We don't need to replace our killers. We need, to use your colloquialism, more grey men."

"You plan for the mission; you prepare for the worst," replied X. "They need to be able to kill, and your geriatrics aren't up to it."

David laughed. "X, they're younger than you."

The senior instructor shrugged. "You can't glue a horn to a horse and call it a unicorn."

"Isn't that exactly what we're doing here?" said David. "Except, with Jacquie's help, we'll make them believe they're unicorns. If Jenny doesn't require additional medical support, I want her to continue."

X shrugged. "As you wish."

"Good. Is there anything else any of you wanted to discuss?"

X scanned the team. They all shook their heads. "Negative."

"OK, keep up the good work. I'll check in again in a few days." He ended the call, and the contestants' rankings replaced his face on the primary screen.

"What are we going to do about Charles? He's being a real pain in the ass about the medical treatment," said Bianca.

"I'll handle that," said X. "I want you guys focused on wrapping up this phase of training. Raj, you all set for tomorrow?"

"Yeah, Boss."

"You'll be running the show while Bianca and I are away. We're taking a crew to the big smoke to set up the next phase. Steve and Jacquie will be supporting you. If you have any more questions, I'll be in the gym."

JENNY DIDN'T EXPECT a round of applause as she entered the dining tent. It started with Nick, then Veronica, and before long, all the contestants were clapping except for Eric and Natalie.

"We thought they were going to take you to the hospital," said Nick. "Are you badly hurt?"

"A bit stiff in the neck and shoulders. Nothing serious," she said, sitting.

"What happened?' asked Brianna.

"I'm not sure. All I remember is driving on the track and then being upside down in the buggy," Jenny replied.

"Eric was behind you," said Nick. "He said your buggy was damaged, and you swerved off the road."

Jenny nodded. "I think one of the red ATVs forced me off the road at the corner." She paused, trying to remember. "Yes, that's right. I hit some large boulders."

"That would have done it."

"A better driver wouldn't have been forced off the road," added Eric. "You crashed because you didn't evade effectively."

The other contestants fell silent except for Nick, who scowled. "Ease up Eric. She's lucky to be alive."

"No, she's lucky to still be in the game. This isn't a popularity contest. If you don't make the grade, you get eliminated."

Jenny met his steely gaze with an unflinching stare.

"You're dead weight, Jenny. You're not going to make it through the next gateway. You'd be better off throwing in the towel before you actually get hurt."

"That's enough alpha dick behavior for one day," said Veronica. "We all know you won the challenge."

Eric laughed before breaking eye contact with Jenny and leaving the tent. Natalie and Mark followed him outside.

"Man, he's an asshole," said Veronica. "Look, I'm glad you're OK, Jenny. I'm going to shower up and get an early night."

Jenny sat with Nick as the others finished their meals and left the tent. Before long, the two of them were alone.

"Don't worry about Eric. He's full of shit," said Nick.

"No, he's worse than that," said Jenny. "I can remember what happened. My buggy might have been damaged on that turn, but it's not why I crashed."

"What happened?"

"Eric drove up alongside me and shoved me off the cliff. He even waved."

"Holy shit. You could have been killed."

She swallowed and nodded. "He knew that."

"But, the crew haven't said or done anything. They would have seen the footage. They'd know exactly what happened. He should be removed from the show."

"I don't think that's how things work around here. X isn't going to cut his star player, and the director, Chuck, he doesn't seem to get much of a say."

"We should tell the others."

Jenny shook her head. "No, he'll deny it and use the accusation to cause even more division."

"Then what are we going to do?"

"We play the game the best we can and we beat him. Now, I'm going to go to the diary room to tell the world how my accident made me look deep inside and realize that I can do this."

Nick smiled. "Everybody loves a loser who comes good."

"Wait, I was a loser?" Jenny feigned shock.

"OK, maybe that's a little harsh. Maybe, underdog is a better term."

"Yeah, well, this underdog will have a little more 'bitch' in her from now on."

Chapter Thirteen

"ONE OF US should get injured more often," said Veronica as the team climbed the stairs to the classroom above the gym.

Their morning training sessions, usually Steve's opportunity to destroy them, had been replaced by an hour of stretching with the psychologist, Jacqui, and a late breakfast.

"Next time, someone else can take one for the team," said Jenny as they entered the room.

"Take a seat, everyone." Much to their surprise, the quartermaster, Raj, stood at the front of the classroom.

As Jenny sat, she noted that a wide range of equipment was arrayed on the front row of desks. A few items were recognizable: drones, optics, and tablets. But others looked far more complex. She glanced at Nick, who was practically drooling over the high-tech buffet.

"During the next training phase," Raj said once they were seated. "I'll introduce you to the technology and gadgets at your disposal. In my opinion, this is the sexiest part of being an operative."

"Do we get a watch that shoots lasers?" asked Eric. "Or a car that drives itself?"

"What? I'm talking about real technology, not James Bond fantasy kit," said Raj.

"So that's a no to the watch. Doesn't sound very sexy to me," replied Eric.

Raj sighed. "This is going to be a long week." He paused. "Right, first things first. What I'm not going to be doing is turning you into hackers. That's well beyond the scope of this program. No, I will train you on employing technology and integrating it into your mission planning."

"Which sounds equally as thrilling," Mark added dryly.

Raj ignored him. "All of you have already achieved some basic tech integration. Nick, you were keen to deploy drones and remote access hardware on your first mission. Great to see and something we will expand on over the next few days."

Jenny caught the sideways glance that Eric shot Nick as Raj continued delivering his introductory briefing.

"Over the next few days, you're going to be expected to process a lot of information," continued Raj in his crisp British accent. "Pay attention because your test of objectives will be the planning and execution of a technology-enabled mission."

"Will that be an elimination mission?" asked Brianna.

"That's a question for X. OK, so first things first. We're going to tackle security systems. Does anyone here know what a back door is?"

The room broke out in laughter.

"OK, innuendo aside," Raj managed while suppressing his smile. "A back door is a way into a system that a manufacturer codes into a piece of hardware. Think of it as a key under a mat."

The Operative

"HOW'S OPERATION EXTREME BOREDOM GOING?" asked X as he entered the production control room wearing a singlet and carrying a protein shake.

"It's progressing well," Raj replied from where he sat with Chuck and Bianca. Around them, video from camera crews, wearable cameras, and drone feeds were displayed on flat panel screens. "The two teams have taken very different approaches, but both have their merits."

"Let me guess. The nerds have gone drone heavy."

"Correct. However, they're also opting to put people on the target. They used a drone to jam the Wi-Fi network and hack the security system. Bravo team opted for drone surveillance and man-packed their jammer." He directed X's attention to the center screen. "Team Bravo, Jenny and Brianna are about to enter the premises."

"Let's tighten that camera shot," ordered Chuck. "I want to capture the tension."

One of his production assistants relayed the order. The drone moved forward a moment later, narrowing in on the women.

Ten miles away, on the outskirts of a small town, Jenny ignored the faint buzz of the airborne camera as she attached a pair of leads to the backup power tabs of an electronic lock.

"I thought the hackers could open these locks?" asked Brianna.

"Not possible. They're digital locks, but they're not connected to the internet. Hacking only works if there is a way in. This facility is off-grid. That's why we've got to get in and install a remote access point."

"That makes sense, I guess."

Jenny plugged the leads into a port on a smartphone then accessed the application Raj had taught them to use. A menu allowed her to select the type of lock. She scrolled through a list till she found the make then chose from pictures of the models.

"Guys, you need to get a move on. That security patrol is looping back around," announced Nick over the radio. He and Veronica were on a small hill overlooking the industrial estate.

She held the phone alongside the lock to confirm they looked identical and activated the hack. Immediately, the image was replaced by a circular progress indicator. "Moving as fast as we can," she said as segments of the ring started turning green.

"You've got twenty seconds before they'll see you."

The ring progressed quickly, filling to the last sector, and then it stalled. They waited.

"You must have chosen the wrong model," whispered Brianna.

Jenny felt panic well. "Should I cancel it?"

"Fifteen seconds," reported Nick.

"We can't start again. There's not enough time," said Brianna. "We need to go. We can wait for the patrol to pass and try again."

"Ten seconds, you need to get out of there."

Her finger hovered over the cancel button.

"Let's go."

A chime sounded, and the mechanism whirred as the final sector turned green. "We're in."

Brianna opened the door and stepped inside as Jenny grabbed her backpack and followed.

"Now that is great TV," said Chuck, as the crew and instructors observed from the control room.

On-screen, they watched as the security patrol rounded the corner and inspected the door where Brianna and Jenny had entered. They confirmed it was locked before continuing their patrol.

Raj turned his attention to one of the other screens and saw that Alpha team was approaching their building as a group.

"Why did they bring the whole circus?" asked X. "Who's the team leader?"

"Troy's in charge, but Eric convinced him that more people on target meant more flexibility to deal with problems. If they can't hack the locks, their contingency plan is to breach the door with a cutting saw."

X stepped closer to the screen and studied the group as they huddled around the door. "Are those long guns?"

"Yep." Raj couldn't hide the disdain from his voice. "Clearly, they haven't grasped the concept of covert intelligence collection."

"Well, at least they're prepared for the worst."

"The nerds brought weapons too. They just chose to leave the heavy artillery with their overwatch."

"Yay for the nerds. How long till this mission wraps?"

"We're on schedule. They should be withdrawing to the RV at around sixteen hundred."

"Excellent, then the real fun can begin."

"Hey, this is fun too. Right?" Raj turned to Bianca, who gave him a thumbs up.

X made for the door. "You keep telling yourself that. We all know how much you're looking forward to what comes next."

"Why does he assume we're all sadists," asked Raj when X was gone.

Bianca laughed. "Because we are."

"NICE OF THE ladies to join us." Mark was the first to greet Bravo team as they arrived at the rendezvous, a vacant, rundown house a few miles across farmland from their target compounds.

"Sorry, stopped off at a day spa," said Nick as he and the team joined the others in the living room. A two-man camera crew was also filming with them.

The contrast between the two teams was immediately evident. Alpha was all armed with assault rifles. Whereas Bravo had opted to conceal pistols under their clothing.

"How did you guys go?" asked Natalie.

"We nailed it," replied Brianna. "You should have seen us. It was *Mission Impossible*. We were cracking locks and dodging security. How about you guys?"

"We got it done," Eric replied curtly from where he was watching through a window. "Did you guys see anything strange on your way in?"

"Define strange," said Nick.

"Anyone watching the house or following you in?"

Nick glanced at his team. "You guys see anything?"

They all shook their heads.

"No, I think we're in the clear. Why? Do you think something else is supposed to happen?"

Eric shrugged. "That all seemed a little too easy."

"Maybe we nailed the mission," said Natalie.

"Nah, that's not how X works."

"I think Eric's right," added Jenny. "Feels like we're being set up."

"Yeah, well, I think that knock to your head has made you paranoid," said Natalie.

"Take it easy, Nat," said Mark. "Eric, what are you thinking? Should we move to the alternate RV?"

"Whatever's coming is going to happen," said Nick. "It's why we're here."

"That's a good point," added Troy.

"Doesn't hurt to be mentally prepared," said Eric. "It's going to be dark soon. That's the time to move." He opened the top of his pack. "I'm going to get some chow and my head down."

The other candidates followed his lead.

Jenny left the others in the lounge and explored the kitchen. Despite its dilapidated state, it still had power and running water. She rinsed a kettle and turned it on before returning to the doorway to the lounge. "I've put a kettle on if anyone wants a hot drink."

"I'd love a coffee," said Nick.

"Me too," echoed Brianna.

The three of them returned to the kitchen, and Jenny rummaged in the cupboards for mugs as the others took sachets of powdered coffee from their packs.

"Do you think we're getting close to the show's end?" Brianna asked Jenny as she rinsed three cups.

"There's still eight of us left. I think the last gateway will start with no more than four of us. Plus, I feel like there's lots more to learn."

The kettle boiled and clicked off.

"What do you mean?"

"Spy stuff. I mean, we've mostly been out here in the sticks," said Jenny as she poured hot water into the mugs. "Surely we've got to do some stuff in the city."

"That's a good point," said Nick.

Jenny stirred a hot chocolate as she gazed out of the

kitchen window. The sun was low and cast a soft glow across the fields that surrounded the house.

"What are all those sheep looking at?" asked Brianna.

Jenny saw that the dozen animals in the field were lined up facing the fence.

"Something has their attention. Might be a deer," said Nick. "There were heaps of them in the hills around *The Station*."

She focused on the distant trees as she sipped her coffee, hoping to glimpse a deer. What she saw sent her heart racing. "There are men in the trees."

"How many?" Nick asked as he placed his mug on the bench and rummaged in his backpack.

"I think I saw two."

"They could be farmers," said Brianna. "Or hikers."

Nick approached the window with a thermal imager. He aimed it at the tree line and looked through it. "Shit! There's at least ten of them." He handed the device to Jenny as he turned to face the living room. "Guys, we've got a problem."

The hand-held device sensed and amplified heat differentiation. In this case, the warm bodies of the people in the tree line glowed black against the cooler vegetation. Jenny counted six figures crouched facing the house. The others looked like they were circling around.

"What have we got?' yelled Eric.

"A dozen men in the tree line," replied Nick.

"They're moving to surround us," added Jenny. "We need to get out of here." She left the kitchen, grabbing her pack. The others had gathered in the living room.

"We need to head to the alternate RV," said Nick, making for the front door.

"Wait," said Jenny. "Shouldn't we work as a team?"

Eric shook his head. "No. We're in Escape and Evasion. We need to bomb burst and head to the RV. If we move as a group, they'll get us all."

The roar of a helicopter shook the building.

"We've got to go now." Eric pushed open the door and ducked outside.

"Eric, wait." Natalie ran out after him, followed by Mark and Troy.

"What do we do?" asked Brianna.

"We need a plan," said Veronica.

Jenny handed Nick the thermal imager. "Yeah, we stick together. Let's check the back door. They may not have surrounded us yet, and Alpha will be a good distraction. They're geared up for a shoot-out."

"Good plan," said Nick as he made for the rear exit. Cracking the door, he gave the garden and woods beyond a quick scan. "Looks clear. Head for the trees on the far side. We'll regroup there and plan our next move."

"WHO'D HAVE THOUGHT that the old geezers would be the last to go down," said Steve, between bites of a roast beef sandwich. He, X and Raj were monitoring the contestants from the control room while Bianca and Jacquie were out on the ground managing the hunter teams.

The status screen showed that all contestants except Nick and Jenny had been captured. They'd picked an extraction route through a heavily wooded and swampy area that negated the hunter's drones and bogged down their vehicles. A moonless night and drizzling rain had also hampered the search efforts.

"They got lucky," replied X.

"Nah, mate, they read the terrain like seasoned pros. That's exactly where I would have gone. You could hide for weeks in that shit show, then, when the hunters get tired, you sneak out and disappear into the hills. We trained them well." He took another bite.

"Well, they've run out of time. Transmit their location to the hunter team and have them wrapped up."

"Can you give me a few minutes?" asked Chuck. "I want to make sure there's a camera crew with the hunters."

X ignored the request.

Steve finished his sandwich. "Bianca has a crew with her. I'll send her team in to bag them." He wiped his hands on his cargo pants before adjusting the mic on his headset. "Delta Sierra Four, this is Delta Sierra Alpha."

"Alpha, this is Four. Send," Bianca replied.

"Roger, I'm sending you the location of the final two contestants. Chuck has requested you take the camera crew for the wrap-up." Steve's fingers tapped his tablet as he transferred Nick and Jenny's location markers to Bianca's device.

"Acknowledged. We'll grab them and get out of this rain."

"I think they'd prefer the rain to what's coming next," Steve said with a chuckle.

"Yeah, but I'm going to be warm and dry. I'll see you guys soon. Four out."

Steve checked the digital map on the wall of the control room. The icons denoting Bianca's team surrounded the two remaining contestants. They'd be captured in minutes and move into the next training phase.

Meanwhile, knee-deep in freezing water and hemmed in by thick brush, Jenny and Nick had no idea they'd been compromised.

The Operative

"Nick, do you think they're closing in?" Jenny whispered, shuddering from the cold.

"Keep moving," he replied. "If we can get to the edge of this swamp, we can reach the hills."

"OK." Jenny was exhausted. They'd been on the run since leaving the house, and it was now well past midnight. They'd seen no sign of Alpha team and lost contact with Brianna and Veronica when a drone had locked onto them, splitting the group.

At the edge of the marsh Jenny attempted to step over an old fence. Something tugged at her pants, a low-hanging strand of barbed wire.

"You OK?" whispered Nick.

"Yeah, just caught on the fence."

A beam of light hit them from a flank. "STOP RIGHT THERE!"

Startled, Jenny tore free of the fence and dashed after Nick. The two made for high ground, seeking cover in a rocky outcrop.

Dogs barked, engines revved and a drone buzzed as they scrambled up the slope. The beam following them as they climbed.

"Keep going," yelled Nick. "Get into the rocks."

The light gained in intensity as an ATV roared toward them.

"STOP!" bellowed a male voice.

A machine gun fired, and Jenny stumbled, falling to her knees. Almost at the rocks, Nick turned with eyes wide and threw his arms in the air. "Don't shoot."

As Jenny struggled to her feet, strong hands grabbed her arms pinning them behind her back. She was shoved to the ground as her wrists were fastened with cable ties and goggles forced onto her face. Before she'd fully registered that she'd been caught, headphones and a hood were slipped on. Panic assailed her as white noise filled her ears. She was hauled to her feet and walked away from the point of capture.

She remembered none of the training Jacquie had given them on conduct after capture as she was tossed into a vehicle. Her heart raced as they moved and she bounced on the floor. It's all a game, she repeated in her mind as she fought to control her breathing. None of it is real, she told herself as she was lifted from the first vehicle and loaded into another. You're going to be perfectly OK. Despite this knowledge, she struggled to convince herself. She was petrified, and knew it was only going to get worse.

―――――

ROCK MUSIC BLARED from hidden speakers as Jenny crouched in her underwear on a plastic mesh grate, her hands cuffed behind her back. She flinched as a cold stream of water hit her body, and she looked up forlornly at the masked guard who held the hose. This was her second watering since she'd arrived at the makeshift prison. She'd lost track of time and hadn't seen any other candidates. She was the only one who'd been captured for all she knew.

Jenny couldn't see the hidden cameras transmitting her ordeal. The video streamed directly into the production truck parked a short distance from a farm complex, now converted into an interrogation facility. Inside, the training and production teams were monitoring banks of monitors. Currently, two contestants were being interrogated by Jacquie's contractors, two were hosed in separate wet rooms, and the remaining four were cuffed in headphones and blindfolds in the holding cells.

The Operative

"Two hours in, and no one has broken. This shit's getting boring," said Steve as he munched a bag of crisps. The former marine was parked on a bean bag in front of the screens.

"Your gear ready?" asked X, from where he and Jacquie were monitoring and directing the interrogation of Eric and Veronica. The psychologist had developed different approaches to suit each contestant's personality, background and observed weaknesses.

"Aye, battle rattle is ready to roll. Although, I reckon we're going to be waiting a while. These cats aren't going to break anytime soon."

"Jac, let's wrap it up with these two. Put Jenny and Nick in the chair," ordered X.

The psychologist nodded, radioing through the orders. Her interrogators concluded questioning and had Eric and Veronica returned to the holding cells.

"I've got twenty bucks that Jenny cracks first," said X.

Jacquie shook her head. "I'll take that bet. She's stronger than you give her credit."

X pointed to the screen that showed Jenny shivering and staring at the wall. "That's the face of someone who wants out."

"I think he's right," added Steve. "She's tough, but damn, she looks miserable."

If Jenny had been able to hear the instructors' comments, she would have wholeheartedly agreed. She was shivering uncontrollably. Her legs ached from squatting, and the soles of her feet felt like they were being sliced to pieces by the hard plastic grating. A sigh escaped her lips as the stream of water ceased.

The guard dropped the hose and gestured for her to stand. A hood was thrown over her head, but there was no headset this time. Jenny stumbled as the guard guided her out of the room. A door was opened, and she was pushed into a hard plastic chair.

"Give the woman a blanket," a female voice calmly ordered. "And take off the hood. Oh, and something warm to drink."

She flinched as the hood was removed, and she was confronted by a woman not much older than her. The stranger was dressed smartly, her grey hair in a high ponytail. Her stern features reminded Jenny of her eighth-grade math teacher, Miss Bailey.

The guard returned and draped a blanket over her shoulders. A mug of steaming brown liquid was placed on the desk before her.

"That's better," said the woman. "You can remove the restraints."

Jenny rubbed her wrists as they were freed, then pulled the blanket tighter. "Thank you," she managed through chattering teeth.

"My pleasure. My name's Helen, and you are?"

Jenny kept her mouth firmly closed. During the classroom training Bianca had reinforced the importance of denying captors information, especially in the first 24 hours. This could assist any uncaptured team members in remaining free.

Helen smiled. Her thin lips turned up ever so slightly at the corners of her wrinkled mouth. "I'm not your enemy. If you work with me, this can be much more pleasant than it has been."

Jenny was still shaking as she clutched the blanket.

"Take the drink. It will help."

She eyed the mug with suspicion.

The interrogator sighed. "It's hot chocolate, not

poison."

Holding the blanket with one hand, she reached for the mug. It was warm to touch. The hot, sweet liquid felt heavenly as it reached her stomach.

"That's better. As I said, this can be much more pleasant than it has been. I'm sure you don't want to return to that room with the hose."

Just the thought triggered a bout of shivering.

"I didn't think so. Now, let's start with your name."

Jenny finished the beverage and placed the empty mug on the table before wrapping the blanket tighter around her. "That was lovely, Helen. Thank you."

Nick wasn't as confident as his teammate in the room next door. He hadn't been offered a chair, much less a blanket or a hot chocolate. He stood in a puddle of cold water in his underwear with his hands cuffed behind his back and an intense light shining directly into his face.

"Who are you, and who do you work for?" barked his interrogator.

Nick exhaled slowly, focusing inwards to distance himself from his extreme discomfort.

"Who are you, and who do you work for?"

His mind wandered back to the start of his reality TV experience. On day one, they'd been forced to jump from a boat into near-freezing waters. It was Jenny who had gotten him through that experience. He wondered how she was doing now. Would she break? Would she sell out the rest of the team? He knew the answer to that. She never would. He lifted his chin and stared defiantly into the light. He wasn't going to let her down. "Bring it."

"Oh, you want to be a tough guy? Yeah, well, we can help you with that. Hose him down again."

X and his crew watched silently from the production

truck as both candidates were marched back to their holding cells.

"I thought you were going to break them," said X. "You went easy on Jenny."

"Her response to a hostile interrogation would be to shut down completely," responded Jacquie. "If we give her a human touch point, she'll reach out for it. One more stress session will motivate her to work with Helen."

"It also gives us variety for content," added Chuck. "We can splice in some of the contestants' backstories."

X ignored the director's comment. "Who's up next?"

"Troy and Brianna," said Jacquie.

"Keep Jenny and Nick in the stress cells and then put them back in with the gators."

"That doesn't seem fair," said Jacquie.

"Yeah, boss. You gotta spread the love," added Steve.

"Are either of you in charge?" he snapped.

Neither responded.

"They're the weak link. That's where we're going to apply pressure."

THE WATER SEEMED COLDER the third time around. Jenny doubled over on the plastic grate, pressing her knees against her chest while her hands remained secured behind her back. She shivered uncontrollably, feet screaming in agony from the rigid plastic digging into her soles.

"I can't take this," she whimpered.

Pain drove every thought from her mind. All that remained was the agony that wracked her body. She had to make it stop. She'd do anything to make it stop.

Then, the water flow abruptly ceased, and the rock

music died. She glanced up at her tormentor, who had dropped the hose on the floor and seemed to be listening to his earpiece.

Shaking uncontrollably, she moved her feet, desperate for relief from the plastic matting. The hood was thrown on her head again, and she was hauled to her feet. The cold cement was smooth and hard, soothing to her aching feet. As she was herded to her destination, she'd already decided to talk to Helen; anything to stop the cold water and stress positions.

A loud explosion stopped her dead in her tracks. Gunfire echoed through the building as she was shoved into a chair.

"Don't move," ordered the guard.

The door to the room slammed shut, muffling the gunshots.

"Hello?" Jenny asked tentatively.

No one answered.

She could hear yelling then a series of single shots. A thump at the door startled her, and the hinges squeaked as it swung open.

"Bravo, Romeo," a familiar voice barked.

"What?"

"Bravo, Romeo."

Then it clicked. Bravo Romeo was the identifier that had been included in their mission orders. It meant the friendly forces were attempting a recovery. She needed to respond with her half of the code. "Alpha Five, Alpha Five."

The hood was yanked from her head and her hands released. She rose from the chair and turned to see that her savior was Steve.

Dressed in combat rig, complete with body armor and a

helmet, the Scotsman shrugged a backpack from his shoulder and took a robe from inside. "Wrap yourself in this, love." He keyed the mic on his body armor. "X, I've got my last one. We're moving to the RV now." He turned to Jenny. "We have to go."

Jenny shuffled stiffly after him as he made for the door. Her legs warmed as they exited down a corridor and through a shattered door. She squinted as they emerged into the sunlight.

"This way." Steve led her from the building to a large black helicopter idling in a field. As she climbed in, she saw that not all candidates were onboard. Nick, Troy and Brianna were absent.

She caught the thumbs up that Steve shot the co-pilot and grasped his arm, yelling over the engines. "We're not all here?"

Steve shrugged.

The helicopter's engines roared, and wind lashed the cabin as they prepared to lift off. Then X jumped into the cabin, dragging someone. He shoved Nick into the seat next to Jenny and slammed the side door shut as the chopper lifted off.

As they climbed, Jenny realized there were only six candidates left. Troy and Brianna were missing. She caught Bianca's eye on the other side of the chopper, and the instructor gave her a nod. Jenny managed a grim smile. She'd cracked, but she was the only one who knew it. She'd been ready to sell out the team and throw in the towel. In her mind, she'd failed and didn't deserve to be on that helicopter.

As Jenny and the others flew west, Troy sat in one of the interview rooms nursing a mug of coffee, dressed in a tracksuit and sneakers. The interrogator had left to check on the commotion outside, leaving him alone. He'd already answered her questions and assumed he wouldn't return to the hose room.

Minutes ticked by, and the interrogator didn't return. He finished his coffee, left the chair, and waved at the CCTV camera in the corner. "Hello…"

When no response eventuated, he tried the door. It was unlocked. Pulling it open, he peered into the dimly lit corridor. "Hey, is anyone there?"

There was a faint response from further down the hall. Tentatively, he opened a side door and found Brianna inside another interrogation room. Like him, she was dressed in a tracksuit and had been left alone.

"What's going on?" she asked.

"No idea. There was gunfire, shouting, and I think I heard a helicopter." He gestured along the corridor. "I'm going to keep looking around." She joined him, and they checked more rooms as they made their way through the building. There wasn't another soul to be found.

Finally, they pushed open a shattered external door and emerged into glaring sunshine in what looked to be a farmyard.

"What the hell is going on?"

"Troy, look." Bianca pointed to two backpacks in the middle of the yard.

He recognized his pack and moved to it. Inside were the things he'd arrived with, including his phone and passport. Additionally, there was an envelope with airline tickets out of Queenstown, a copy of the non-disclosure agreement they'd signed, and a cheque for twenty thousand dollars. "We've been scrubbed," he murmured.

Bianca's bag contained the same. "This is crap. Why us and not someone else?"

Troy spotted a vehicle driving along a track that snaked through the farm's fields toward the facility. "Because we broke first."

Chapter Fourteen

"WELCOME to the urban operations phase of training." X had assembled the six remaining candidates in the living room of the sweeping mansion that was their new training facility.

Having been extracted from the enemy farm stronghold, the team had returned to *The Station* where they'd been afforded a half day of rest and recovery. Then they'd been bused to a small airfield and flown by business jet to New Zealand's largest city, Auckland. It had been another short drive to the luxury estate where they'd been allocated individual rooms, complete with ensuite bathrooms.

"Over the next few days," X continued. "We'll consolidate what you've been taught and adapt it to the urban environment. Then, working together, you will plan and execute your operation." He paused. "Your performance on that mission will decide if you progress to the final phase." He glanced at his watch. "First lessons are scheduled for fourteen hundred. I'll see you after lunch."

"Now, this is more like it," said Nick as he and Jenny

followed the others into the estate's dining room. A sumptuous buffet of fresh fruits, sashimi, sushi, and seafood had been laid out.

"Do you think they're setting us up again?" asked Jenny as she eyed the feast.

"I wouldn't put it past them," replied Veronica before tucking into a Californian roll.

"Every time we've lost people, the conditions have improved," added Mark. "I think this is the new normal. We've got this far and earned a little luxury."

"Imagine how good it's going to get when we cut away the rest of the dead wood," said Natalie as she shot Jenny a smile, casually flicking her long blonde hair over her shoulder.

"Give it a rest," said Veronica. "We all got this far on our merits, even you." Jenny was surprised the African American wasn't attempting to form alliances with stronger contestants, a testament to her character.

"Whatever." Natalie moved off to join Eric and Mark, leaving Veronica, Nick, and Jenny to sit at a separate table.

"They've cut back on the crew for this phase," observed Nick. Through the dining room's floor-to-ceiling windows, they could see the production team working around a new van. It was almost half the size of the truck they'd used down south.

"If we're doing lots of urban fieldwork, they're probably going to rely more on body and car cameras," said Veronica.

"Let's hope it's slightly less physical. My knees need a break," said Jenny.

"That's probably why they've given us real beds," added Nick. "The show wouldn't be that interesting if we're all hobbling around like geriatrics."

"Well, you guys pretty much are," teased Veronica.

Nick snorted. "Well, one thing we do know. If there's less crew, there will be fewer teams to cover. Someone's going to be going home, and soon."

As the contestants continued their lunch, a short distance away in an adjoining residence, X and his team were making their preparations. The schedule for the next three days was projected onto a white wall. Raj had come forward a few days earlier to establish the base and drove the presentation as X, Bianca, Steve, and Jacquie sat at a long table with coffee and iPads ready.

"Where the fuck is he?" asked X.

On cue, there was a knock on the door, and Chuck burst in. "Sorry, guys. Been dealing with some technical problems."

X's steely gaze didn't leave the screen. "Right. Bianca, run us through the program for the urban phase."

Bianca glanced at her tablet. "Sure, as you can see on the board, all the training has been locked in. We're starting with basic foot surveillance and then stepping up to vehicles. From there, we're going to cover safe houses."

"Staging locations!" X interrupted. "There's no such thing as a 'safe house'. Let your guard down, and you're dead."

"Good point," agreed Steve as Raj amended the wording on the program.

"Safehouse sounds cooler," said Chuck.

X turned and glared at him.

"But staging locations works fine," back-pedaled the director.

"The final piece of training will be a planning activity," continued Bianca. "Then, we kick off into the full mission profile."

X's phone vibrated on the desk. He glanced at the screen. It was David. "Team, this all looks good. Deconflict the details and back-brief me in five."

He took his phone and stepped outside. "What's up?"

"I just spoke to Hartman. He'll be ready to receive the final four candidates by the end of the week."

"We're on schedule at this end. Is he sending one of his people to tie up the loose ends?"

There was a pause. "Do you think that's necessary?"

"Yeah, and it needs to be done professionally."

"Is there any reason your team couldn't deal with it?" the lawyer asked.

"We're a training team supporting a reality TV show, not an expendable asset."

"Good point. I'll have Hartman take care of it."

"Additionally, it'll be myself and Jacquie that will be going on to the next phase. Let's keep Steve, Bianca and Raj clean. Make sure Hartman knows that I'm running the show. I don't want that madman challenging my decisions."

"Anything else?" David asked sarcastically. "Maybe you'd like me to book you a hire car and late checkout?"

X laughed. "You'd make a shitty personal assistant. Too much sass and not enough action."

"Fuck you. Check-in when you've got your final four."

"You don't want to know the plan for the next week?"

"No, you've got it in hand. I briefed the board yesterday. They're impressed by your progress. We'll talk soon."

X ensured the call had been terminated and returned to the briefing room, where a disagreement had broken out between Bianca and Chuck.

"What's the problem?" he asked, returning to his seat.

"I don't have enough crew to capture three lots of surveillance training," the director whined. "You can't run it simultaneously. You'll have to move from pairs to two teams of three."

"Tactically, that doesn't work," said Bianca.

"Well, physically, we don't have a choice. I don't have enough crew to cover the activities," declared Chuck. "The other option is to push filming right, and have one pair rest."

"No, our schedule is tight. Make do with what you've got."

Chuck shook his head. "You guys are killing this production. We're close to the end. This is where we need all the footage we can get. We're running out of opportunities."

X fixed him with one of his legendary stares and spoke very deliberately. "Make do with what you've got."

FOG FORMED inside the hire car's windshield as rain lashed it. Jenny cracked her side window an inch to try and clear the glass.

"Damn this rain," said Mark from the passenger seat. "I can't see a thing."

"Could be worse. We could be out in it like the others," she replied.

"Yeah, they certainly drew the short straw."

The covert earpiece in Jenny's ear crackled. "Any sign of our contact?" asked Nick. He was the team leader for the mission and was a few hundred yards away in a white delivery van. The rest of the team was on the ground, positioned throughout a public park.

"Negative," reported Veronica.

"Nothing here," confirmed Eric.

"All I can see is rain, rain and more fucking rain," moaned Natalie.

"Yeah, we're also having trouble with visibility," reported Jenny.

This phase of the mission was relatively simple. A contact would meet them and provide information regarding a local criminal group's hierarchy, activities and locations. The team's task was to recover a stolen smartphone.

"Team, the weather is severely impacting our ability to maintain security," transmitted Nick. "All the remote cameras have fogged, leaving gaps in our coverage. Jenny and Mark, I'll need you out on the ground to give us better awareness."

"I knew this was too good to be true," Mark said adjusting the radio under his jacket. "Time to get wet."

"Jenny, you take the northwestern approach to the park," Nick ordered. "Mark, you're in the parking lot."

They confirmed acceptance of their tasks, donned their wet weather gear, and headed to their allocated zones.

Heavy raindrops slapped Jenny's jacket hood as she walked along a path that skirted the park. Nick has made the right call, she thought. Visibility was rubbish, and without the cameras, they were vulnerable. Arriving at her area of responsibility, she gave it the once over.

There was a cafe at the entrance to the park, a kiosk-type arrangement with outdoor seating protected by large umbrellas. From there, she would be able to watch the primary access route.

"I'm in position," she transmitted, before ordering a coffee and taking shelter from the rain.

Moments later, Mark checked in, confirming the security perimeter was set.

The Operative

Jenny spotted their contact as her coffee arrived. The figure was dressed in a blue anorak, as briefed, with the hood up. She waited for the waiter to leave before keying her radio. "Possible target has entered the park and is heading west."

"Roger," replied Nick. "Natalie, confirm when you have visual."

She contemplated tailing the target when she noticed two people a hundred yards behind them. As they approached, she got a better look.

"Guys, there's two persons of interest heading through the park. They might be tailing our contact."

"Might be?" replied Natalie. "Can you be more specific? Any suspicious behavior?"

"They're heading in the same direction. Middle-aged couple sharing an umbrella." What had been an almost torrential downpour when she left the car had petered off to a drizzle. Jenny finished her coffee and watched the couple heading deeper into the park, moving in the same direction as the target.

"Keep an eye on them," ordered Nick.

"I've got visual on the contact," Natalie announced. "He's following the protocol and heading for the bench."

"Wait for all security to report in before approaching," transmitted Nick.

Jenny rose from the table and casually left the cafe, nursing her takeaway coffee. As she walked, the other security elements reported in. She was the last. "I'm watching the couple."

"Don't you dare spook the contact," barked Natalie over the radio.

Jenny bit her lip, fighting the urge to snap back a response. If anyone was going to scare off the gang member, it was Natalie. She'd bullied her way through every challenge so far. But that wasn't Jenny's problem. Her responsibility was to ensure the security of the meeting.

Ahead, the couple had stopped to lower their umbrella. Jenny could see Natalie sitting on a park bench with their contact a few hundred yards away. Nick would be monitoring the conversation.

By her recollection, and she'd seen all the *Daniel Craig* James Bond movies, 007 had never wandered through a park watching a middle-aged couple giggle as they battled with an umbrella that refused to fold. This wasn't going to make for exciting television. That thought reminded her that she had yet to spot a camera crew.

The crews had been constantly present during training and on their missions. Now, they were noticeably absent. Glancing skyward, she expected to spot one of their camera drones. All she could see was dark clouds.

Her earpiece crackled. "I've got the information," reported Natalie. "We can extract."

Jenny saw that the contact had left the park bench and was heading directly toward her, past the couple and their umbrella.

"Good job. Once you're clear, we will collapse security and return to the RV."

Jenny continued her stroll, sipping her coffee as she headed toward the exit on the opposite side of the park. As the contact passed, she noticed his head was down. On the other hand, the couple had managed to secure their umbrella and were heading toward the same exit as Jenny.

Stopping to drop her cup in a trash can, she watched as they exited. Despite looking harmless, something about them drew Jenny's attention. She continued observing as they moved to a grey sedan, climbed inside, and departed.

Jenny committed the number plate to memory, just in case.

"Guys, the intel we've recovered is time-sensitive," transmitted Nick. "We need to move fast."

Jenny fought the urge to run as her heart raced. This was the *James Bond* stuff that made it worthwhile.

―――

X WOULD NEVER ADMIT it to the candidates, but he was impressed by how far they'd come in such a short period. Standing at the back of the living room that had been re-rolled into an operations center, he watched as they planned their next mission, a short-notice operation to recover a smartphone stolen by a criminal gang.

He listened as Eric outlined their Actions On, deviations to the plan that considered outcomes ranging from 'unlikely' to 'almost certain.' They'd come up with a solid response to most of them. However, their plan lacked consideration for a crucial piece of information. Intelligence that wouldn't be revealed to them until they first encountered the opposing force (OPFOR). Up until now, their opposition had consisted of actors and role players. Tonight, that was going to change. Tonight, their OPFOR was an actual criminal gang.

He gave Steve, mentoring the planning, a nod and left the trainees to their devising. Tonight would be complex, and he needed to ensure all the pieces were in play.

"X, we need to talk." The director, Chuck, ambushed him as he walked through the mansion.

He exhaled before replying. "What now?"

"I got fuck-all footage today, and Bianca just told me I won't be able to put camera crews on the job tonight."

"Correct, you'll have to rely on body cameras."

"You're kidding, right?"

"No. I'm deadly serious. I won't have camera crews compromising the integrity of this mission." X turned his back on the director and made for the kitchen.

"This is unprofessional and total bullshit," Chuck yelled after him. "How can I film a reality TV show without cameras?"

"You'll work it out," X quipped over his shoulder. "Adapt and overcome, mother fucker." He left the director fuming in the corridor and swept into the kitchen, where Raj and Bianca were talking.

"Did Chuck find you?" she asked.

"Yep. Where are we at for tonight?"

"We've got surveillance feeds throughout the building and full network coverage. As long as the perps don't decide to bug out, the mission should be a win," replied Raj. "We've also hacked the police network. I've got real-time access to all reporting and dispatch."

"Any sign of firearms?" X asked.

Bianca shook her head. "Local cops are all over these guys. They're low-level crims that get a bit stabby now and then. If the candidates can't wipe the floor with them, they've learned nothing."

"Time will tell." X checked his watch. "They're back briefing their plan in an hour. Failing significant changes, they'll be executing around zero two hundred hours. Keep monitoring the target location. I don't want any surprises."

Bianca smirked. "Come on, boss, you love surprises."

He shook his head. "Not ones that get a project burnt and our bonuses torched. We need this to go smoothly."

The Operative

"FIVE WEEKS AGO, we were on a flight to Queenstown," observed Mark as he adjusted his tactical vest. "Now, we're gearing up to raid a gang house at two in the morning."

"Been a wild ride," agreed Veronica.

"Challenging, that's for sure," added Jenny, double-checking the taser holstered on her vest.

The three candidates sat in a hire car parked in a dark alley. Nick, Eric and Veronica were closer and hidden, providing overwatch. All were dressed in dark colors with bulletproof vests adorned with various pouches, holsters, and body cameras.

"Are you nervous?" Jenny asked Veronica.

The athletic African American shook her head. "Not really. I think I'm getting used to all this. How about you?"

"Same. Don't get me wrong, I'm excited but not feeling the nerves like I used to."

"Don't get too cocky," said Mark. One thing is for sure. Someone's going home, and soon."

"That's the nature of the game," said Jenny.

"Yeah, well, it's zero one five nine," said Veronica. "That means it's game on." She triggered her radio. "Overwatch, any sign of movement on target?"

"Negative," reported Eric. "The place is a graveyard."

"Perfect, let's get it done."

They exited the vehicle and approached their target, a three-story brick building previously used as a hotel. Veronica, the acting team leader, was on point. From their intel, they knew that the device was in an office on the second floor. They'd selected a fire exit as their egress point. It gave them access to an internal service staircase.

Jenny's first task was defeating the lock on the fire door. It was a basic tumbler. Locks and technology were not something she'd previously performed well in. So, when she was allocated the breacher role, she immediately hit Nick up for assistance. He'd taken her through the basics and shown her some neat tricks.

She inserted a thin tool into the lock, jiggled the internal pins into place and turned the mechanism. The door opened with a soft click.

"Nice work," murmured Veronica as she slipped inside.

Jenny waited for Mark to enter then took her position at the rear.

It was dark inside. The only illumination spilled in through grubby windows from street lighting. As they made their way up a debris-strewn stairwell, Jenny gagged. The stench was vile, a blend of mold, vomit, garbage and urine.

"Holy fuck, that stinks," said Mark as they reached the third-floor landing.

"Keep it down," hissed Veronica.

The door to the third floor was unlocked. Mark took point, lighting the way with a compact flashlight as they entered a wide corridor with a slightly less offensive odor.

"Last door on the right," Veronica whispered.

"I know," said Mark.

Light spilled into the hallway as a door opened, and a figure appeared. "Who da fuck's that?" an accented voice barked, the man squinting as Mark lit up his oversized features.

"Keep your hands where I can see them," ordered Mark.

"Fuck you, brah."

Jenny caught a glimpse of a leather vest and silver chains as the hulking figure lunged at Mark, punching him in the face. The candidate stumbled and was shoved aside as the juggernaut slammed into Veronica, smashing her to the ground.

That was as far as he got. Jenny flicked off the safety bail on her taser and fired the device directly into his chest. Electricity coursed through his massive body, and he collapsed a few feet from Veronica, convulsing as Jenny released the trigger.

"Mark, are you OK?" Veronica asked.

"Been better," he moaned.

"Let's get the phone and get the fuck out of here," said Veronica.

Jenny gave the groaning assailant another dose of voltage. "I'll keep him down."

"GO, GO, GO!" ordered Veronica. It took her and Mark less than a minute to enter the office, break into a locked desk and recover the phone. In that time Jenny gave their assailant two bursts of high voltage to keep him immobilized. She ejected the spent cartridge and replaced it with a fresh one as they reappeared in the corridor.

They were halfway down the stairwell when all hell broke loose.

"Guys all the lights are coming on," reported Nick from outside via the radio.

"Good one. The whole fucking building is awake," transmitted Eric.

"Shut up," snapped Veronica. "We've got the package, and we're heading out."

Shouting echoed through the stairwell as they reached the ground floor. Jenny was the last out. She slammed the door behind her and toppled a bin in front of it.

Veronica and Mark reached the car fifty yards ahead of her. She could see them climbing inside as a vehicle's headlights backlit them. Their sedan's lights came on, and she paused by the road, expecting them to swoop her.

Suddenly, blue and red lights flashed, and the wail of a

siren filled the air. Jenny ducked into a side alley as their car's engine roared, and it sped past her with a police car in pursuit.

"Jenny, we're going to ditch these guys," Veronica transmitted, her voice panicked. "Get to the others and extract with them. We'll see you back at the safe house."

She waited till the police vehicle had well and truly passed before continuing along the street, putting distance between her and the target compound. "Nick, where are you guys?"

"Two blocks north, we're parked up," he replied over the radio.

"You got two minutes, Jenny," added Eric. "You don't make it; we're leaving you behind."

Another police car appeared as Jenny made her way along the street. She ducked in behind a parked car as it passed. Checking back toward the target building, she spotted a single figure standing on the road.

Pulling her jacket tight to hide her vest, she made a beeline along the dark street, heading north. Since joining the show, she'd faced her fears, but nothing compared to how she felt now, alone in a rough suburb in the dark morning hours. A glance over her shoulder confirmed the figure was following.

"Guys, I've picked up a tail."

"Ditch them before you get to us," transmitted Eric. "Or find your own way back."

The sound of footsteps spurred her into a trot, and she checked over her shoulder. Grasping the taser, she sprinted across the street and ducked into an alley alongside a boxy building. Turning, she crouched, and held the taser ready.

A moment later, the figure appeared. She aimed the taser and began to squeeze the trigger. The flash of a vehicle's headlights illuminated the target. It was a late-night runner.

Holstering the weapon, she took a moment to steady her nerves. "Who the hell runs at three in the morning in this neighborhood," she murmured.

She waited till the runner had passed before continuing. A few minutes later, she spotted the white sedan that Nick and the others were using. "Thirty meters out, off your six. Flash twice to confirm," she transmitted.

The car's hazard lights blinked twice.

"Rear left door, hurry the fuck up," said Nick.

Jenny followed his directions and joined the others in the car. Eric was behind the wheel and pulled away from the curb, accelerating down the street.

"Tell me, you get the phone?" asked Natalie from the front passenger seat.

"No, Veronica has it," replied Jenny.

"That's not good," said Nick from the seat opposite. "Have you heard anything from them? We can't raise them."

She shook her head. "What are we going to do? Head back to the RV?"

"No," replied Nick. "Have you checked your watch? We've had a mission update. We're to head to a new location south of Auckland. Looks like a private hangar on an airfield. Hopefully, Mark and Veronica will meet us there."

"Or," added Eric, smirking in the rear vision mirror, "they've been eliminated.

"OK, people, we're initiating contingency plan Zulu." Despite the severity of the situation, X's voice was calm. He sat in the converted living room command post nursing a mammoth cup of coffee. All the training team were present.

"Boss, you sure? I mean, that's the end of it, right?" Steve asked.

"Yeah, that's what Zulu fucken means." He sighed. "Look, it is what it is. Ya'll have done a great job. It's been a pleasure. Hopefully, we'll get to do it again sometime soon. Maybe even in a country with decent fucking internet."

"Amen to that," added Raj.

"Fuck the internet," said Steve. "I want to know if I'm getting my bonus."

"Same here," added Bianca.

X laughed. "You did the job. You get the coin. Right. Let's get this shit show wrapped up." He rose, taking his tablet and headset with him. There was a pelican case on a table beside the door. He dumped the devices inside and left the building. Crossing from the staff residence to the mansion grounds, he made a beeline for the production van. Pulling open the door, he stuck his head inside. "It's over. Pack up your kit."

"Wait a second," said Chuck. "What the hell has happened? First, you cut us out of the live feeds, and now this?"

"Take it up with the management. They're the ones who have pulled the pin."

"Yeah, because you didn't listen to me, and now we're all screwed."

"You'll be taken care of. You've got nothing to worry about." X slammed the door and returned to the staff house, where Jacquie was waiting with her go bag.

"What happens to Mark and Veronica?" she asked as they walked down the drive to a hire car.

"Nothing. They're burnt. They're done." X popped the trunk. His gear was already inside.

"Oh, that must be a bit of a disappointment." She tossed her bag in the trunk.

"Why?"

"Because that means, despite your best attempts, you didn't manage to get rid of the oldies. Nick and Jenny are still alive and kicking."

They both climbed into the vehicle, and X started the engine. "They're going to wish they weren't."

THE DOOR to the interview room swung open, and a police officer dressed in plain clothes entered the room with a large cardboard box in his arms. He placed it on the table in front of Mark and Veronica.

"Mark Dunstan and Veronica Bloom, here are your things. You are free to go. However, in the future, if a law enforcement officer signals you to stop, I suggest you do so immediately. What's more, it is highly recommended that you provide the officer with your name and identification."

Mark rose and grasped the box. "We appreciate the advice."

"So, there's no charges or anything?" asked Veronica.

The officer shook his head. "No. Consider yourselves very lucky."

He led them out of the secure part of the station and left them in the foyer.

"Where the hell did they get our names?" asked Veronica as they left the building. "We were in there for five hours and didn't say shit."

Outside, Mark placed the box on the footpath and

looked inside. "Our tactical gear isn't here." He pulled two backpacks from the box, the backpacks they'd brought with them when they'd first arrived.

"Shit!" She grabbed her bag and unzipped the main compartment. Inside was an envelope with her name on it. Tearing it open, she found her passport and a business-class ticket home. Fighting back tears, she slumped to the ground. "It's over."

Turning to Mark, she saw he was clutching similar documents. "Fucking assholes. They hung us out to dry."

"What could we expect. I mean, we got picked up by the cops. How else could that pan out."

"We said nothing. They gave our names to the cops. We played the game exactly how they taught us." He fished around in his backpack and pulled out his phone.

"What are you going to do?" she asked.

"I'm getting an Uber to the house. I will tell that asshole X exactly what happened. Are you coming? Or are you going home with your tail between your legs?"

"I'm in."

It turned out that the police station was only a twenty-minute ride to the oceanside mansion that served as their training base. They stormed up the drive, anger building with every step.

There was a single van parked in front of the entrance. Emblazoned on its side was the branding of a cleaning company. The doors to the house were open, and they walked inside.

They searched rooms until they found a cleaning crew.

"Where is everyone? asked Veronica. "Where did they all go?"

One of the men turned from a window he was polishing and shrugged. "Look, lady, we just clean. That's all."

The Operative

They searched the gardens and found nothing. Every trace of the contestants, staff and the TV crew was gone.

"What do we do now?" asked Veronica.

Mark shrugged. "We could dig around, find out who rented the house. Or, we could head home." As he spoke, his phone pinged. He glanced at the screen, and his eyes went wide.

"What?"

"You should probably check your bank accounts. Because someone just deposited a hundred grand into mine."

———

CHUCK TOSSED his backpack into an armchair and made a beeline for the self-service bar at the airport business lounge. Throwing ice into his glass, he doused it with a hefty slug of bourbon.

"Bit early for the hard stuff, mate," observed another of the lounge's guests.

He shrugged. "Been one of those months."

Returning to his backpack, he took a sip of the amber liquid and savored the burn as it slid down his throat. Sitting in the chair beside his bag, he placed the drink on a low table and took out his iPad. Scrolling through his emails, he noted he was still waiting for a response from David, the producer.

"Assholes," he murmured, checking his phone for messages. There was one from his agent but nothing from anyone attached to *The Operative*. Tossing his phone onto the table, he grabbed the drink and downed it in one gulp.

He didn't believe the show had been canned for even one second. That asshole 'X', or whatever his real name was, had most likely brought in a new director. They had all his material, and he had nothing to show for a month's work. That wasn't entirely true. His bank account looked very healthy. But that was beside the point.

He contemplated his next move as he went to the bar for another drink. When he returned to LA, he'd have his agent dig up everything he could on X, David, and their people. Then, he'd give an exclusive to TMZ outlining the dangerous behavior on the show. He might even be able to track down some of the contestants. He'd show those bastards how it was done in Tinseltown.

Turning from the bar, he ran into a solidly built man dressed in a suit. His drink was knocked from his hand, the contents soaking into the carpet.

"I'm so sorry," said the man. "Was totally in dreamland."

"Accidents happen," said Chuck.

"The least I can do is replace your drink." The man recovered the empty glass and placed it on the bar. "Smells like bourbon."

"Well done."

"You American?" he asked, pouring Wild Turkey into a clean glass topped with ice.

"Yeah. Heading back to LA. You?"

"British, on my way back to London." He handed the glass to Chuck. "Sorry again for the inconvenience. Have a good flight."

"You too."

Chuck took a swig as he returned to his seat. His plan of action against *The Operative* team was solidifying. He'd schedule a meeting with his lawyer to review the contract again. Find out if there were any loopholes that he could exploit. Additionally, he'd hire a private investigator to dig up dirt on all the staff.

His bourbon seemed to burn a little harsher than the last, and he rubbed his chest. A spark of genius hit him as he took a bottle of water from his backpack. He would pitch a documentary to reveal the dark underbelly of *The Operative*.

When a swig of water failed to ease the burning sensation in his chest, he exhaled, thumping it with his fist and coughing. Feeling lightheaded, he took another swig from the bottle, struggling to contain his anxiety. The pressure in his chest had increased to the point where it felt like someone was sitting on him.

He rose from the chair. "Help me," he managed as he staggered toward the concierge but only managed a half-dozen steps before he collapsed, passing out.

An off-duty airline staffer was the first to reach him and correctly identified that he was having a heart attack. She checked his pulse before starting compressions and screaming for someone to call an ambulance.

The airport's first responders took less than four minutes to reach the lounge. They replaced the airline staff, attaching a defibrillator and oxygen mask to the unresponsive patient. Only minutes later, a paramedic team arrived. They administered adrenalin but to no avail. After twenty minutes, Charles 'Chuck' Chen was declared deceased. He was lifted onto a gurney with his belongings and wheeled from the lounge.

His body was being loaded into an ambulance as lounge staff rearranged the table. His now empty glass was placed in a tray, taken into the kitchen and washed in a high-powered sterilizer, destroying any trace of the poison used to kill him.

Chapter Fifteen

PRIOR TO *THE OPERATIVE*, Jenny had never been in a helicopter. In the last six weeks, she'd lost count of the flights, of which this was the latest. She exited the business helicopter behind Nick with a backpack slung over her shoulder. She followed him to a railing, feet ringing on the raised steel platform. X, Jacquie, Eric, and Natalie were already there. The senior instructor was talking to someone who had met them.

"Holy crap, we've landed in *Pandora*," yelled Nick over the helicopter's roar as it departed.

"Pandora?" she queried, gazing out over the vista of green jungle and mist-shrouded mountains as the chopper's sound faded. In the distance, she spotted what looked to be a village with metal-roofed buildings among the trees.

"Yeah, from *Avatar*."

"Oh, the blue people. It does look like that jungle. Although, hopefully, it's a little friendlier."

X led them down a gantry that plunged through the

lush green canopy. As they descended, a base emerged from below.

The steel gantry was the facility's center and had a concrete structure beneath. Around it were at least a dozen transportable buildings ranging in size from a single shipping container to a large warehouse. Footpaths of plastic matting ran between the buildings.

"Right," said X once they'd reached ground level. "This is home for the next few weeks. Find a cabin, stow your kit and meet us in the dining room. You've got five minutes."

A sign pointed the way to the accommodation, and Jenny followed the others toward a row of cabins. She opened the door of one and stepped inside. It was spartan, with a narrow bed against one wall, a desk with a metal chair, and a tiny bathroom. She dropped her pack on the desk and sat on the bed.

This was a long way from the extravagance of the New Zealand-based production chapter. So far, she hadn't seen a single camera operator, much less a production assistant. It was as if the entire premise of the show had changed. It left her feeling a little uneasy.

"You ready?" Nick asked from the doorway.

She let out a snort. "Ready for what? Nick, this doesn't feel like a reality TV show anymore."

"What do you mean?"

"There are no cameras. No crew."

"I think they're using tech now. Lots of hidden body cameras. But I guess we're going to find out." He smiled. "You should be very proud. No matter what happens from here, you made the top four. At the start, no one on that boat would have even dreamed that you and I would be here."

"You're right."

"Now come on. We're going to be late."

They joined Natalie and Eric in the building that housed a basic kitchen and dining room. A moment after their arrival, X, Jacquie and a third man entered.

"Team, welcome to the final phase of *The Operative*," said X. "You might have noticed we're down on staff. That's because most content here will be generated in a virtual reality environment. This facility has a lab that delivers the latest in ultra-realistic VR training." He paused to let the information sink in. "But it won't be all make-believe land. Operating in the jungle takes a special kind of human and our head of security here is an expert. Ain't that right, Hartman?"

The man who'd arrived with the two instructors nodded. He was shorter than X with a lighter build and a narrow, clean-shaven face. Like the others, he wore combat boots, lightweight cargos and a T-shirt. His belt carried a radio, pistol and spare magazines.

"Something like that. Team, while you are guests here, you will remain inside our security fence unless directed by staff. The jungle here is a nasty bitch and there's plenty of shit out there that wants to kill you. My crew will be keeping them out. Follow their instructions at all times."

"Your intro VR session is in two hours," said X. "Get some rest. Things are going to get intense."

"PLEASE CONFIRM THAT YOU ARE READY," said a voice over Jenny's headphones.

She reached up with gloved hands and made a minor adjustment to the headset that covered her eyes. "I'm ready."

The Operative

This was her first experience with virtual reality, and she was a little nervous. Her mission was to neutralize the leadership of a criminal gang terrorizing villages. She'd planned the operation in total isolation from the other candidates, selecting infiltration routes, weapons, and exit strategies with only limited guidance from Jacquie. Then, a technician took her plan and entered it into the simulation.

"You're going to be dropped at your insertion point as per your plan," the technician's voice informed. "Any equipment requested will be in location. Are you ready?"

She took a deep breath. "Yes."

"You're online in five, four, three, two, one."

The display before her eyes flickered and exploded into high-definition graphics, revealing a clearing in a heavily forested area. She was blown away by how real it looked and sounded, from grass swaying in the breeze to birds chirping in the distance.

She stood in awe momentarily, turning on the rolling mat beneath her feet to take in the digital vista.

"This is amazing," she murmured.

"Yeah, it is. But you've got a mission to run," prompted the technician.

"Oh, yeah."

She searched her immediate area and spotted a parachute caught in a tree. In the bushes below it, she found a plastic equipment case. As she grasped the handles, her gloves provided feedback, enough to convince her the item was genuine.

Inside, she found the equipment she'd included in her planning: a sniper rifle, a chest rig, and a submachine gun. She donned the rig, checked the weapons were loaded, and slung the rifle over her shoulder. Mission planning had revealed an opportunity a short distance from her infiltration point. Her target, a gang boss, was known to frequent a coffee seller most mornings. With only a small security detail, that was her opportunity to strike.

Jenny was being watched from the virtual reality control room as she approached. Jacquie sat with the technician, staring intently at the wall of screens, monitoring every aspect of the virtual mission.

"Did you want to throw anything to upset her plan?" asked the tech.

"No, let's keep this mission fairly straightforward."

The technician didn't know that this mission was a small piece in a mental conditioning program designed to manipulate Jenny into a mindset enabling her to take a human life. It was the first step in a ruthless journey that Jenny had no idea she was on. This was Jacqui's area of expertise. It was why she'd been included in the program.

Jenny's mission was complex enough for her to feel challenged but simple enough that she couldn't avoid the task of neutralizing her target.

Jacquie had previously used virtual reality training environments, but nothing as realistic as this. Additionally, the VR suite was able to give her in-depth neurological feedback. The headset monitored Jenny's brainwaves, giving her a more detailed understanding of how the trainee was thinking and, more importantly, feeling.

Jenny, oblivious to the level of scrutiny she was under, had reached the sniper position she'd identified during her planning. Positioned on a forested ridge three hundred yards from the roadside stall, it offered concealment and a rapid escape into the jungle.

Setting up her rifle, she lay behind it, finding her aiming point through the scope. The roadside cafe resembled the image supplied in her intelligence pack, a dilapidated building cobbled together from sheets of tin and salvaged wooden planks. A tall tree shaded a bench with stools where a young woman was sweeping leaves from the ground into a pile. Jenny was blown away by the realism of the simulator. She could make out the intricate details of the woman's clothes through the high-powered scope of her rifle. Then, when the girl turned, she could see her face, which took her breath away.

Lifting her head from the scope, she spotted a black SUV on the road in the distance, the target. Forgetting the woman, she lowered her gaze to the scope and centered it on the truck. It pulled off the road directly in front of the stall.

She'd memorized the target's features and recognized him as he climbed from the rear of the vehicle. Racking the bolt on the weapon, she chambered a round and centered the reticle on his chest. She already knew the distance, from her planning. At five hundred meters, the boat-tailed, high-velocity round would drop almost six feet. She adjusted the turret accordingly.

Jenny was more than a little scared by how methodically she'd calculated the adjustments required to kill the man, even if he wasn't real. That wasn't a normal thought process.

"It's not real," she whispered to herself. "It's all a game."

Her target sat on one of the stools, and the girl disappeared inside to fetch his order. Security personnel left the car and stood casually around him.

"It's not real," she whispered as she exhaled, gently squeezing the trigger.

There was a loud crack, and her gloves jarred, simulating recoil. The target was blown off his stool in a cloud of flesh and blood a split second later. Jenny froze, shocked by the gore.

Something hissed through the jungle to the right, followed by a cacophony of gunfire that echoed off the hills.

More rounds slapped the trees and bushes around her, but she couldn't move. She was transfixed on the scope and the bloody, crumpled body sprawled on the ground.

"Wraith, this is Banshee, we're inbound," a voice crackled in her ears. The extraction platform was approaching. Ignoring the incoming fire, she rose and ran into the jungle, abandoning the sniper rifle.

Heart pounding, she tore through the jungle, her mind racing. A chopper roared overhead as she ran. Her boots slapped the treadmill under her feet. Bursting into the clearing, she leaped into the helicopter, and the world went black.

"Simulation complete," announced the technician.

She tore the goggles from her face and let them drop onto the multi-directional treadmill.

"Hey, easy on the gear," said the tech as he appeared from a side door.

She ignored him, tearing off the headset and gloves. Then she left the lab and stood outside, staring through the security fence into the jungle.

"You, OK?"

She turned and saw that Nick had appeared. She shot him a tight smile. "I'm alright."

"How did you find the simulator?' the lawyer asked, sitting on the steps to the lab.

Jenny exhaled. "It was a little overwhelming."

He nodded. "Pretty intense, but it's important to remember that the targets aren't real people. They're just packets of data."

"They looked real to me. Not sure why it had to be so graphic."

"I guess they want to see our reaction to it."

"Except there's no cameras here to capture it."

Nick fell silent.

Jenny continued staring through the high-security fence at the jungle beyond. "And now we're in a cage." She turned to face him. "Nick, something's not right."

"WHERE ARE WE GOING?" asked Jacquie as she followed Hartman and X along a track.

They'd left the secure compound where the VR lab and accommodation were located and headed into the thick jungle.

"We need to get our heads around the next training phase," said X.

Jacquie slapped a mosquito on her arm. "And what phase is that?"

"Live fire," said X.

"They've done plenty of that," said Jacquie.

"Not like this," added Hartman.

They walked silently until the jungle canopy opened, and an array of buildings appeared behind a tall, electrified security fence. Hartman swiped them through an access control point, and they entered what seemed to be a disused industrial site. Large warehouses, silos, and structures punched up through the jungle. Vines and creepers adorned rusted walls and beams.

"It used to be a cement factory," Hartman told them as they moved through the camp. "The place went bust. David picked it up for a penny on the dime, established the VR lab and kept this place for specialist training."

Hartman led them into what looked to have been a site office. They were met by two muscle-bound mercenaries sporting the same pistol belts he wore.

"How are our tangos?" Hartman asked the men.

"Living their best lives," responded one of them. "They're in here."

They followed the mercenaries through another door into a large warehouse decked out with creature comforts. There were comfortable beds, refrigerators, couches, and a massive television screening an action film. Six men watched the movie intently while nursing beers and packets of crisps.

Jacquie and the others looked on as a gunfight erupted on screen, and the men cheered. She noticed they were all dark-skinned with broad noses and black hair.

"Any problems?" asked X.

One of the guards shook his head. "Nope. They're all keen to earn their get out of jail free card."

"And a lump of cash," added Hartman. "Everybody loves cash."

"What exactly are they doing here?" asked Jacquie once they'd returned to the office.

"The trainees are going head-to-head with them," said X.

"They're the OPFOR? I thought you said this is live fire."

"It will be," he added. "Well, at least it will be for the trainees. The tangos will be shooting paint."

Her jaw dropped. "They're going to kill them. They're going to shoot actual people? Who are they?"

"Rapists, murderers and child molesters. Absolute scum

who will end up in the bottom of a hole in the ground, one way or another."

"Jesus, this is a huge step. I mean, today they were playing computer games, and tomorrow, you expect them to kill?"

"End of the week. They'll make their first kill on Friday. You need to make sure they're ready."

"X, that's not enough time, especially for Jenny. She's going to need a lot more work."

"Yep, I've been saying that all along, but here we are. You've got three days to get it done. Otherwise, they will end up in the same hole as this lot. And that means no bueno on that hefty bonus from David."

"Yeah, so get that shit squared," added Hartman. "I don't wanna hang around in this fucking jungle any longer than I have to."

"Well, you two better turn them into killers then," said X.

Chapter Sixteen

JENNY'S HANDS trembled as she took the VR headset from the padded ring surrounding the omnidirectional treadmill. As she slipped it over her head and adjusted it to her eyes, she concentrated on breathing deeply and smoothly.

It's only a game, she told herself as the goggles flickered and the scenario commenced loading. It's only a game.

The VR activated with a flash of light, and she found herself in a familiar setting, a weapons range. She looked left and right and saw that avatars of the other contestants were also in the sim.

"Listen up. Things are about to get serious." She recognized the booming voice as Hartman's. "Today, we're covering the art of the kill."

A table appeared before them, laden with carbines, pistols and submachine guns.

"The most effective way to neutralize an organic target is to destroy the nervous system. We achieve this by accurate shot placement in the T zone."

The Operative

A figure appeared down range. A Caucasian male with short dark hair, a tight-fitting T-shirt and jeans. A red T appeared as he walked towards them, linking his eyes and extending to the center of his chest.

A shot rang out, and the figure jerked as the digital bullet smashed into his face. Jenny gasped as blood and gore blossomed from the back of his head and froze.

"As you can see. This target is completely neutralized." As Hartman spoke, the target slowly rotated. "The bullet has destroyed the spinal cord and brain interface. No signal is being transferred to the vital organs or limbs."

The graphic representation was so realistic it left Jenny feeling queasy. She was physically relieved when the target was reset to an unviolated state.

"Bullet placement in other body parts can be equally lethal," continued Hartman. Gunshots rang out, and the body seemed to flinch as it was hit. Blood sprayed from the chest, stomach and groin. "However, the T zone is the golden solution."

The target disappeared, replaced by four individuals, one in front of each candidate. Jenny's was a hulking white man dressed in jeans and a T-shirt. He wore an aggressive scowl and glared at her.

"Select a weapon and practice engaging the T zone," ordered Hartman.

She joined the others at the table, taking a submachine gun and loading it. The weapon felt comfortable in her hands, a reaction that chilled her almost as much as the thought of killing someone.

Gunfire echoed through her headset as the others commenced firing. She focused on her target, avoiding the carnage happening to her right. "It's only a game," she murmured, raising the weapon to balance the red dot aiming point in the center of the man's chest. "It's only a game."

She squeezed the trigger, and her aim was true. The target shuddered, dropping to the ground like a puppet with its strings cut.

"It's only a game," she whispered again.

"Good shooting," barked Hartman.

Her target leaped to his feet, wounds miraculously healed.

"Let's hit it again," added Hartman.

They engaged targets of differing sizes, sexes and ethnicities for another hour. Jenny focused on her accuracy, concentrating on shot placement rather than the damage inflicted on the digital humans. With every target neutralized, she became more resilient to the blood and gore, to the point where she was almost enjoying the challenge of hitting the T zone.

That evening, as she entered the dining facility Jenny was confronted with Eric's viewpoint on the training. "This is unreal," he declared to Natalie as they finished eating. "We never had anything like this in the Army. This has got to be some Special Forces-level shit."

She listened to their conversation as she collected her meal and sat at a separate table. Eric and Natalie enjoyed the training and were excited about what would come. They finished their meal and left as Nick entered.

"I think you're right," said Nick as he joined her. "Things have taken a dark turn. That VR killing will never be allowed on a reality TV show. I'm not exactly sure what the play is, but I know it's not what we signed up for. I mean, why the hell did we change countries?"

"We should leave," replied Jenny.

"You want to throw in the towel and let Natalie and Eric win?"

She shook her head. "I don't care who wins. I want to leave the camp and go home."

"Well, they let the others leave. Why shouldn't it be any different for us?"

"Nick, the others weren't taken to a remote location in an unknown country to be trained as killers."

He was silent for a second. "You think that's what they're doing?"

She shrugged. "Why else?"

"Shit. OK, but we need to come up with a plan. We'll need equipment and a way out."

"I've got the gear covered. I need you to work out how to get through the electric fence."

"That's easy. The generator and breaker box are on the far side of the VR bunker. We flick the isolator and cut a gap to slip through."

"CCTV?"

"From what I've seen, the only cameras are outside the helicopter platform. I don't think they anticipate much of a threat from the outside."

"There could be ground sensors?"

"Not likely. The wildlife would always set them off. I've heard monkeys whooping, and there's got to be ground-dwelling birds."

"I wish we knew what country we were in."

"Well, the jet we flew in was a Gulfstream G650. They fly at close to a thousand miles an hour. We were in the air for about three and a half hours. And when we took off, we seemed to head northwest. That would put us in the Southwest Pacific or maybe Australia."

"Why would they leave a developed nation to head to another?"

"Good point. Then I'm guessing we're in the Solomon Islands or maybe Vanuatu."

"The people there are friendly, right?"

"Yeah, lots of tourists."

"When we landed, I saw a town out to the west. It didn't look very far. We could probably find a road and get there quickly."

"What about the others? Do you think we should take them?"

Jenny shook her head. "No, you should have heard Eric, he's loving this. He'd sell us out in a heartbeat."

The door to the dining room swung open, and Jacquie and Hartman entered. The pretty psychologist and the hired gun made a beeline for their table. "Hey, team, how did you find today's training?" Jacquie asked.

"Pretty intense," Jenny replied.

"But rewarding," added Nick.

Jacquie offered a thin smile. "Plenty more of that to come. We're going to take you guys to the next level."

"That's one way of putting it," added Hartman with a snicker. "Come on. I'm starving."

"We go tonight," said Jenny as the instructors left them and they vacated the table.

"I'll meet you at the fence just beyond the VR bunker on the western side," Nick replied as they left the dining facility and walked toward their accommodation.

"What time?"

"Moonrise. Zero two thirty." Nick's voice was low and calm. "That gives us a little light. But we need to move fast. By zero-nine, they're going to know we're missing. We need to head for that town and find help. Have you got any money?"

She shook her head. "We've got our kit bags. We can swap the gear we've collected."

"Good idea."

"We've got a good plan,' Jenny added, reassuring herself.

"That's what they've taught us," said Nick. "I'll see you at zero two thirty."

Jacquie and Hartman were dining together as the candidates headed to their rooms.

"What's the go with those two?" asked the former CIA contractor.

"How do you mean?" asked Jacquie between mouthfuls.

"I don't get an operator feel from them. The others, yeah, maybe. But not those two."

"That's the point. We need people who can blend in and not look like they've just stepped out of a *CrossFit* box."

Hartman took a bite from his burger and chewed as she continued. "The four of them are clean skins, no previous links to the organization or any other intelligence services. Jenny sells insurance, and Nick is a lawyer of some kind. If we can turn them into operators we can tap an unlimited supply of field agents."

He swallowed. "Yeah, but what if they can't kill?"

"They're not going to get a choice in that. They all have the mental resilience to get through that level of trauma. They'll be fine once they come to terms with the situation."

Hartman licked his fingers. "Yeah, and if they're not cool with it, then we roll out the blackmail. Threaten their families, you know the drill."

Jacquie sighed. "We will offer them significant remuneration and the ability to change the lives of those they love. Neither of them have significant financial resources."

He winked. "Blackmail and bribery. Can't say I'm hearing anything innovative going on here."

"There's a little more to it than that."

"I'm sure there is. I tell you what, I've got a nice bottle of bourbon in my room. We could wrap this dinner up with a nightcap, and you can tell me all about it."

Jacquie shook her head in disbelief. "You're married."

"Not in PNG, different hemisphere."

"Operators," she said, her voice laced with disgust. "You're all the fucking same."

UNABLE TO SLEEP, Jenny had turned her attention to triple-checking the contents of her gear bag. Emptying the black nylon pack onto her bed, she inspected each item before stowing it. A fleece and lightweight rain jacket went in first. She doubted they'd need them in the jungle, but it was best to be prepared. Energy bars, water, spare clothes and a compact survival shelter filled the main compartment, along with a small drone in a tactical case. In the pack's side pockets, she stowed another bottle of water, multi-tool, survival kit, compact binoculars, and a medical pouch. All the candidates had been issued the same gear. The instructors referred to it as basic rig; the core equipment to conduct a simple surveillance job or, as it happened, escape and evade capture. She contemplated stashing a three-inch survival knife in her pack but instead strapped the plastic sheath around the top of her boot and hid it under the cuff of her pants.

Sitting on the bed, she checked her watch. It was almost time to meet Nick. Despite the enormity of what she was about to undertake, she felt deathly calm. If there was one positive she'd been able to take away from the whole experience, it was confidence. Confidence in her ability to handle almost any problem, even the bizarre situation in which she'd found herself.

There was no doubt in her mind that something sinister was lurking beneath the surface of the alleged reality TV show. They'd been whisked away to an unknown country without production staff and taught how to kill people. By any measure that wasn't normal.

Once again she contemplated inviting Eric and Natalie to join them. But she knew they'd never agree to leave and would no doubt betray them to the staff. Checking the time on her smartwatch, she unclasped it and tossed it on the bed. For the last six weeks, the device had run her life. Not anymore.

Shouldering the pack, she stepped out of the air-conditioned cabin into the darkness and humidity of the jungle. Her eyes adjusted to the gloom as she made her way to the western side of the VR bunker. On arrival, she scanned the surroundings. There was no sign of Nick.

Minutes passed. He's changed his mind, she thought. She went to check the time but remembered her smartwatch was still in the cabin. Her plan to escape relied on Nick helping her breach the fence. She had no idea how to kill the power. Without him, there was no chance. Then, as she was about to return to her room, a figure appeared from the direction of the fence.

"Hey, I've prepared the breach," whispered Nick. "The fence wasn't live."

Jenny followed him through the darkness to the fence. Below a sign proclaiming High Voltage, he'd cut a flap four feet high. Peeling it back, he gestured for her to crawl through. Once on the other side, she returned the favor, before folding the wire back to its original position.

She half expected alarms to wail and lights to flash on, but nothing happened as they put the camp behind them and made their way into the jungle.

It took forty minutes to push through three hundred yards of dense undergrowth in almost pitch-black darkness. They dared not use their flashlights, and the moonlight barely penetrated the upper canopy. Nick kept them on a straight path using a tiny button compass from his survival kit.

Jenny was drenched in sweat and breathing hard when they finally punched out of the dense jungle onto a narrow footpad.

"Let's take a quick break," Nick managed between breaths.

She sipped water from a bottle and gazed up through the canopy at the cloudless sky. "Do you think they know we've gone?"

"Not yet. Our first activity isn't until zero-seven hundred."

Jenny slung her pack. "We need to get moving then."

They hiked along the narrow trail, making much better time. They reached a single-lane track within an hour and headed west. They'd walked less than two miles before the sound of a truck penetrated the jungle, and headlights flashed behind them.

"Do we hide?" asked Jenny as the vehicle got closer.

"This could be a chance to reach a town," said Nick. "It's too early to be anyone from the show."

"So, we try to wave them down?"

"I think so."

Nick took a flashlight from his pack and waved it from side to side as a battered pickup came into view. The truck crashed through its gears, brakes screeching as it came to a stop with the pair fixed in its headlights.

Then, as the pair approached, doors swung open, and figures appeared. Voices shouted in a strange, almost English language. Jenny's heart dropped, and panic assailed her as two men moved forward with weapons aimed. They'd stepped out of the frying pan directly into the fire.

JENNY FOUGHT the urge to vomit as diesel fumes spilled into the enclosed bed through missing tailgate glass. Lying on her side, hands bound behind her back, she desperately hoped this was another one of X's scenarios.

"Jen, can you reach my hands?" The men had also detained Nick, restrained him, and shoved him into the pickup. "Jen, can you hear me?"

"Huh, yeah." She felt Nick touching her hands with his. They were lying back-to-back.

"I can loosen the cords. Try to get them as slack as you can."

She jammed her wrists together as Nick worked the knot with his fingers. "I think I can get it."

The truck swerved, and they were thrown to one side of the bed. Jenny struggled against the nylon rope binding her wrists. She almost had enough slack to slip the cord over her hands.

With a shudder, the dilapidated pickup came to a halt. Jenny continued to fight her bonds until the tailgate was dropped. "Please don't hurt us. We have families," she cried out as she was dragged out and forced to her feet.

Thankfully, the men hadn't blindfolded her. She could make out a cluster of ramshackle huts in the morning gloom.

"We're tourists," said Nick. "If you contact the US embassy, they will reward you for helping us."

"Shut up!"

One of the men shoved Jenny toward a dimly lit hut. She turned her head and saw that Nick wasn't with her. That wasn't surprising; they'd been told to expect isolation after capture during their training. Except, she reminded herself, this wasn't another scenario. This was real life.

The man shoved her through an open door headfirst onto a bed strewn with filthy blankets. Terror gripped her as he grabbed the back of her pants and tried to force them down. Her belt held firm. He grunted, roughly rolled her over and tore at her shirt, exposing her sports bra. The stench of his breath was overwhelming as he bore down on her. He found her belt buckle and managed to unclasp it as she wriggled her hands against the bonds behind her back.

"Please don't do this," she whimpered as he stripped the belt from her waist.

Then, as he grabbed her pants, she slipped one of her hands from the bonds behind her back.

She struck with speed and aggression, driving her thumb, like Steve had taught them, into the eyeball of the attempted rapist. Then, as he recoiled, she slipped from under him and made for the door.

He roared with pain but reacted quickly, shoving her sideways into the wall.

Pain shot through her shoulder as she stumbled and

dropped to a knee. Her right hand slid to the knife she'd strapped to her ankle.

"You die, bitch," he bellowed, one hand cupping his injured eye, the other a clenched fist.

Jenny managed to dodge a blow as she lurched to her feet, the short knife gripped in her hand.

"Get the fuck away from me," she yelled, thrusting the blade toward him.

Snarling like an animal, he pounced. He plowed into her like a bulldozer, smashing her back onto the bed. All air was driven from her lungs as he crushed her, his forearm pressed against her throat. She released the knife and clutched his arm.

Even with both hands she couldn't find enough space to breath, or scream. She flailed at his face to no avail. Darkness gathered in the edges of her vision, and her hands grew weak.

Then, as she made one last ditch effort to claw his face, her hand hit the knife handle, sticking from his neck where she inadvertently stabbed him.

Grasping the handle, she wrenched it free and tried desperately to stab again. Warm liquid poured across her as she fought to stay conscious. Her last thought as she plunged into the abyss was that she'd failed Nick. These men were going to kill them both.

JENNY WOKE IN AN ABSOLUTE PANIC. She was trapped underneath her assailant, but he'd released the pressure on her throat. Gasping for air, she tried desperately to maneuver out from under him. Her arms were weak, and he was a brute.

It took her a moment to realize he wasn't moving and a split second longer to register the warm liquid drenching her shirt. Fighting the urge to scream, she pushed him again. The body finally budged and slid onto the floor with a dull thud. Springing to her feet, she moved to the other side of the room.

Her attacker lay on the floor, eyes wide, lifeless and staring. The absolute horror of the situation hit Jenny like a blow to the head. She'd stabbed the man in the neck and killed him. Legs like jelly and heart racing, she staggered toward the door.

"No, stop," she murmured to herself. "He was trying to rape you. He would have killed you."

In that split second, she remembered Nick and the severity of the situation. A man was dead, but a friend would die if she didn't move fast. She needed to bury her emotions and get on with the job.

She pulled a blood-soaked blanket from the bed and tossed it over the body. Then, she quickly searched the room. She found a battered pistol and magazine containing two rounds in a rusted footlocker. Not ideal, but a weapon nonetheless.

After extinguishing the light and with the pistol in hand, she tentatively pushed open the door to the hut and moved outside. Beyond the pickup, she spotted another, larger hut. Weapon held ready, she advanced cautiously and peered in through the window.

Nick was sitting on a chair with his hands tied and blood flowing from a cut above his eye. The two men looked to be drinking, and one was threatening Nick with a machete.

She tried the door handle. It was unlocked. She slowly turned the handle and placed her shoulder against it. Then, with a shove, she burst into the room, pistol held ready.

Machete guy saw her and froze, a look of terror on his face.

Splattered with blood, her hair matted, and her eyes wide, she resembled something from a horror movie.

The shock didn't last long. He raised the machete and yelled a war cry as he lunged.

Jenny's battered pistol boomed, the bullet smashing into the man's thigh. He went down screaming, the machete clattering on the floor as he clutched his leg.

She pointed the pistol at the other man. "Untie him, or you're next."

He swallowed then complied, releasing Nick from his bonds.

"You, OK?" she asked as he walked stiffly to her side of the room.

"Yeah, what about you?"

"I'm alive." Her eyes never left the unwounded assailant. "Help him with his leg," she ordered. "If you try to follow us, I'll kill you."

They left the shack and ran to the rusted pickup. It was sunrise, and dawn had cast a soft glow across the jungle. Nick checked the back, saw their packs still inside, and jumped into the driver's seat. The keys were in the ignition.

Jenny made it as far as the passenger door before the situation caught up with her. Her body shook, tears streaming from her eyes as her chest constricted. She stared at her blood-stained hands, letting the rusted pistol drop.

"Jen, everything is going to be OK," said Nick. "But not if we don't get out of here. I need you to get in the truck."

"Nick, I killed a man," she sobbed. "I stabbed him in the throat."

"Jenny, get in the damn car!"

She stared at him and then climbed inside, slamming the door.

Nick turned the key and pumped the gas. Still warm, the motor sparked to life, and they roared along a rutted track.

"Jenny, we need to focus," Nick yelled over the truck's rattling engine. "How long were we traveling before we arrived at the huts?"

"It wasn't long. Not more than a few minutes."

They bounced along the track, Nick working the throttle to keep the worn engine from stalling. Moments later, the single-lane track reached a wider dirt road.

"Is this the road where they found us?" asked Jen.

"I think so. We were heading downhill."

She exhaled. "Then that's the way we go. We need to find a village and work out where we are."

"I think they were speaking a kind of pidgin English," said Nick as he turned onto the road. "We're somewhere in the South West Pacific."

"Will there be an embassy?" asked Jenny.

"Most likely. If not, we can find a phone and contact the authorities."

"WHERE ARE THEY GOING TO GO?" X asked as he ran a gloved hand along the vertical cut that Nick had made in the perimeter fence.

"They're heading east. They'll have intersected the main access road less than a kilometer from here. It leads down to Biatava and then to the coast road," replied Hartman.

"From there?"

"Road goes to Port Moresby, where they'll head for the US embassy."

"And we've got people there?"

"Yep."

X let out a sigh. "I told him these two wouldn't work." He rose and turned to face Hartman, who was waiting with Jacquie. "Six weeks work flushed down the toilet."

"We could still salvage this," said Jacquie.

"How?" he snapped. "We ain't got no goddamn leverage, and they're on the fucking run. No, those two are done. Hartman, get a vehicle ready with two of your best. I'll take care of this myself."

"Sure, boss."

"What do you want me to do?" asked Jacquie.

"Put the other two through another day of simulator work. We'll blood them tomorrow."

STEAM BILLOWED from the engine bay of their stolen pickup as Nick popped the hood and fumbled with the support strut. "Jen, check in the back for water."

She found a battered orange plastic container in the truck bed. Once she'd wrestled the lid off, she carefully sniffed the contents. It smelt of dirt and organic matter, definitely not fuel.

"Is it going to keep running?" she asked, passing the container to Nick.

"We should be fine if we give it time to cool."

She left him working on the engine and walked further down the rutted road. In the distance, through the trees, she could see tin roofs, smoke, and, beyond them, the ocean.

The growl of a diesel engine caught her ear, and she turned, looking back up the track.

"Get in behind the vehicle," said Nick. "It could be a search party." He had their backpacks ready if they needed to duck into the jungle.

Jenny joined him, taking her pack and slinging it over her shoulder.

The vehicle that appeared from around the corner was a small truck. As it approached, she saw that the back was filled with people. As it passed, she realized the smiling faces peering through the wooden slats were children. One of them spotted her and waved.

The girl couldn't be much older than Jenny's youngest niece. She fought the urge to wave but couldn't hold back a heartfelt smile. The first thing she would do when she reached the US embassy was call her sister.

The truck came to a shuddering halt a car length past them, and a smiling male face appeared from the passenger side window.

"Do you need help?" he asked, with a thick accent.

Nick stood. "We're waiting for it to cool down. It should be good now. How far is it to the closest big town?"

The man's eyebrows rose. "Big town?"

"Yeah, the capital."

"Pot Mosebi, yeah, that four hours." He glanced at their pickup. "In that. Maybe six. You sure you not need help?"

Nick shook his head. "No, we will be fine. Thanks for asking."

"All good. We love America," said the man as the truck's engine revved and the load of waving kids departed.

"Well, at least we know where we are," said Nick, checking the radiator cap. "Port Moresby is the capital of

Papua New Guinea, and I know for certain that there's an embassy there. We could call them from the next town."

Jenny shook her head. "No, if X has people in the embassy, they might tip him off. We need to drive there as fast as we can."

"That's a good point. OK, but we are going to need more water. We can find some in the town and then head to Moresby."

Chapter Seventeen

X ACKNOWLEDGED the knock on the window of his SUV by lowering it.

"Boss, you're going to want to see this," said Hartman.

"You got them?"

"Not exactly, but they were definitely here."

He led X from the vehicle to a ramshackle hut. Inside, the senior instructor found a blood-drenched murder scene. A local man lay in a pool of blood, sightless eyes gazing up at the ceiling.

"Which one of them did this?" he asked.

"I'm still putting the pieces together. There are two more of them in the other hut."

X spotted a knife on the floor and squatted to investigate. "Dead?"

"No, still alive. They said the woman killed this guy and then shot one of them."

"No shit!" he murmured.

He left the hut and made a beeline for the larger dwelling. Inside, one of Hartman's men was guarding another two locals. One of them had a makeshift bandage wrapped around his leg. X gave them a once-over before stepping outside to talk to Hartman. "So these pieces of crap snatched them on the road. The stiff gets himself one-on-one time with our girl, and she sticks him in the throat. Then, she busts in on the other two and rescues her offsider."

"Looks that way," said Hartman. His security team had tracked Jenny and Nick through the jungle to a dirt road. From there, they'd found where they'd been abducted and followed the suspect vehicle tracks to their current location.

"Never would have thought she had it in her," added X. "We couldn't have planned this better."

"Hartman, I found a weapon," one of the men reported. "Over by the vehicle tracks. Looks like an old .45."

"Don't touch it," ordered X.

"What are you thinking, boss?"

"I want a complete forensic collection on the site. Milk the two idiots inside for everything they've got. I want fingerprints, DNA, and a crap load of high-res photos."

"Blackmail?"

"Leverage."

"And then?"

"Use the gun; keep the prints. Then burn it all." He dialed David as he returned to the SUV.

"Did you find them?" the lawyer asked once the connection was secure.

"We'll pick them up in Moresby. I'll take a team down in the helicopter," reported X.

There was a pause. "And you want my permission to terminate them?"

"Not today. There's been a change in circumstances. They made their first kill."

"What?"

X gave him a quick rundown of the situation.

"Wow, we go to the effort of setting this all up, and they slip out through the wire and stab some local scum bag. The live targets we had for them cost us a small fortune."

"We'll use them training the other two," said X.

"How are they going?"

"On schedule."

"Keep me in the loop." David ended the call.

"Hartman, your team can wrap this up. We need to get down to Moresby."

FOR FIVE HOURS, Nick nursed the battered pickup along the pot-holed coastal road that linked Papua New Guinea's capital to the ramshackle fishing villages on its west coast. They'd stopped no less than a dozen times to top up the leaky radiator and let the engine cool. Then, as they reached the outskirts of Port Moresby, Nick had managed to limp into a gas station as steam billowed from the front grille and the temperature gauge rocketed into the red.

"I think this might be the end of the road for this old girl." He popped the hood latch and left the cab to check the engine.

Jenny climbed out and joined him.

"Radiator hose has split," he said.

"The gas station might have a spare," she suggested.

"I doubt it. Place looks like it sells gas and crisps. I vote we get a map and walk the rest of the way. It can't be far to the embassy."

"It would be good to get off the main roads," said Jenny. "X will have people looking for us."

"They'll be watching the embassy. We need a map so we can conduct a recce and come up with a plan."

The attendant at the gas station knew a good deal when he saw it. The teenager happily swapped snacks, water, and a map of Port Moresby for the tactical drone Jenny had in her pack. He'd even thrown in a small amount of the local cash, called Kina.

They left the pickup at the gas station and headed down the coast. They examined the map in the shade cast by a patch of shrubs.

"I think we're here." Jenny used the tip of a twig to point at the edge of a waterfront suburb on the city's outskirts.

"Poreporena Village," read Nick. "Yeah, you're right. He gestured down the beach to the east where, in the distance, they could see lines of tiny structures built out over the water.

"And the embassy is here." She pointed to an area on the map beyond the village where the US facility was marked along with a yacht club, apartments, and restaurants.

"The village offers great cover. There will be plenty of people going about their daily routine," said Nick.

"But, they might not be particularly friendly to outsiders. The area looks poor. Is crime in this area a problem?"

"I'd say so. We'd want to stay off the streets after dark."

"We also need to avoid the highway and main roads. Which means we need to get moving." Jenny folded the map and slid it into a thigh pocket.

Shouldering their packs, the pair trudged off along the

shorefront, following a path between the narrow beach and the highway built above it.

X USED his fingers to expand the digital map of Port Moresby displayed on his tablet. He and Hartman had positioned their hired SUV a block from the US Embassy. Their ground team, icons on X's map, were set to intercept Jenny and Nick if they made for the official entrance to the compound. Another pair was patrolling the highway that led in from the west, searching for the pickup whose description had been provided by a now-dead criminal.

"Boss, you happy with the coverage?" asked Hartman. "I can probably whistle up a team of local cops."

"No, let's keep this in-house. We know they're not armed. So, they'll do exactly as they're told if they've got a Glock shoved in their face."

"And if they try to run?"

"Taze the fuckers."

One of the icons on X's map flashed, indicating that the team was transmitting via digital radio. He wasn't monitoring the network. Hartman had that in hand.

"They've found the pickup," reported Hartman.

X zoomed in on their icon and saw the team was at a gas station less than two miles away. "If they're on foot, they will follow the coast and enter the village."

"I'll push the team in there?"

"Negative. I want them at the choke point near the yacht club." He tossed his tablet on the dash and started the engine.

"Where are we going?" Hartman asked.

"To the other entrance to the Embassy."

"Other entrance? There isn't another entrance. It's surrounded by a twelve-foot fence."

X let out a snort as he accelerated the car. "And that's why you're not on the instructing team."

THEY SPOTTED the hulking grey office building of the US Embassy as they made their way through the coastal village of Poreporena. To their right the trash-laden town extended into the polluted waters on boardwalks and stilted homes.

"We're close," said Nick as they passed four young men sitting idly in front of a hut.

"Hey, drink with us," one of them yelled.

"No, thanks," Jenny replied firmly.

The man leaped up and grabbed her arm. "No, you drink with us."

Nick didn't have a chance to come to her defense. She executed a move that Steve, the mad Scotsman, had taught her. Spinning the assailant off his feet, she flipped him onto the ground. The move was finished by dropping a knee onto his chest, driving the air from his lungs. Then, she sprung to her feet, ready to run.

Peals of laughter caught the pair by surprise as the man's colleagues remained seated. The assailant gasped for air, on his back in a puddle of beer. He reminded Jenny of a fish flapping on the deck of a boat.

"Let's go," insisted Nick.

They jogged away from the men, who continued their laughter. Locals had given them curious looks before the incident. Now, they appeared downright hostile. Fortunately, they'd reached the edge of the village and jumped off the path, onto the beach.

To their front, the coastline curved to a breakwater that jutted out from the shore. A high concrete wall topped the first hundred yards of the rock structure. According to the map, that was the edge of the embassy, and the entrance was beyond it where the coast road passed in front.

They moved quickly and soon reached where the beach met the breakwater. A copse of gnarled trees filled the corner, their roots and trunks festooned in plastic litter. Moving cautiously, they used the scrub as cover, climbing out of the beach and moving to a point where they could see along the road.

"That's the entrance," said Nick. The beach trees ran into a narrow park that paralleled the road till it hit a wide drive that led into the walled compound. They could see the cameras and security outpost at the main gate. "We could make it." He leaned forward.

"Stop." Jenny raised her binoculars. "They're waiting for us. In that grey SUV." She passed them to him.

Nick spotted the two men inside. They were fair-skinned and tough-looking. He swore he'd seen them in Hartman's team at the jungle facility. "If we get to the gates the marines will protect us."

"I doubt it. Not if we're on the outside."

"What are we going to do? We need to make a move."

"This is too risky. Let's try to find another way in. A back door."

"OK."

They carefully backed out of the trees onto the beach. Then, they scrambled across the rocky breakwater and slipped around the corner of the embassy wall. Jenny found a gap in a rickety wire fence and sneaked through into an adjacent construction site.

"It must be the weekend," observed Jenny as they moved through the empty site.

"Probably going to be an apartment complex," added Nick as they moved in behind a pallet loaded with bags of cement.

The building was three stories of open concrete levels that stretched the entire length of the embassy's razor-wire topped security fence. Jenny estimated it was less than twenty yards between the two structures. "There's a crane," she exclaimed.

Sure enough, peeking over the edge of the top floor was a yellow boom with a hook hanging from the end.

"What are we going to do with that?"

"Haven't you ever seen the Bond movie?" said Jenny as she made for a scaffolding staircase.

"I was afraid you were going to say that." He followed her up onto the third floor. Half of the level had a concrete roof over it. The section where the crane was working was uncovered but laden with walls and beams being emplaced to support the next level.

The crane was situated at the end of the building, with its boom positioned to lift materials from the yard below.

"Do you think it will reach the compound?" asked Jenny.

"Pretty risky move," a deep voice spoke. They both turned as X stepped out from behind a wall, his massive arms folded across his chest.

Jenny turned to run, but Hartman appeared, blocking the exit. The operator had a pistol on his hip and was holding a taser. He smiled, and Jenny saw more men either side. It was over; they had no more moves to make.

"But exactly the sort of solution I'd expect you to come up with."

Hartman and his men closed in. There were now four operatives facing off against them, two armed with tasers.

"You know the drill," said Hartman. "We can do this the easy way or the hard way." He smirked. "Please choose the latter."

Chapter Eighteen

"SO, WHEN DID Y'ALL KNOW?" asked X from where he sat, one leg crossed over the other, on a dark blue couch.

Jenny sat opposite on the furniture's twin. Between them was a low table on which one of the Hartman's men had placed a tray of donuts and a coffee, made to her order. Beside the tray lay a large white envelope. The hoods and cuffs hadn't lasted long. She'd been driven a short distance from the point of capture before being guided into this room and released.

"Where's Nick?"

"He's fine." X took a sip from his coffee. "Now, answer the question. When did you work it out?"

Jenny hadn't expected this. She'd feared being taken into the jungle and shot in the back of the head. She hadn't anticipated a casual sit down with the boss. "When we dropped to the last handful of contestants. Probably the raid on the gang house. That was a little too real."

He laughed. "That's because it was. Probably my favorite moment in the whole clusterfuck. You tasering the shit out of that big bastard. That would have made for great TV."

"Except, this was never about TV," she stated.

He winked. "I had my doubts about you and Nick, but you guys have something that the others don't."

"What's that."

"Humility. Nothing gets someone killed quicker than ego."

"The others?" She swallowed. "They're all dead?"

The big man laughed again. "No. They're not dead. They've been compensated and sent home."

"What's going to happen to Nick and I?" she asked tentatively.

He smiled. "Well, that's where it gets interesting." He gestured to the envelope. "Inside that envelope is a first-class ticket back to the US."

"So, I just leave?"

"Kind of. I mean, yeah, you get to leave PNG, but no, technically, you never get to leave. You work for us now."

"Work for who?"

"It's better not to ask."

"It's the CIA, isn't it? This has all been a giant black ops recruitment and training program."

"Sharp as a fucking tack."

Jenny shook her head, laughing. "What makes you think I would agree to work for the CIA?"

"Because you don't have a choice," he replied, deadpan. Behind him, a flat screen flickered to life.

Jenny felt like the floor had dropped from under her as images of the man she had killed appeared on the screen.

"My team completed a full forensic analysis of the crime scene. We've got your prints and DNA on murder weapons and the crime scene."

Jenny shook her head. "It was self-defense, and only one man died."

The image on screen changed from the body in the hut to high-resolution photographs of the two men who'd tortured Nick. Both men had been shot between the eyes.

"I didn't do that. You killed those men."

X shrugged. "The evidence certainly suggests otherwise."

"This is blackmail."

"You call it blackmail. I call it a backstopped employment contact. Either way, you work for us now. That is unless you want to spend the rest of your life inside a maximum-security prison?"

Jenny shot him a look of pure hatred.

"If you need additional motivation, I could always remind you that we know everything about you."

"What's that supposed to mean?"

"Jenny, this is not an organization you want to cross."

She sat in silence, contemplating her options. "So, what do I tell people?"

"You tell them you were part of a reality TV show and are under a Non-Disclosure Agreement."

"And what happens when it doesn't air?"

He took another sip of his coffee. "You tell them Netflix cut it. Happens all the time."

"And I just go back to my life and wait for what? You guys to send a secret message?"

"I'll brief you on the protocols."

She shook her head. "I'm not cut out for this."

"That's what I told the head shed. But, here we are..."

"What happens to Nick and the others?"

"That's not your concern."

"I think it is."

"They're being offered the same opportunity." He finished his coffee. "We need to run through your communication protocols." He glanced at his watch. "Then you've got a flight to catch."

JENNY HAD EXPECTED a look of disgust or perhaps surprise when she presented herself at the VIP lounge at Port Moresby International Airport. However, the young lady behind the counter smiled and presented her with a high-quality carry-on suitcase.

As promised, X's crew had dropped her at the airport. She'd passed through ticketing and immigration with zero fuss. Someone must have doctored her passport with inbound flight and visa details.

"There are bathrooms on the right-hand side as you enter," the airline employee added.

"Thank you." She took the bag and entered the lounge. It was a pleasant setting, considering where she was. The individual bathrooms were nicely appointed, spacious, and had large mirrors. Jenny locked the door and placed the suitcase next to the sink. Inside, she found a well-appointed toiletries bag and the clothes she'd brought to Queenstown. They'd been freshly laundered.

She removed her boots and stripped off her filthy cargo pants and T-shirt. Bundling them into a bag, she dropped them in a trash can.

She stopped before the floor-to-ceiling mirror and made for the shower in her sports bra and briefs. The woman she saw was not Jennifer Murphy, who investigated insurance claims. This new woman cut a leaner figure with muscular arms and legs. She barely recognized the killer, who stared back at her. That woman had taken a life, killed to defend herself and save a friend, but killed nonetheless. Jennifer Murphy would never have been able to do that. She would have died in that filthy hut, raped by a criminal and murdered; her body thrown into a ditch. But, this woman, this trained operative, had fought back and lived. At that moment, she realized she was no longer the Jennifer Murphy she once was. In the future, no matter what happened, she was a new woman. A stronger woman who would not be manipulated and who would find a way out from whatever web she was now entrapped.

X AND HARTMAN took the helicopter back to the camp. Jacquie was waiting on the edge of the landing pad when they touched down.

"Update me on Natalie and Eric," X said as they descended the stairs.

"Eric is good to go. The live engagement scenario didn't faze him, and the pitch was well received," replied Jacquie. "Natalie will need a little more time to process the severity of the situation."

X stopped. "What the hell does that mean?" He glanced at his watch. "I've got a call with David in less than three minutes. What am I going to tell him? Do we have three operatives, or do we have four?"

"You can tell him we've got four."

X gave her a thumbs up. "Good job. You just increased our bonuses by fifty grand."

"Fuck yeah," said Hartman.

"I'll take the call with David in the VR lab. Hartman, what's the go with the bodies?"

"Blast furnace. The remains get mixed in with concrete. They'll be part of a school by the end of the week."

"Efficient. Jacquie, get your gear packed and warn out the new operatives. As soon as I'm done with David, we're heading back to Moresby and getting Stateside."

"Roger."

He took his satellite phone from his pocket as he entered the VR lab. Sensor lights flickered on, revealing an empty building. Hartman's technician had already packed away his gear. It wouldn't be needed until the next class of trainees came through in six months.

There was a couch against a wall, and he slumped into it as he dialed David and established a secure call.

"X, what's the final SITREP?" asked the lawyer.

"Four agents across the line. Nick and Jenny have been fully briefed and dispatched. Eric and Natalie will be outbound on flights first thing tomorrow."

"And your final assessment?"

"They're raw, but if they survive the first nine months, they'll be good to go."

"Even the geriatrics?"

"If they don't have a stroke or a heart attack. I'll finish my final report on the flight home."

"Who's your top performer?"

"Why? You got a job?"

"Possibly, the board's pretty keen to field test this little experiment of ours."

X sat up on the couch. "They're paying the bills. If I was going to send any of them, it would be Jenny."

David laughed. "That must hurt to say. I really should have put a wager on her."

"Good training can bring the best out of anyone."

"That's not what you said at the start."

"Yeah, well, I got them across the line."

"That you did. Right, I'll update the board. I look forward to seeing your final report."

"Aren't you forgetting something?"

"What do you mean?"

"The money!"

David snorted. "Fucking mercenaries. If you check your accounts, you'll see it's already there. Fly safe." He ended the call.

X opened a secure banking app on his device and logged into his Swiss account. "Fuck yeah," he murmured as he read the balance, enough to buy the cabin cruiser he'd always wanted.

Chapter Nineteen

"DAMN GIRL, you look fit as all hell." Ben wrapped his arms around Jenny and bear-hugged her. Her best friend had been waiting at the arrivals gate. "What the hell did they do to you?"

"They worked us hard," said Jenny. "It's so good to see you. How have you been?"

He released her and shrugged. "Same old, same old. Buffalo and I have been watching lots of movies together. Did you know he's a big Harrison Ford fan? Seriously, we've watched all the Indiana Jones movies twice. Anyway, give me all the juicy details. Did you win?"

"I can't say. They made me sign an NDA."

"Oh, come on. You have to give me something. I mean, you've been gone eight weeks. Surely that means you're one of the finalists?"

Jenny shook her head. "Ben, I can't say. Like everyone else, you'll have to wait for it to air."

"And here's me thinking I was special, but it looks like I'm just the cat sitter."

"There's so much I wish I could tell you," said Jenny. "But you'd never believe any of it," she added as an afterthought.

"All good, I'm just happy you're home safe and sound," said Ben as they exited the airport.

"Yep, safe and sound."

JENNY'S INBOX had over three thousand emails when she logged into her work computer. It took less than an hour to flag those of importance and delete the rest.

After eight weeks of pushing her body, mind, and emotions to the limits, emails relating to insurance investigations didn't exactly get her pulse racing. She wondered whether Nick would be back at his desk at his father's law firm. Opening a browser page, she logged into her Facebook account. In moments, she'd found a Nick Lui, based in New Jersey and an associate at *Lui Family Law*. As she contemplated messaging him, she realized someone would likely monitor their accounts. No, it would have to be face-to-face if she wanted to talk to Nick.

She checked the pending insurance claims and saw a warehouse flooding transaction in Trenton. She noted that the account was allocated to her supervisor, Neville. Leaving her cubicle, she went to his office, stepped inside, and shut the door behind her.

He glanced up from his computer. "Jenny, can I help you?"

"Yeah, the Windsor account in Trenton, New Jersey. I'd like you to reallocate the investigation to me."

He exhaled. "Jenny, you can't take two months unpaid leave and then waltz in here making demands."

She sat in his spare chair and crossed one leg over the other. "Neville, I've been working here for four years. I've closed out more insurance claims than any other agent in that time. I've uncovered over a dozen fraudulent transactions. What's more, I've never said anything about the excessive travel you take to cover up your affair with Susan from accounting."

He swallowed. "I don't know what you're talking about."

Jenny smiled and winked. "It's OK, your little secret's safe with me. Now, about that Trenton job?"

"I'll allocate it to you, but this is a one-off. Don't think anything is going to change around here."

Jenny rose, offering him a coy smile on her way out. "Oh, Neville, of course things have changed. Everything has changed."

"MAGDA, I'm off to the gym. I'll be back in an hour," said Nick to his assistant on his way out of the office. "Let me know if you need anything."

He scanned the parking lot as he left the building that housed his father's law firm. Ever since he'd returned from Papua New Guinea, he'd felt like he was being watched. He wouldn't put it past X and his team to monitor his movements to ensure he complied with their directives.

The gym he'd joined was a short walk from the office. Along the way, he executed a number of the counter-surveillance techniques that they'd been taught. He paused at a shop front and used the reflection to monitor the people passing. Then he doubled back and entered a coffee shop where the barista prepared his usual, a double shot espresso with a teaspoon of honey.

Standing before the cafe, he sipped his coffee as he watched the street. Then, comfortable he was free from surveillance, he tossed his cup in a trash can and walked the final few hundred yards to the gym.

The health facility was a twenty-four-hour access club with change rooms, a cardio facility, a weights room, and a boxing lab. In line with the training they'd conducted with Steve at *The Station*, Nick opted for a ten-minute warm-up before hitting the weights room. He selected a rowing machine, cranked his Bluetooth headphones up, and went to work.

Minutes passed, his heart rate rose, and his focus sharpened. He concentrated on his split timing, pushing hard to beat his previous five-minute distance of one thousand four hundred and twenty yards. He was so focused that he didn't register someone using the rower beside him. Pushing hard, he fought the urge to vomit as the timer hit five minutes. Removing his headphones, he fought to catch his breath.

"Crushing it," said a voice next to him.

He turned to see Jenny sitting on the rowing machine next to his. "Oh, my god. What are you doing here?" he managed, between gasps for air.

The two of them jumped off their rowers and embraced.

"I wanted to talk to you," said Jenny. "And this is the only way I could do it safely."

"Wait, did you follow me?"

She nodded. "I staked you out for a few hours first. I wanted to make sure they didn't have you under surveillance."

"I knew someone was watching me."

She shrugged. "Just me, as far as I could tell, and I was pretty careful."

"How are you?"

Jenny managed a thin smile. "Still coming to terms with what happened."

"That might take a while. After we were captured, they told me I could never see you again. They'd terminate you if I attempted to make contact or didn't follow directions."

"They told me they'd take me down for murder, and if that didn't work, they'd go after my family."

"Yeah, and I don't think that's the sort of behavior the US Government would condone."

"What do you mean?"

"I don't think X and the others work for the CIA or any other government agency. They must have in the past, but not now."

"What makes you say that?"

"It all seems a little too dark and a little too slick. Why would the CIA run a fake reality TV show to recruit agents? We've all seen the movies. They can recruit whoever they want, and they have access to remote training facilities. Why expose themselves to the risk associated with the program we just finished? No, I think this has to be a private venture."

"Who would do something like this?"

Nick glanced over each shoulder. "I don't know. But I sure as hell want to find out."

"We need to stay in touch," said Jenny. "That way, we can share information."

He nodded. "I'll sort out secure communications. There are lockers at the main bus terminal in town. The code for the locker and the phone will be ten triple six. Ensure the VPN is active and only communicate using an app called

Dust and always over the cellar network. They might be monitoring Wi-Fi nodes at your house and work."

Jenny hugged him again. "I'm so glad I'm not in this alone."

"Hey, they've underestimated us the whole way through. Together, we'll find a way out."

Chapter Twenty

JENNY FINISHED her notes on the Windsor insurance claim during the short flight from Trenton back to Charlotte. The case was cut and dry. A fire investigator had confirmed that an electrical fault in an old junction box had sparked the inferno that had torched the warehouse. A structural engineer and two builders had confirmed that it wasn't worth salvaging. All she needed to do now was type up the claim report and send it to Neville. She closed her laptop; that was a job for tomorrow.

Relaxing into her seat, she contemplated messaging Nick on the burner phone. The device had been exactly where he'd said. She'd picked it up that morning on her way to the airport. Nick had replied to her test message and reminded her of the protocols they'd agreed to. They weren't dissimilar to the ones she'd been briefed on before leaving PNG.

She never wanted to see that place again. There was barely a moment in her day when she didn't think about the man she'd killed. Over and over, she relived the horrific incident, fixating on the moment she drove the knife into his neck. She had saved her life and Nick's in that instant, but it didn't matter how often she told herself that. He continued to haunt her thoughts and dreams.

Her phone vibrated in her pocket. Unlike the burner, she'd connected it to the aircraft's complimentary Wi-Fi. Unlocking the screen with her face, she checked the notifications. Someone had sent a message to her Instagram profile. As she opened the app, her mouth went dry. The message received contained a key phrase indicating she had been activated. X had told her that contact would be made through social media. Then, according to her protocol, she was to log into a remote server to access her mission profile. That required her to remember a ten-digit alphanumerical sequence. After three attempts, she was able to connect. The briefing was a short message.

PDX, Ace Car Rental KV6745

She assumed that PDX was a designator for an airport. Google quickly confirmed that it was Portland International. The additional code was a booking reference for a hire car.

A part of her wanted to ignore it, but X had made the ramifications of that all too clear. If she didn't carry out the mission, her life, Nick's and potentially her entire family's would be forfeited.

She used the phone to book a flight to PDX as her plane touched down. Then, she activated the burner phone and waited for it to acquire a signal before messaging Nick via the secure application. She wanted him to know that she'd been allocated her first mission. He messaged back before they'd taxied clear of the runway.

Do you want me to come with?

The message gave her a certain amount of comfort. No, he couldn't go with her. The risk of compromise would be extreme. As far as they knew, this could be another test, a fake mission designed to test her compliance. If the organization detected Nick, it would see they were working together and terminate them. She responded accordingly, reassuring him that she'd keep him in the loop and see what she could dig up. Worst case, she could find out who paid for the hire car.

———

THE ACE CAR hire attendant at Portland International Airport was a spotty-faced twenty-something more interested in his phone than providing anything that resembled customer service.

"My booking reference is kilo victor six seven four five," Jenny repeated for the third time.

"Right, yeah, it will be in here." He dumped a box filled with envelopes on the countertop.

Jenny shook her head and flicked through the records until she found one marked with her reference number. Tearing the top of the envelope, she found a rental agreement and a key fob for a white Corolla.

"Do you need to see my ID?" she asked.

"You're hardly underaged." He snickered.

Ignoring the jibe, she inspected the document and found it was blank.

"Can I get a receipt or an invoice?" she asked.

"Nah, it will be emailed once you return the car."

"I'd like a copy now."

The kid looked up from his phone. "Serious?"

"Deadly."

"Right, hang on a second." He slapped his hand against a keyboard, waking his computer. Fingers raced over the keys, and a moment later, a printer behind him hummed. He wheeled his chair over, grabbed two pages as they were spat out, and thrust them in her direction.

"Thank you."

"Whatever." His eyes were already back on his phone.

Jenny found her Corolla in the furthest corner of the parking lot. Unlocking it, she tossed her bag onto the back seat. She climbed behind the wheel and inspected the document the kid had supplied.

The rental agreement was made out to a corporate entity that sounded as fake as they came, *Modus Consulting*. She was about to message the name to Nick when she caught herself. The car may have been wired with technology that allowed them to monitor her communications. No, she'd wait till she was clear of the vehicle before contacting him.

Folding the papers tightly, she jammed them into her pocket. She'd dispose of them later. Sitting in the car, she realized she'd completed all her tasks and still had no idea what her mission was. She had transport but no destination. Leaning across the passenger seat, she opened the glovebox. Inside, lodged under the car's operating manual, she found a smartphone in a leather case. There was a credit card and a micro-USB tucked inside.

The screen lit up as she handled it, prompting her to place her thumb on the device's base. Access revealed several apps on the home screen. One was marked with the universal symbol for information, and another with a chat bubble.

She tapped the information app, and a briefing appeared on screen, revealing her mission and target. As she read, a weight was lifted off her shoulders. Her task was recovery, not assassination.

The mark was a software developer who worked from home. According to the file, he kept his work on a secure server in his house. Her job was to locate it and plant a device.

Her briefing was comprehensive. It included floor plans of the house and possible locations of the server. However, it needed more detail on exactly who the developer was and what he was working on.

She contemplated googling him from her burner phone but thought better of it. First, she would conduct a recce of the suburb where the house was located, and then she would find a hotel from where she would contact Nick.

THE MESSAGE PINGED to David Martin's secure phone with only moments to spare. He read it as he left his office and made his way through the sterile corridors of the consulting firm. Smiling, he dropped the phone into a plastic container marked electronic devices and entered the company's secure board room.

There was no one inside. He took his place at the monolithic polished wooden table that dominated the room and slipped on a pair of VR goggles. Technically, the device was an augmented reality headset, but that level of detail was lost on David.

Despite the absence of people in the room, the lawyer was no longer alone. The headset had filled the other chairs with figures. Six men and two women formed the board of

The Entity or *Carmen Associates Consulting* as its cover organization was known. The Eight rarely physically met, running the organization via secure communications, including augmented reality for board gatherings.

The meeting's agenda was short, and the lawyer's pet project was the centerpiece.

"David, what was the final cost for your four recruits?" asked the Chairman.

"Twelve million," he responded.

"Christ, three million each. Surely, we could have recruited replacements for cheaper than that," added one of the others. He was one of three who initially opposed the concept.

"Your budget was eight," the Chairman reminded him.

"There were some initial costing discrepancies. However, future programs will benefit from this. I anticipate our costs halving."

"Future programs," said the skeptic. "You've cost us twelve million and delivered nothing. You'll be lucky if we don't terminate your contract."

David swallowed. Termination at *The Entity* had a more permanent outcome than in a traditional corporate workplace. He composed himself. "I understand that some of you have had apprehensions regarding the program. However, I can now report that it has been successful. In the last forty-eight hours, one of our recruits executed an asset extraction."

"What asset?" asked the skeptic.

"Target A43, an artificial intelligence program designed to consolidate and allow for rapid dissemination of excess food products. A program that a corporation has paid us four million dollars to recover, effectively covering the development costs of that single agent. I'll post the after-action report in the next few hours."

"A positive outcome," said the Chairman.

"That's one agent. What about the other three?" asked the skeptic.

"With the board's endorsement, I'd like to advance the program to include the full spectrum of activities," said David.

"You think they're ready?" asked the Chairman.

"I do."

"Give us a moment."

David's sound was cut off as the board discussed the issue. He already knew the outcome. Twelve million was a lot of capital, and they would be keen to put their new agents to work to recover the rest. Having the Chairman question the program's cost was all part of the strategy to bring the doubters on board.

"David," the Chairman reopened the audio. "Your request is endorsed. The usual mechanisms for mission selection and approval will be enforced. You can hand off all four agents to Operations at your earliest convenience."

"Excellent, I'll have that done within the next twenty-four hours. Thank you for your time."

"That's not all. We've also approved the next iteration of selection and training. Funding of eight million has been approved. What's the time frame for commencing the program?"

David had yet to anticipate this move. He'd assumed that the board would want to put all four agents through their paces before approving another iteration of *The Operative*.

"There are some operational security factors to consider. We will have to change the host nation. I'd estimate four to six months to establish training facilities and conduct initial screening."

"Make it happen. Team, I've got a meeting with a client. I'll see you at the next meeting if there isn't additional business." The Chairman paused for a second before terminating the session.

David removed his headset and placed it on the table. He sat momentarily and contemplated how he would convince X to rerun the program. Money, he'd offer him more money.

Chapter Twenty-One

NICK LUI WIPED his hands on his shirt for the third time in fifteen minutes. Guatemala was oppressively humid, but that wasn't what was causing him to sweat. The source of his gurgling stomach, sweaty hands, and heightened senses was his mission. More specifically, the task verb neutralize. This wasn't the first task he'd been issued. He'd completed two surveillance tasks within the US, but this was the first time he'd been ordered to kill a man.

His hide was in an abandoned factory a short distance from where his target, a local doctor, resided in a shabby second-floor apartment. He'd watched the man for three days before developing his plan of execution. Then, once the doctor had gone to work in a local clinic, he'd broken into the apartment and made a subtle adjustment to his gas-fired oven, adding a tiny remote control to its igniter. Then he'd worked the aged flexible hose back and forth until it fractured. Happy with his handiwork, he'd retreated to his hide and waited.

The target had been remarkably punctual over the last

three days, arriving home on his bicycle at five fifteen sharp. Nick had worked the math on the gas flow against the apartment's square meterage. He was confident that the explosion would be sufficient to obliterate the structure.

His target package hadn't outlined who wanted the doctor silenced or why, but Nick's research had led him to believe it was a pharmaceutical company. He'd hacked the doctor's email account and found an email to a health official telling them that an anti-malarial drug trial was causing severe side effects that could have long-term health implications. The response had been blunt; the trial was to continue, and the doctor was to keep his opinions to himself. Nick could only assume the official was on the pharma company's payroll.

Nick regretted his research. The job would have been much easier if he thought the doctor was a child molester or a murderer. Now, he faced a dilemma: kill an innocent man or forfeit his own life and the lives of his family and friends. He only saw one way out.

Through an open window he spotted the doctor as he cycled along the street. Nick wiped his hands dry again and opened a rugged plastic case that contained his makeshift firing system. A rocker switch illuminated a red LED, indicating the system was armed. He waited for the man to chain his bicycle and disappear into the building. Then he started his countdown. Thirty seconds was more than enough time for what needed to happen.

His heart raced as he reached the final ten seconds, and he wiped his hands again. Five, four, three, two, one. He flicked the ignition switch. Nothing happened.

He flicked the switch back and forth. There was a flash, and the roadside wall of the upper-story apartment seemed to jump away from the building. A deafening boom shook

Nick's position as a wave of heat and debris-laden dust slammed into him.

Coughing, he fumbled for the smartphone he was using to record the mission. As the smoke cleared, he focused it on the wreckage. His calculations were on the money. The doctor's apartment had been obliterated, its contents smoking on the street below. As he panned the camera over the destruction, he spotted a smoldering corpse among the rubble.

"Mission accomplished," he murmured as he rose and gathered his equipment into a backpack. His car was parked a block away. He kept his head down as sirens wailed and emergency services vehicles flashed by. Leaving the small town he drove for half an hour before reaching his intermediary staging location, a small hacienda deep in the jungle. Entering the house, he made for the bathroom to wash the dust and grime from his face.

When he emerged, a second vehicle with two occupants had pulled in beside his. He walked to the front door and opened it.

Jenny greeted him with a broad smile. "Mission success." She led her companion in, and Nick closed the door behind them. When they were inside, she introduced them. "Nick, meet Doctor Luis Guerra, your target. I briefed him on the situation on the way over."

The doctor grasped Nick's hand with both of his own. "Mr. Nick, I cannot thank you enough for saving my life."

Nick blushed. "I don't think you can exactly call it saving. To everyone outside this room, you're very dead."

"Yes, your friend said that. But I don't understand. When they don't find a body, they will know I escaped."

"They'll find a body."

The man frowned. "How is that possible? Did you..."

"No. We borrowed a corpse from a mortuary. A man who died in a car accident earlier in the week."

"We're counting on the fact the police around here won't put much investigative effort into a tragic accident," added Jenny.

Luis Guerra shook his head. "Why you would do all this for a stranger? You don't know me. Wouldn't it be easier to… I mean, that's what you do, right? That's why they sent you."

Jenny shot Nick a sideways glance before responding. "We can't go into it, but no. That's not what we do."

"We're not the bad guys," said Nick.

"You just work for bad people."

"Something like that." Nick took an envelope from his pocket and handed it to the doctor. "You've got to promise that you'll lay low for a few months, change your name and never return to the clinic. Because if you don't, they will send someone else to make sure you keep quiet."

The doctor opened the envelope and saw it was filled with cash. "You want me to take this money and hide? What about the people whose lives are being ruined so someone can test a treatment that doesn't work? They don't get to hide."

"How does your being dead help them?" asked Jenny. "You go anywhere near that trial, and you'll get us killed too."

His shoulders slumped. "I understand."

"You can stay here for a few days," said Nick. "There's a third car in the garage; it's clean. We purchased it with cash in Zacapa. Do you need anything else?"

"No, you've done so much already."

"All right, good luck."

Nick and Jenny left the doctor in the hacienda and

moved outside. "Do you think we will get away with this?" Jenny asked.

"I don't see why not. As long as the doc holds up his end of the bargain."

"I guess. I'm just worried about the next job and the one after that." She looked at him with fear-filled eyes. "Nick, we need to get out from under these people."

He reached over and grasped her hand. "We will. We need to stay ahead of them until we get all the pieces together."

"And then what?"

"Then we need to find allies. Someone to help us burn the bastards down."

X'S PHONE rang as he was cresting a ridge on his favorite horse, deep within the bounds of his five-thousand-acre ranch. The view from the hill was one of the best on the property. From high in the saddle, he could see as far west as his boundary fence.

He fished the device from the pocket of his flannel shirt and glanced at the screen. It was David.

"What the fuck do you want?" he asked gruffly once the call was secure. "You gave me a month before we kick off again. Any changes are going to cost you."

"Hold your horses, cowboy. This is a courtesy call. I wanted to let you know one of your kids made their first kill."

X's eyes narrowed. "Which one?"

"That I'm not going to share. But I wanted you to know they've reached full operational capability."

"Confirmed?"

"Multiple sources and video proof from the operative."

"So that ticks off my final bonus," added X.

"It certainly does. Well done. I'll have the amount deposited in your account today."

"That all?"

"No, I've also got confirmation that the host country for the next training iteration will be Spain."

"Cool, now leave me the fuck alone."

"Always a pleasure doing business with you X."

The hulking former operator terminated the call and dropped the phone into his pocket before turning his horse for home. As he rode, he contemplated which of the team could have made the kill. At the start of training, he would have put his money on anyone other than the two oldies. After seeing what they'd achieved in PNG, he had them pegged as the favorites.

Reaching the bottom of the hill, he dug his heels and urged the quarter horse into a canter. Unlike the trainees, the beast didn't need much prompting; it lived to run. That was the one thing about the program that didn't sit well with him. Over the years, he'd worked with operatives of varying skill and talent, but they'd all had one thing in common. They'd all executed their missions willingly. Differing motivations, but always voluntary. The 'Operatives' were different, blackmailed into their new occupation by threats to their lives and the lives of those they loved. X did not doubt that, eventually, it would come back to bite them in the ass.

Urging his horse to a gallop, he pushed the thought from his mind. That would be someone else's problem.

Also by Jack Silkstone

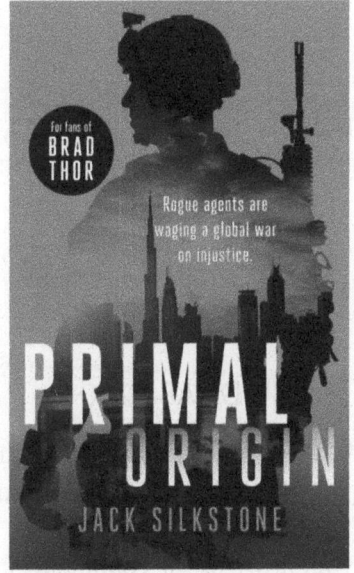

vinci-books.com/primal-origin

They are the unseen guardians, the avengers of the innocent, the destroyers of evil.

In a world where governments fail, PRIMAL delivers justice with a dose of fury. This is the first book in the PRIMAL Origin thriller series, a page-turning, gripping tale of vigilante justice against evil.

Turn the page for a free preview…

PRIMAL Origin: Chapter One

ABU DHABI, 2004

THE US EMBASSY in Abu Dhabi didn't impress Vance. Like so many other buildings in the Emirates, it was a monstrosity of steel and glass, chilled to almost arctic temperatures by an army of air conditioners. A CIA paramilitary officer, the solidly built African American wasn't bothered by the heat of the Arabian Gulf. He'd been in the country for over a month and was fully acclimatized. So much so, he was shivering as he waited for an audience with the ambassador.

"They always have it up too high," the secretary said.

Vance attempted a smile. "Yeah, it keeps the penguins working."

The pretty blonde laughed and returned her attention to her computer.

He scanned the room again. It was lavishly furnished, some new vogue designer's attempt to give it some warmth. The marble floor was laid with ornamental Persian rugs.

Expensive paintings graced the walls on either side of a pair of solid mahogany doors that barred entry into the ambassador's office. It was nothing like the rough compound he'd called home for the past five weeks.

Vance and his offsider, a former Marine known as Ice, were working with a World Health Organization team in an industrial sector of the desert city. They had established a health clinic to support thousands of the city's impoverished workers. In a US Government–sponsored initiative, the team was currently checking for any signs of a superflu pandemic.

From Vance's perspective, the WHO team was providing cover for the CIA to track down a terrorist group. In the last month, a spate of suicide attacks had rocked the Gulf States, targeting Western expatriates and government officials. CIA analysts had assessed that the attacks were linked to the recent US invasion of Iraq. However, one of the suicide bombers had been identified as Bangladeshi, recruited from the UAE's immigrant workforce.

Vance and Ice had been sent to Abu Dhabi to track down the recruiters and follow the link back to the terrorist command structure. So far the few leads they'd uncovered had been dead ends. Despite this, Vance's experience and gut instinct told him they were hunting in the right place.

A buzzer sounded on the secretary's desk. "Sir, the ambassador will see you now." She rose and walked across to open the solid wooden doors.

Vance extracted his muscular frame from the sofa and followed her into the ambassador's office. The opulence of the waiting area was magnified tenfold in the huge room. Tall, blast-proof, tinted windows reduced the sun's glare but allowed a sweeping view of the malls, hotels, and high-rises that had sprouted from the oil-rich sands of Abu Dhabi.

This was the office of a man at home with wealth and power.

Howard D. Beecroft sat behind his antique desk and examined Vance with a critical eye. He noted with scorn the dusty boots, grubby khaki cargo pants, and faded blue shirt. His gaze lingered on the weathered features of the CIA veteran.

"So this is the renegade running black ops in my Emirates," Beecroft said.

"I'm sorry: black ops?" Vance returned the scornful gaze, equally unimpressed with the bureaucrat.

Beecroft sported a portly frame and ruddy complexion, the result of years on the cocktail circuit. "Yes, the CIA didn't seek my approval for your little mission." His chins wobbled as he spoke.

"Last time I checked, the CIA didn't work for the State Department."

Beecroft tipped back in his soft leather chair. His belly strained against a tailored waistcoat under a dark blue suit. Vance almost expected to see a gold chain disappearing into the vest pocket.

"I don't think you understand, Mr...." The ambassador paused, unable to recall Vance's surname. "I don't think you understand just how important the Emirates is to America. The lifeblood of our nation flows through this relationship and it is my job to ensure that nothing damages that. That no obstacles block the flow. Obstacles like you."

Vance's brow furrowed. "Don't get me wrong, I understand the situation. But what I don't get is how a discreet CIA operation could be considered an obstacle."

"Discreet? Is that what you think your little mission is?" Beecroft selected a manila folder from a pile on his desk. "If it is so discreet, then explain to me why the head of the

Special Tasks Branch is sending me reports warning that you are, in fact, the next target for the very terrorists you're supposed to be hunting?"

He threw the folder on the desk. "Your operation has the potential to severely embarrass my standing with the Emir. I can only hope that he isn't aware of your activities already."

Vance stepped forward to pick up the folder. It contained a single-page police report. He skimmed it and dropped it back on the desk. "How the hell did they find out we're here?"

"Evidently your World Health Organization cover isn't as good as you think."

"I call bullshit on that, Mr. Ambassador."

"How it happened doesn't matter." Beecroft waved his finger as he spoke. "The simple fact is you've been compromised and now you're out. I'm sure you can hunt terrorists in Iraq or Afghanistan. My aide has arranged tickets for you and the—"

"Get the WHO team out, but I'm staying."

Beecroft pushed back his chair and struggled to remove his corpulent frame from its clutches. He finally got to his feet, drawing himself up to his full five feet nine inches. "You will do no such thing. This is my post and I will—"

"You will sit the fuck down, Ambassador!" Vance growled from a height advantage of almost six inches.

Beecroft shrunk like a deflated balloon, dropping back into his chair.

"The only way we could have been compromised is through this office."

The ambassador opened his mouth to object but Vance cut him off again. "Now. You're probably not harboring Bin

Laden and co, so my guess is you blabbed to one of your buddies at poker."

Beecroft opened his mouth to protest, but thought better of it.

"Now usually I would get very, very upset about that, but this time I'm gonna let it slide. What I won't be doing is getting on any airplane."

The ambassador's face turned a brighter shade of red. "You will get on that plane. Otherwise I will submit a report to Washington."

Vance smiled. "You go right ahead and do that, Mr. Ambassador. By the time your report gets read and someone takes notice, my job here will be done. So you just get back to protecting the flow of oil and I'll get back to tracking down our nation's enemies." He turned and walked toward the door.

"This will be the end of you, Vance. I'll make sure of that."

"Take your best shot, Mr. Ambassador. Better men have tried."

———

ICE WAS WAITING in the parking lot when Vance exited the building. He wore similar clothes to the senior CIA operative: tan cargo pants and a loose-fitting shirt. The former recon Marine was chatting with a member of the Embassy's Marine security detail. The guard was a big man, at least six feet, but the paramilitary operative towered over him. With short blond hair, a square jaw, and the build of an NFL quarterback, Ice was a formidable-looking individual.

Spotting Vance, he shook hands with the Marine and

walked back to their Toyota Land Cruiser, starting the engine.

Neither man said a word as Ice drove them from the embassy, until the battered four-wheel drive had merged into Abu Dhabi's hectic traffic.

"Where we heading, boss?" Ice asked.

"Find a place to park. I need to make a few calls."

"That bad?"

"Yes and no." Vance gave him a rundown on the conversation with the ambassador. "If the police report is accurate, we've been compromised and now the hunter has become the hunted," he concluded.

"There's more good in this than bad," Ice said after a moment.

"How's that, big man?"

"The way I see it, the ambassador's done us a favor. Now we know for sure that this terrorist group has links to the Emirates government. We just need to flush them out."

Vance looked sideways. "Ice, you're nuts. I tell you a bunch of jihadist douche bags are gonna try and blow us to hell and you think it's a good thing." He shook his head and laughed.

The corner of Ice's mouth turned up in a slight smile. His eyes never left the packed highway.

Vance continued. "Only problem is that pompous cocksucker has given us the boot. It won't take Langley long to follow that up and shit-can us."

"Means we need to move fast."

"Yep. First things first, we get the Doc and his crew out." Vance pulled out his phone and scrolled through the contacts, looking for the physician in charge of the WHO team. "After that I'll arrange a meeting with Tariq and find out how Special Tasks were alerted to the attack. You check if the gear has arrived."

Ice pulled into the parking lot of one of Abu Dhabi's shopping malls and slotted the four-wheel drive into a free spot. Vance was already talking to the head of the WHO team. Ice jumped out of the vehicle and dialed the FedEx Custom Critical depot to check if the extra equipment he'd ordered from Langley had arrived. With a direct threat to the team, he'd be happier packing a little extra heat.

**Grab your copy...
vinci-books.com/primal-origin**

About the Author

Jack Silkstone grew up on a steady diet of Tom Clancy, James Bond, Jason Bourne, *Commando* comics, and the original first-person shooters, Wolfenstein and Doom. His background includes a career in military intelligence and special operations, working alongside some of the world's most elite units. His love of action-adventure stories, his military background, and his real-world experiences combined to inspire the no-holds-barred PRIMAL series.

www.ingramcontent.com/pod-product-compliance
Ingram Content Group UK Ltd.
Pitfield, Milton Keynes, MK11 3LW, UK
UKHW020449240925
463234UK00004BA/118